# FROM A HOLE
# IN THE GROUND,
# IT ROSE . . .

Wanda reached for the flowers, pulled them. The tough stems resisted. She had to brace herself and yank hard.

The roots came loose quite suddenly, tearing the earth and bringing up clods of dirt, releasing a stench so thick it could almost be cut with a knife, an odor of rot and death and decay.

Wanda fell backward, throwing the flowers as far away as possible. She scrambled to her feet, scrubbing her hands frantically against her pantsuit, backing unsteadily toward the car as a mist rose from the hole where the flowers had been. It rose up, and up, twenty feet over her head, and began to take a shape that looked almost human. The translucent misty figure reached out one stinking, dripping hand to her, and a sound came from somewhere, a moan, a cry . . .

# UNEARTHED

## ASHLEY McCONNELL

DIAMOND BOOKS, NEW YORK

UNEARTHED

A Diamond Book / published by arrangement with
the author

PRINTING HISTORY
Diamond edition / March 1991

ISBN: 1-55773-476-3

Diamond Books are published by The Berkley Publishing Group,
200 Madison Avenue, New York, New York 10016.
The name "DIAMOND" and its logo
are trademarks belonging to Charter Communications, Inc.

PRINTED IN THE UNITED STATES OF AMERICA

10  9  8  7  6  5  4  3  2  1

This book is dedicated,
with love and sorrow,
to the memory of my mother.

## ACKNOWLEDGMENTS

Among the people who helped to make this book possible are Mike Zimmerman and the troops; Jerry McCorkle and Tex Samuelson; Nora Hakala; Andrew Phillips; Charlie Grant; the Thursday Night Gnaw & Nibble Club; and Kathryn Ptacek, who has *always* encouraged me in my writing. Thank you all!

"Nevada is peculiarly a surface-known country. . . ."
—**Mark Twain**

# Prologue

## 1

Deep in the guts of the earth, a small group of men press themselves back against walls of earth to make room. A gigantic iron bucket clatters to the floor, the pulleys two hundred feet overhead shrieking like damned souls echoing down the shaft. The men do not hear. One man clambers out of the bucket. He is not tall, but even in the unsteady candlelight that provides the only illumination, his yellow eyes glare out from under heavy brows like a hawk's. The men shrink out of his way. Ignoring them, he strides to the blackened wall where blast powder has ripped a gaping hole.

Somewhere deep in the mine shaft, a rumbling. The men are too busy watching as the hawk-eyed one examines the rubble. He picks up a shard of rock, rubs it on his pants, holds it up to the candle. His eyes glitter. He licks the burned rock, scrubs it again. The cleaned place shows white, with a heavy blue-gray streak. The man's lips twist into a feral grin. The men around him start to cheer.

And the walls of the mine open.

# 2

Deep in the earth, a presence stirs. Irritated. Invaded. It can feel damage, piercings and explosions in its guts, acids soaking into its skin, and many many demanding noises from those living things which are and are not a part of it. Noises it cannot ignore.

It can hear a summons, an old summons, a once-powerful summons; but its pain is very great. The pain is a violation of old agreements. And also, it may once again be more powerful than those who call upon it, and that is something to think on most carefully.

It considers, and it takes a shape.

# 3

The double-wide had two small bedrooms at one end, for the children, and the master bedroom at the other. Jeremy walked very softly down the hall to the front door. His hand was on the knob when he heard the whisper behind him.

"Jeremy?"

The boy grimaced.

"Jeremy, what're you doing? Where you going? It's—"

"Shut *up*, Tessy!" he snapped voicelessly. "They're gonna hear you!"

Tessy, his eight-year-old sister, stood in the middle of the living room, rubbing one foot against the back of the other leg and yawning. She was wearing bright yellow pajamas; in the shaft of moonlight coming through the partially open venetian blinds she looked like an out-of-season daffodil. "Where are you going, Jeremy? It's real late."

The boy stalked over to her, jaw stuck out determinedly. Mustering all the authority of a twelve-year-old big brother, he said, "That's none of your business. You go back to bed."

Tessy didn't intimidate easily. "You better tell me, or I'm gonna tell Mom."

"Go to bed!"

"I'll yell!"

Jeremy sighed; he never won arguments with his little sister. "Okay, okay. You promise you'll go back to bed if I tell you?"

Tessy chewed on her lip. "Well—okay."

"And you won't ever tell Mom and Dad?"

"I promise."

"Cross your heart?" Jeremy regarded such superstitions as kid stuff, but Tessy was still a firm believer. It was handy sometimes. She might stretch things a little, but she'd never break a cross-my-heart promise.

"I'm going out to Heartbreak."

"Daddy said he'd spank us if we went there!"

"All the guys are going. We're gonna see if we can find the mule stable."

"Daddy's gonna be mad if he finds out." A gleam of speculation entered her eyes. Jeremy winced, visualizing blackmail for months to come. The possibility had to be quashed at once.

"That's why you promised," he reminded her sharply. "You promised, right?"

Tessy hung her head. She wasn't really a tattletale. "Yeah. What mule stable?"

"There was some place in the mine where they kept the mules that pulled the ore carts. They had food and water for them and everything. They kept them underground and they never came outside at all."

Tessy's eyes, bluer than her brother's, were huge in the moonlight as she looked up again. "You're gonna go *inside* the mine? Daddy's gonna kill you!"

"Not if he doesn't find out. Now you promised. Come on, go back to bed. I'm gonna be late."

She started back to her room, the brilliant yellow of her pajamas fading as she stepped out of the moon's rays. Jeremy was halfway back to the door when her voice stopped him. "Jeremy?"

"*Now* what?"

"I thought you didn't like those guys. How come you're going with them?"

Jeremy just stared at her. "Who else is there around here to hang out with?"

He vanished out the door. Tessy paused a moment, looking after him, and then scrambled for her room, stripping her pajama tops off as she went.

Jeremy had taken the flashlight, she discovered a few minutes later. It made no difference. The streets were almost as well lighted by the moonlight as they would be in the early morning sunshine. She guided her bicycle down the dirt road that served for a side street. A brief relay of barking began until the neighborhood dogs caught her scent and subsided again.

Her brother was nowhere in sight. She stopped at the corner of the street and looked around, getting her bearings. Nintucca had one paved road that cut directly through the center of town, with no signal lights, no stop signs to slow traffic down. Her parents had warned her about riding her bike along that road, but there was a well-worn path alongside that would go at least to the last house. Past that, it was another two miles to the mine turnoff. Nintucca was a town of trailer homes and ramshackle buildings from the twenties scattered against a series of abrupt, naked hillsides; the street bobbed up and down like the frame of a roller coaster, hiding the lights in some of the houses, throwing others into prominence against a silvery horizon.

She took a deep breath and looked behind her, then to both sides. The town was absolutely silent; she couldn't hear even an echo of the country-western band from the tiny casino whose lights glared half a mile up the street. Nintucca might be abandoned, empty of human life. It wasn't right. Even at one in the morning, there were supposed to be *some* noise.

Tessy bit her lip and pushed the bike into motion. The card stuck into the spokes of the front wheel provided a comforting rattle to inhabit the silence. If she pumped hard enough, she should catch up to the boys before they actually went into the mine. She wasn't sure what she'd do then, but Jeremy wasn't going to have an adventure without her.

Gravel spattered up from the tires. She settled into a relentless rhythm, humming to herself, using the sound of the card as her percussion section.

There was a rumbling behind her.

She braked abruptly, swerving half-around to look, expecting to see the lights of one of the big trucks that sometimes passed through town, heading for somewhere else.

There was nothing.

She held her breath, listening.

Nothing.

Not even the wind.

Tessy stuck out her lower lip and blew, fluttering the fine golden veil of bangs away from her eyes, and decided she must have just made up that sound, after all. She wasn't afraid of the dark. Jeremy was afraid; he had to have a night-light in his room. She used to hide it to tease him, but one time when Mom and Daddy were out he'd even cried, so she stopped doing it any more. That was a long time ago.

She straightened out the bike and set out again. Three yards down the road she stopped and took the card out of the front wheel and listened harder. There wasn't anything behind her, but she could listen better without that noise all around.

The road dropped as it left town, climbed one last gradient, then dived between the shoulders of two barren hills, twisting away from all the light of the town, all sight of human habitation. She coasted down the slope toward the rise, listening hard. The last house on her left spun away behind her, lightless, and she struck the pool of shadows at the low place and began to pump hard again to the crest of the hill.

Her tires hissed as she steered back onto the road. There wasn't any path to follow any more; the roadside was deceptive sand, dotted with sage and salt grass to bump against and twist control out of her hands. It was colder than she expected, and a night breeze licked at the back of her neck.

She wasn't that far behind the boys, she thought. She'd see them any second now. And if they didn't let her stay, boy, would they be in trouble.

Gasping for breath, she stopped at the top of the hill, looking back at the lights of the town, listening.

Her stomach gurgled, and she jumped. "Quiet!" she ordered herself, whispering.

Nothing.

Turning forward again, she peered down into the shadows between the hills. Something seemed to move down there.

"Prob'ly just a dumb cow," she muttered. It couldn't be anything really bad, or she'd have met those boys running back to town, Jeremy in the lead. "Scaredy-cat," she added. It wasn't clear whether she was referring to the cow, or Jeremy, or perhaps herself. Pushing off, she pumped down.

The hills rose up around her, seeming to enfold her in cloaks of granite and depleted, silver-bearing quartz. Her eyes adjusted quickly, allowing her to swerve away from the darker holes where the lighter concrete had crumbled, the edges where half the roadbed was eroded away. There were places two cars couldn't pass each other without going into the shoulder and miring themselves in the sand.

The bike picked up speed as she went, legs churning, deeper into the pass. She was gasping as she hurtled along, not daring to glance to either side, not daring to think what would happen if that dumb cow picked right now to wander into the road in front of her, or some ol' coyote or badger or rabbit was lying there, soaking up the warmth the road retained long after the sun disappeared and the rest of the world grew cold. Down through the pass and the dark place, and then she'd be going out past the hills and into the desert, next to the great white dry lake bed, and there wouldn't be anything there for miles and miles until she caught up with the boys on their way to the mine.

She heard the rumbling again, and the bike jolted suddenly, almost twisting the handlebars out of her hands. She squealed as the brakes grabbed and stuck, and bicycle and girl went spinning, end over end over end.

The rumbling got louder.

Tessy lay crumpled on the shoulder of the road, still conscious, too shocked to cry.

The earth rumbled again.

Before her nose, a crack opened in the earth, and sand fell hissing into it, whispering.

She tried to get up.

The crack got larger, wormed its way to her crumpled machine, paused beside it; and then widened to a chasm, and with a sibilant whoosh her brand-new bike followed the sand into the earth.

Tessy got up on her hands and knees, staring at the crack and then all around her, as if her bicycle had crashed somewhere else and she could see it if she only looked hard enough.

The earth rumbled again, deeper, almost in a growl. The sound seemed to come from behind her.

She turned around on her bottom and looked up at a sky frosted with a million stars, and a brilliant white-gold moon;

and then a shadow fell over her, a massive shadow bigger than the hills, and the shadow thrust its head at her and snarled, and the earth snarled with it and split open beneath her, and swallowed her screaming.

And the sand whispered after her in gritty sheets, and the rumbling came again; and the earth closed over and sat empty under the stars.

# SUNDAY

# One

## 1

David Esher was drinking a midmorning Diet Pepsi in a diner/bar in Beatty, Nevada, when the nuclear bomb exploded.

At first he thought it was an earthquake. It felt as if the booth he was sitting in, the table in front of him, the whole building lifted, rolled, settled without a sound, as if it rested on the skin of a giant cat stretching in its sleep. A hanging lamp over the bar swung back and forth, casting odd glares and shadows into the corner of the room.

He looked up wildly from the ice dancing in his glass—the glass dancing in his hand, no matter how hard he tried to hold it still—to the bartender, a skinny, dried-up woman in a pink housedress, a green scarf around her head. He was just in time to see her glance significantly from her watch to the man at the next table. "Got it off at last. Told ya they'd do it on a Sunday if they had to."

They must have had a bet on it, he thought. Do they bet on earthquakes here? Why isn't anybody panicking?

Then: That was over awful fast.

"What was that, about eighty kilotons?" the bartender asked. "Didn't feel as big as the last one."

The man at the next table sniffed. "Read it in the paper, Donna. They don't tell me nothin' either."

David's gaze dropped to the tabloid-sized newspaper the

previous patron had tossed into the corner of the booth, the *Tonopah Times-Bonanza (and Goldfield News for a Greater Nevada)*. It bore yesterday's date, and told him about the dedication of the local brothel museum, primly giving no address; the Tonopah Parrots had won another game and were sure bets for the local softball championship; the June bunco held in the community center was a great success; the local Catholic church had bingo scare cards available for next Friday; and above the fold, a nineteen-year-old boy had disappeared in a mine shaft the day before. Search-and-rescue efforts were proceeding.

June bunco? Scare cards?

He found himself searching the newspaper for something about kilotons. He understood about kilotons; scare cards were alien artifacts. He hoped it was a typo.

" 'Nother drink?" the bartender asked. She had to say it twice before he looked up. Her voice was raspy from cigarettes or allergies and hard to hear.

"Huh? Sure. Another Diet Pepsi. Say, what *was* that a couple minutes ago?"

"Scared you, did it?" She grinned. "They set themselves off another nu-klur bomb down to the Test Site. Usually don't on Sunday, but they postponed this one six times because the wind wasn't right and I guess they just got fed up waiting.

"Feels like an earthquake, don't it? We had one of them not too long ago. Damn near tore my trailer in half." She grinned at his expression. "Tourist, are you? Goin' up to Scotty's Castle? Bet they felt that one clear up there." She paused in the act of wiping down the chipped plastic-finish table, cocked her head like a robin zeroing in on a worm. "You know about the Test Site, doncha?"

"Uh, yeah. Yes, of course. That's where—that's where they do the underground nuclear testing, isn't it? I guess I never thought I'd ever feel a bomb go off. A big one." His mouth felt parched suddenly. A nuclear bomb?

"Yep," she chuckled. "Those Greenpeacers, they keep trying to stop'em, but they just go and go and go. You visiting fam'ly here?" She was abruptly curious again.

"Uh, no. I'm a writer."

"A writer! Well, whaddaya know about that. You write books?"

David shook his head, unwilling suddenly to talk about it. Books? No. Not lately. Not for a long time.

The woman left him alone then, and he paid for his drink and stood up, stretching mightily as he took another look around the room. Plastic and chrome chairs as one might find in a cheap kitchen set. Row upon row of baseball caps nailed to the walls, hundreds of them, each with an insignia, too many to read. In the corner, the inevitable slot machines, and one dried-up old man steadily feeding in nickels, pulling the lever, pushing in more nickels automatically, as if he were as much a machine as the one he played. Wide-plank wooden floors, dusty and sagging, in contrast to the polished bar. Booths covered in splitting green plastic, tufts of yellow sponge erupting out of it.

He took a deep breath and went out the door, telling himself that this was Nevada, and it wasn't all Las Vegas. The early June heat and the glare of the sun off the white-yellow desert had him gasping in four steps. He dived into the Nissan, more grateful than he had ever been for tinted windows and air-conditioning.

The map provided by the rental car agency was still fresh and crisp. There weren't that many highways in the state; take 95 north to Tonopah, then go east, north—follow the only roads there were, endless straight stretches of two-lane highway interrupted by nothing, no houses, no trees, no color. Sometimes a truck would flash by, going in the opposite direction, carrying cattle or refrigerated food or timber (and where did they get the timber? he wondered. Not from the Joshua trees). Or a car would pass him, going at least ninety, blithely ignoring the speed limits set for lesser mortals, the natives gambling that the State Highway Patrol was somewhere else this day. They must be, he thought. They certainly weren't anywhere he could see them.

He had highlighted the road to Nintucca. It didn't look that far on the map, but he had learned already that the distances were deceptive. If he had driven this long back in New York, he'd be in Maryland by now. Large sections of the state were shaded gray, completely blank except for natural landmarks (Shoshone Peak, el. 7058 ft). The gray sections, the legend told him, belonged to the United States Government. And if they had set off a nuclear bomb at the Nevada Test Site that morning, he'd been driving right by it for the last hour and a half. No wonder it was so damn hot.

The map listed towns along the route with populations of 0–250, and a sprinkling of brothels that looked, as he passed them, absolutely nothing like what he thought a brothel ought to look like. He'd imagined glitz. He saw cinderblock buildings, trailers, truck turnarounds; maybe the glitz was all inside.

The road glared and shimmered before him.

He stopped again in Tonopah, having swept through Goldfield (*News for a Greater Nevada*) in less than a minute and a half, getting another Diet Pepsi. He wanted a Scotch, or at least a beer. Something wet, that was all. Just something wet, and maybe cool. Just a beer to take his mind off—

No you don't, he told himself, and told himself that it was easier this time.

He got back in the car and kept on driving. The road unrolled beneath him, east then north and on and on, and the sun climbed and dropped back toward the horizon. The land was broken now, ripped and twisted and crumbling, hills rearing up before him and falling behind, all the same shade of brown and blue and yellow.

# 2

"Bet the little brat fell in," the short man said. He kept one hand casually on the thick worn rope as he moved down the ladder.

The ladder was bolted against the side of a shaft about four feet square. Walls of rock, nearly perpendicular, leaned in above the men. The nearest daylight was more than a hundred feet up.

The other man, above him on the ladder, did not respond.

They came to a five-foot-wide, uneven ledge rimming the hole into which the ladder plunged. The short man stepped onto the ledge and strode forward, the light from the miner's lamp on his hard hat lancing through the dark.

"Those pussies would never come down this far," he said, peering up the shaft. The light faded out some long distance up. "Too far down." He set up a battery lantern, and a globe of bright white illuminated a cave perhaps thirty feet across into which the ledge opened. The second man stood back, deferential.

"Yeah," he added to himself, his voice rich with satisfaction. A pause. "Hey, Roy, come look at this!" He examined an outcropping of stone, rubbing at it. "Let's set it here."

"Harry, that's awful damn close to the shaft." The second man came up beside Harry. Roy was several inches taller, but he hunched his shoulders standing next to the other.

"Come on, damn you." Harry snapped his fingers hard, twice. He didn't bother to look around. "Set it here, I said. Break off this stuff."

Roy took a small drill out of his backpack and looked over the part of the tunnel wall Harry indicated, studying the veins of white and gray twisting through the dark foundation rock. After a moment he whistled. "Shee-it, Harry. You're sure right. This is a good'un."

"This is what I need to show those assholes come Friday. I can take a sample down to Tonopah, get it assayed, have the report all ready to set down on the table. It'll *prove* it's worth it. Come on, blow it!"

Roy slid him a glance, shrugged, applied the drill. The noise was painfully shrill in the enclosed area, and sound vibration showered dirt from the tunnel roof above them. After a few moments he withdrew it, blew the dust away from the hole.

"That's not enough."

"Christ Almighty, Harry, you trying to blow us both to kingdom come? We haven't surveyed this tunnel yet. We don't know where the stress lines are. We'd be better off taking it out with a pick—"

"God damn you, do as you're told. You're my foreman, you take my orders."

The other man jerked as if hit with a lash, but he didn't look around. He applied the drill again, hesitated. And then, reluctantly, withdrew. Harry hovered as Roy tamped powder, set up fuses.

"Over there." Roy waved at an old ore cart some distance the other side of the shaft. "Behind the cart." His voice assumed a thread of authority.

Harry turned, the light from his helmet intersecting that from Roy's, until both touched the cart. "All right." He started over, stopped again to wait for Roy to reel out fuse. He was swearing under his breath by the time Roy had set the fuse to his satisfaction and joined him, crouching behind the rusty equipment.

The blast reverberated through the earth and air like a hammerblow. Both men gasped and choked at the smell of brimstone, the dust and smoke; but Harry was out from behind the cart again before the dust and noise had cleared away, scrabbling for pieces of rock, dropping the ones too hot and picking them up again, bouncing them in the palm of his hand until they were cool enough to handle.

"Oh, man, oh, man, oh, man." He rubbed the rocks against the leg of his jeans, spat on them, rubbed again. A glitter of specks shone against a dull gray stripe.

"Silver," he said reverently. "And gold." He spun around, looked back at the gaping hole in the ledge. "Silver! Silver, dammit! Mine!"

His roar of triumph echoed in the cavern, up and down the mine shafts.

Far away, a rumble answered.

# 3

It was dusk, and nearly nine o'clock, when David Esher arrived in Nintucca. If he hadn't seen the sign just before he came around the curve, he probably would have kept on going, dismissing it as his destination, wondering what it might have been. He had an image of Nintucca that hadn't been shaken by the long empty roads and tiny clusters of towns; he expected streetlights, neon lights, a business district. But he saw the sign, reflective white letters on a standard highway green background, and slowed down.

What struck him first was the darkness. Dark corrals, dark sheds. Dark houses. No yard lights. No streetlights. No people. He slowed the car down to a crawl, looking for the people. The sound of his tires whispered loud against the pavement.

The sign for the Rowdytown Hotel and Casino swung from an improbable pair of cattle horns at least ten feet from tip to tip. The building itself was built into the side of a hill, its solitary lights glittering over the nearby abandoned-looking brick and stone buildings, sounds of live country music squalling from between swinging saloon doors and bouncing off the deliberately old-timey wooden sidewalk. A rib-high hitching rail, built of the same silvery gray wood as the walls of the hotel, separated the sidewalk from the dirt parking lot. A few tiny shops, equally antique, shared the walkway; what looked like a grocery store, dark at this hour, anchored the other end of the block.

He parked the car, got out, and stretched mightily, working nine solid hours of driving kinks out of his shoulders and breathing deep. A second later he sneezed even more mightily, the dry, dusty air shriveling the inside of his nostrils.

Two men perched on the hitching rail looked over at him, their expressions invisible in the gathering darkness.

One of'em's gonna spit any second now—he grinned to himself—and then they'll say, "Howdy stranger, new in town?"

He walked back to the truck of the little Nissan, still chuckling to himself at the overpoweringly Old West flavor of the place—Texas itself would be proud of those horns—when he heard an odd clopping sound. Pulling out his bags, he hitched the case for the laptop onto his shoulder and looked around.

"Oh, come *on*!" he burst out. The men sitting on the hitching rail were deep in conversation with a third man, who sat comfortably on the back of a horse.

The three men looked over at him. "Kin we he'p you?" one said politely.

"Ah—" David stepped up onto the sidewalk. It was a real horse, white with a black mane and tail, lazily twitching an ear in his direction. The man on his back looked like he might be in his early twenties—still a kid in Esher's eyes, making him feel ancient even as he formed the thought. He was dressed in boots, jeans, and a Grateful Dead T-shirt. He was incredibly skinny. One long leg was hooked casually across the horse's neck, in front of the horn of a battered, weatherbeaten saddle.

If this is the local color, somebody's bought this town some different kind of palette, he thought. I hope I can make Steve believe this. "Ah, this is the Rowdytown Hotel?"

"Yes sir, it is. Only one in town." The young man was curious, not sarcastic, with a surprisingly deep voice for such a skinny frame.

"You just come in from Reno?" one of the others asked.

"Nope, drove up from Vegas." It was remarkably easy to fall into that laconic drawl, not Texan, not quite like anywhere else in the West. "I'm here to write some articles about the mine opening up again."

The three men looked at each other significantly. "You workin' for Mistah Kostner?"

Innocent curiosity was gone, replaced by something else too ephemeral to identify. David balanced the computer on an end post of the rail and chose his words carefully. "I'm free-lance. I'm not working for anybody, except the magazine that wants to buy the story. They think it's pretty interesting. They've got some mines in Ohio and Pennsylvania that might be opening up too."

"They got silver back East?" Doubt was palpable in the young man's voice.

"Not silver, coal. But I'm more interested in how the town feels about it. I'll be talking to people, seeing what they think about things. See if I can find—"

"Old-timers" might not be the word to use here, he thought suddenly, and shifted gears. "Do you know anybody who was around when the mine was open before?"

The three men glanced at each other. "Not too many," one of them said, and the two on foot hopped off the rail and stalked away without another word.

The man on the horse stared after them a moment. "You sure you're not here about the little girl?" he asked.

"What little girl?" David was honestly bewildered. He'd had lots of interviews end abruptly, but not as abruptly as this. It didn't bode well for his stories. And now, "the little girl"?

"Had a little girl come missing the other day. We've all been out looking for her. You sure you don't know anything about that?"

"First I've heard of it," David assured him. "I hope you find her okay." Maybe a sidebar, he thought. How a Western community comes together to protect one of its own. But I'm not here to do true crime. "I read about a boy falling into a mine shaft."

"Ah, that's down in Tonopah." The man's expression said that just about anything could be expected from those folks in Tonopah. "We heard Kostner hired some writer from back East."

Kostner. Not "Mistah Kostner."

"He talked to my editor, sure. But I don't work for him. Why? Does it make a difference?"

The rider grinned and slid off. The horse snorted but did not otherwise react. "Up to lately, most everybody round here worked for Kostner. He liked that a lot." The boy reached down to pick up David's bag. "My name's Rick Zimmermann."

"David Esher." He glanced back at the horse, then at Rick, who was waiting for him by the saloon-style doors. "Uh, will he stay there okay?"

Rick looked at the horse and laughed. "Hell, yes, she's dog meat if she don't. C'mon. Settle you in and you can tell me what it's like writing for magazines."

Rich showed him into the hotel lobby, a long hall with trophy cases lining one side and the doors to the inevitable casino on the other. He was getting used to the ubiquitous sound of coins crashing into the metal bowls and slot reels whirring, croupiers calling roulette, and the occasional shriek as someone hit a big one; after a while one could block it all out, like low-level static or white noise. The music from the far end would take a little more concentration to ignore. He stopped to examine the contents of the cases.

Rusty teakettles, carefully labeled by hand, a word misspelled here and there; pickaxes, still wickedly sharp. Photographs of the old Heartbreak and Silver Badger mines. Main Street, back when Nintucca was one of the largest cities in the state of Nevada, with a population of nearly ten thousand. Mule harness. A big chunk of white rock, oddly grooved in long parallel lines, with a narrow dirty gray streak running through it—ore from the mine, the label said.

"You really interested in all that old stuff?" Rick said at his elbow.

"Sure. Look at those old guys in the picture. Imagine what it was like for them back in those days. I wonder how many of them got rich."

"Only one." Rick nodded toward the registration desk, tucked away in an anteroom.

"Which one was that?" David gave up and followed, grateful to lower the computer to the floor beside the bag Rick had dumped. The clerk, a teenager in flannel shirt and jeans, smiled prettily at him, snapped her bubble gum, and gave him a form to fill out. Rick grinned at her, and she turned her nose up in the air with an audible sniff and marched over to the key board, making a great deal of fuss over finding a room key.

"Only one rich man in this town," Rick said a little too loudly, still grinning. "Harry Kostner. And he's gonna get even richer if he can get that mine opened again."

Overhearing him, the desk clerk slapped a key down in front of David and glared at Rick. "You're just jealous, Rick Zimmermann. You'd just like to have as much money as my daddy. You and those dumb friends of yours in the bar."

Rick shook his head. He was deliberately exaggerating his drawl to irritate the girl, David saw. "Now Sherry, honey, I got a job that does me just fine. Don't you go getting mad at me just because I won't work for your daddy."

"You're just scared. You'd rather sit around guarding that dumb government man than get your hands dirty."

Rick leaned across the desk and made a face at her. "Don't want to get caught by those *monsters,* honey!"

Sherry snorted in an unladylike fashion and said to David, "It's room 712, towards the back so you won't be hearin' the band. Hope you enjoy your stay, Mr.—" she skimmed the registration card—"Esher. The stairs are just inside the casino there."

"Thank you." He heaved the computer to his shoulder again and balanced himself with the suitcase. "Tell you what," he went on to Rick, "why don't you join your friends and I'll be down in a couple minutes."

"Sure thing. What're you drinking?"

Bars in Nevada were open on Sunday. Everything in Nevada was open on Sunday. He wasn't going to get a day off from temptation this trip.

His smile was only a little forced. "Ginger ale is fine for me."

Rick shrugged and vanished through the doors. Sherry spoke up once more. "Don't you pay no mind to Rick, Mr. Esher. He tells stories."

"That's all right," David said. "So do I."

# Two

## 1

The pickup pulled up in the driveway of the frame house and sputtered to a stop in the rapidly increasing darkness. Roy Evans got out and looked around him, searching; the curtains were drawn in the next house down the hill, and nothing stirred in the night except the mongrel hound that came up to greet him, tail whipping lazily. "Hush there, old son," he muttered unnecessarily. The dog snuffled at his hands and went back to the blanket on the porch to sleep.

Evans reached back into the car and pulled out a burlap sack filled with heavy, irregularly shaped objects. The wind sprang up behind the truck, and for a moment he thought he heard the dog on the porch growl; he stood clutching the sack to his chest, sweating, trying to penetrate the darkness. The contents of the sack grated together like broken bones.

He could hide the sack in the shed. Or he could just leave it in the truck, behind the seat, and take it on in to Reno. He had a friend there who would assay it out, pay him quietly. And Harry would never know. Nobody would know.

Especially Harry, who'd left him behind at the mine, staring at a fortune in ore scattered on the ground.

Another rumble from the porch, and he spun around. "Who's out there?"

The wind whistled, and from the darkness, down the road or perhaps echoing off the opposite hill, came an answering *rumble*. The dog yelped.

"Hey! You!" His voice quavered and cracked. The curtains in the house next door twitched.

He panicked. They would see him with the sack—

He opened the car door again, and was in the act of tossing it onto the passenger seat when the hound leaped up underneath his arm. He cursed and reached for the dog's collar, and the animal spun and snapped, fighting its way into the vehicle.

The curtain next door opened, and a face appeared in the window.

Careless of his arm, he hauled the frenzied animal out and threw it across the yard with more strength than he knew he possessed. He could hear its body hitting the shed, the *yawp* as air was forced out of its lungs by the impact; but by that time he was in the truck and the motor was started, and he skidded out of the driveway again.

Behind him he could hear a shifting, and a rumbling, and a dog's despairing howl.

# 2

The old man stood on the crest of the hill, silhouetted by the rising half-moon, his arms raised, singing in a cracked, quavering voice a song whose words, in a language long dead, were seized and swallowed by the night.

Before him the land unrolled to the invisible horizon, pale gray stippled with sagebrush, wide stretches of salt flats gleaming white, the shadows of hills both man-made and natural a solid black. Above him, the stars were washed out around the moon, regaining their brightness again halfway across the sky. A whisper of wind shook the branches of a lone Joshua tree, rippled in the patches of thin salt grass.

The old man sang. The hoarse voice rose and fell, warning, pleading. The wind died away, leaving the song the only sound. The desert held its breath and listened. The moon cleared the horizon. Climbed a quarter of the way up the sky.

The voice wavered to a halt. He lowered his arms, waiting; the desert waited with him, as if curious to see what would happen.

His mouth worked, trying to bring up saliva against the dryness. After some effort he shrugged, pulled a flat bottle out of a pocket in the faded vest, twisted off the top, and took a drink. Putting the bottle away, he looked around as if indignant.

"Spirit of Earth!" It was an old man's yell, but there was still power in his lungs. "Spirit! You there? You awake? You wake up now!"

No response; unless the whisper of wind was a response. Evidently the old man thought so; he wheeled to face into the gust of wind, ignoring the pat of dust against his face. He spoke as if to a living presence: "Spirit? I know you there. I feel you there. We all feel you. Wind, Coyote, Antelope, Tree, Stone, Badger . . ."

The wind died away. In its place a presence, a sensation of sharing space with another, a vast other who was invisible, providing no obstruction to the view of sand and scrub and sky. It waited, as if listening. The old man smiled, and his voice became stronger.

"I sing for you, Spirit. I sing you calm, I sing you quiet. Man comes for you, comes into your den . . ."

No response from the presence, no sound no acknowledgment. Nothing.

"You leave us alone, Spirit."

Then, finally, something. A sensation, that was all—not even so strong as a feeling—of release, relaxation. A half mile down the hill, shadows moved, formed themselves into a band of wild horses; the coughing bark of a coyote signaling its mate. A lifting as if of a great weight, relief from a burden whose weight has not been fully realized until it is set aside, or removes itself. The presence was gone.

And the old man was angry. "Spirit! You come back! You listen!" And when nothing happened: "Hear me! You are the Beast and you must obey!"

But there was nothing out there to obey him, and after a time he admitted it, and stumbled down the side of the hill to an old pickup truck, where he curled up in the front seat and drank from his bottle and muttered to himself for the rest of the night.

# 3.

Esher had a choice: a rickety-looking elevator in front of which an older couple stood, looking as if they'd been there ten minutes too long already, and the stairs. He took the stairs.

To reach them, he had to enter the Rowdytown Casino and edge past a bank of slot machines. An older, not unattractive woman wearing a dark blue pantsuit sitting at the end caught his eye, and he watched her as he went up the stairs; she was sitting hunched over, staring at the video poker screen, one hand holding a smouldering cigarette and the other hitting the buttons in front of her, *snap, snap, snap,* and another five quarters into the slot, barely waiting to see if the previous hand had won. She wore her dark sable hair in a huge beehive out of the Sixties, and her eyes were outlined in heavy black kohl. He wondered, as he turned the corner and she disappeared from sight, if she'd been sitting there for the past twenty years, throwing quarters into the slot machine, ignoring the passing of time, staring at the screen and willing a jackpot to appear.

The "second floor" was a series of risers, each four steps high; a stretch of hallway with two doors on either side; then four more steps up to the next stretch of rooms. He counted seven landings before him to the end of the hall. The motel was built against the side of the hill, he remembered. Perhaps built into the hill itself. His room was almost at the end, away from the sound of the casino and the country and western band in the bar.

The bar. He thought about going down to the bar, ordering a drink, tasting it, feeling it slide down so smooth—*No.*

Fumbling for his key, he swung open the dull beige door to his room, slapping on a wall switch. A lamp on the bureau came on, and he set the computer and his suitcase beside it with a sigh of relief, feeling as if he was unburdening himself of the entire long aching trip, starting in Cleveland early in the morning and ending now, finally, at last. He was so tired he wasn't even hungry; more than anything, almost, he wanted to collapse and sleep.

Except, of course, that he'd promised to meet Rick in the bar. The damned bar. He hadn't set foot in a bar in thirteen months. Other than that place in Beatty this morning, and that was really more a restaurant. It hadn't been hard to think of it as a restaurant, and ignore the bottles.

It was a problem that had to be dealt with sometime. It might as well be now. At least, he thought he could deal with it. He'd already told Rick what he would be drinking.

The room was dark. There were two king-size beds, each flanked by two reading lamps, but no overhead lights. He surveyed the room as he hung up his suit coat, thinking that he wouldn't be putting it back on until he left Nintucca. The walls were too dark a shade of beige. The drapes were a heavy, artificial material, dark maroon to match the bedspreads. Not exactly a Holiday Inn.

Pushing the drapes back, he found himself looking out the window to the main highway, across the narrow parking lot. Rick's gray horse was hitched at the far end of the hotel, apparently half asleep, one hind leg cocked up under itself. A semi pulled in behind it, the roar of the diesels not disturbing the horse's nap at all, and parked over by the gas pumps. Across the road the outline of a hill was barely visible against the night.

It was so—empty. And yet there was a feeling of life out there, wrapped up in the darkness. A shiver crept up his spine.

Shaking it aside, he unpacked, putting clothes away in the bureau, setting up the computer and modem. He would be writing his articles here and transmitting them directly, so that if Steve wanted changes he could oblige on the scene. The beds, he noted with amusement, felt like cardboard boxes instead of mattresses. He thought about bouncing, but that would probably break them. The pillows deflated at a touch. He wondered what Steve would think about an article about roughing it in a central Nevada tourist haven, and decided his editor wouldn't believe him anyway. But he'd have to get some of this in. Local color: drab.

He changed his shirt and tie for a pullover and washed his face, and came out of the tiny bathroom to look around again, making sure everything was done.

Procrastinating, he corrected himself. There was nothing left to do here. His tape recorder was up and running, transferred from his suit pocket to his pants pocket. There was nothing else to do but go.

Down into the bar.

He licked his lips, thirsty suddenly, and shook his head. The hell with it. He'd order a ginger ale, and if the locals didn't like it, the hell with them. He wouldn't drink.

He would *not* drink.

The woman with the beehive hairdo was still hunched over her machine as he passed her going into the casino. He glanced down at the plastic bucket she propped in her lap as he went by; it held a few dollars' worth of loose quarters and six or seven rolls of wrapped coins. Clearly she was settled in for a long evening. It was a small casino, with only one wheel and two craps tables surrounded by the ubiquitous slot machines against the walls and in four rows down the middle. Off in one corner, separated from the rest by a dusty gold-colored rope, four poker tables were huddled for the serious players. The change cage was built into one wall next to the doorway to the restaurant. No mirrored ceilings. No fancy fixtures. No threat to Steve Wynn.

The bar was off to one side of the casino area, opposite the hotel restaurant. Esher stepped down, spotting Rick almost immediately on the side farthest from the band, sitting at a table with his arm around a girl and talking animatedly to two other men. Waving Esher over, he slid against the girl, who gave him a glare but didn't appear too unhappy at the greater proximity.

"Hey, man, what you drinkin'?" the lean youth said hospitably, apparently unaware he was repeating himself. "Lees will be back here in just a minute. Marianne, this is Dave Esher. That's Gil and Mikey. Sit on down."

Esher took the indicated space and smiled at Marianne. She looked about twenty-two, with blonde hair and serious gray eyes, wearing jeans and a plaid blouse. Even seated at the table he could tell she had a figure that explained why Rick's arm tightened casually around her shoulders. With an effort, he pulled his attention away before it became offensive and acknowledged the greetings of the others.

Gil and Mikey looked a few years older than Rick. They too were dressed in jeans and knit shirts and wore scuffed and weathered cowboy boots. They had evidently been there a while, judging from the litter of beer bottles and cigarette butts mashed into foil ashtrays, but no one appeared drunk.

"They just got in from looking for that little girl," Rick went on. The band obscured his next words, but with that final blare went on break. Esher breathed a sigh of relief. At least from this distance he could hear himself think over the sounds from the casino.

"That little girl? Did you find out what happened?" He looked up to find a waitress at his elbow placing a napkin in front of him.

"Getcha a beer?" she said. She had good legs; her brief black uniform, while positively chaste by Vegas standards, showed enough for that. Her name tag read "Lisa."

Just one? he thought, breathing deep the rich malt smell of the drinks before the others. One?

"No thanks," he said. "Ginger ale, please."

"Ah, c'mon, have a drink," Mikey invited.

Esher shook his head firmly. "Thanks, but no. Can't handle the stuff. I'll stick to ginger ale." He was aware of Gil's eyes on him, sharp with interest, but went on, "What about this little girl?" He told himself firmly, *You're doing the right thing. Stick with it.*

"Disappeared two nights ago. We've all been out looking. Mom thinks she might have fallen down a sinkhole." This was Marianne, who picked up her mug, took a long swallow, and set it down again on the other side of her, some two feet away from him, shifting temptation that much farther out of reach. She didn't look at him as she did so; it might have been an accident instead of a courtesy. He wasn't sure if he was disappointed or not.

"Mom's the sheriff," Rick remarked, filling in. "Thing is, she took her bike, and we can't find that either."

"How old was she?"

"Just eight," Mikey said. Mikey was a bear of a man with longish dark brown hair, heavy sideburns, a full moustache, and a wide, friendly smile that faded out as he talked about the missing child.

Esher winced in sympathy. Eight. He remembered a child, eight years old, holding up her arms to him and laughing. And he firmly quashed the memory. He would not let the past get to him. "They don't have any signs at all?"

"Nope. We'll find her, though. She can't just have evaporated." The big man's smile came back and he took a deep draft of beer, licking white foam off his moustache.

Mikey was an optimist, Esher thought. He shook his head, sipping at his ginger ale, as much at the cheerful naïveté as at the idea of the girl gone missing. In a town like this one, he supposed, with so few people, it must be quite a shock to have a child disappear. Little places like this were supposed to be safe for kids.

He asked about the search parties, and where they'd looked, what they thought might have happened. Mikey was full of theories. Gil was silent, listening. Rick and Marianne put in a comment or two, mostly bringing Mikey back into the realm of the probable.

"What do the little girl's parents do?"

The four young people glanced at each other. "Kostner's tame geologists," Rick said finally, an edge of distaste in his tone. "New in town."

"Does everybody around here work for Kostner?"

Gil snickered, the first contribution to the conversation he'd made. "Practically."

"Do you?" Esher challenged. The other man smiled thinly, shaking his head. Gil was a dark and muscular man, Indian or Hispanic, with flat brown eyes that had assessed Esher, identified him, and filed him away before he'd even sat down. He reminded Esher of a big-city cop, looking out of place in this small-town bar, and Esher wondered what his story was. He'd find that out too before he left Nintucca, he decided.

"Gil and Mikey, they work for the government," Marianne said. "And Rick. Out at the site. Security."

"The site? You don't mean the Nevada Test Site, do you? What's this one all about?"

The three men looked at one another. "Well, you know how it is," Mikey said at last. "Nevada's mostly government land.

The Test Site down south, Navy, Air force, BLM. Whole damn state's a 'government-owned and -operated facility.'" He quoted the phrase with relish and great familiarity. "We call ours 'White's Site,' or just the site. They do drilling and— stuff."

"So there's testing going on near here, too? Bombs and stuff?" This had nothing to do with mining, but David found it interesting nonetheless, especially considering his experience in Beatty. Maybe he didn't want to spend a full week here after all, if there were going to be exploding nuclear bombs next door.

Rick laughed. "Hell, no. Nothin' so fancy. They're just drilling holes in the ground, that's all. They've been losing some equipment, so they hired a bunch of us to keep an eye on things. No big deal. But it's better than working for Kostner."

The crisp bubbles of the ginger ale snapped against the inside of his mouth as Esher sipped and thought about that. Rick seemed adamant that he wouldn't work for Kostner— actively disliked the man. He wondered if Mikey and Gil felt the same way. He wondered too about the site, and what impact it had on Nintucca's economy. Obviously it was providing jobs, and jobs never hurt.

"What else do people do around here? They work out at this drilling site of yours—how many people does that employ?"

The three men exchanged glances again, uneasy. "Twenty or thirty, maybe," Rick admitted at last. "Mostly people work at the mine offices. Some businesses around here to support the ranches, but not too many."

"Where *are* the ranches, anyway? I didn't see any fences."

Marianne giggled, sliding him a sideways glance. "Aren't any."

The band came back and swung into a spirited semi-rock version of "Ruby."

Esher arched an eyebrow, trying to decide whether the girl was teasing him or trying to get a rise out of Rick, or both. He had to raise his voice to be heard over the music. "Right, they let the cattle just run out in the road."

The men burst out laughing. "He thinks they *don't!*" Mikey snorted. "Listen, I lost a damn fine truck last Christmas making hamburger out of some steer. This ain't back East, with neat li'l fences and stuff. Nobody's gonna spend the money to fence off the damn road." Mikey finished his beer in one massive swallow, leaving a wisp of foam on his moustache. "You're never gonna understand this place if you keep thinking like somebody from back East."

Ouch, Esher thought. I'll take that as a friendly warning, I guess. "You were born in Nevada, then?"

"Born and raised in Nintucca," the big man said proudly. "M'daddy worked in the mine office after they shut things down. M'granddaddy used to have his own mine, but he sold it out and then died in the big disaster. Now we run a couple hundred head out east of town. Somebody's gonna have to feed the mines when they open up again."

"So you grew up with the mines, but they were all shut down. Ever seen them up close?"

More laughter, not abrasive but forgiving. Clearly green-horns couldn't be expected to be too smart. "Hell—sorry, Marianne—heck yes, we played in'em all the time. Once a bunch of us took lamps and went from one end of town to the other under the ground. Caught holy you-know-what from our daddies for it, too. But you know kids, never have any sense. They blocked up nearly all the tunnels after that."

"And that kept everybody out, sure enough," Rick said drolly.

Marianne chuckled, a soft, pleasant sound. "We've all been exploring, one time or another."

Esher smiled, imagining a smaller version of the big man standing hangdog before an outraged parent. He liked these people, he decided. They were good folks. "How much difference will it make to have the mine open?"

"Everything," Mikey said, slapping his hand down on the table. "Kostner opens up the mine, brings people in, we'll have a bigger tax base, get more state funding for the schools. We'll have stores again. There'll be money in town. My wife, she runs a gift shop, but hell, nobody has any money to buy but Kostner and his pet geologists. She wants to expand, get some more tourist trade. People heading up to Winnemucca."

"The only people going through here to Winnemucca got lost on the road," Rick said. Mikey grinned as if he'd heard the line before, reached across to swipe at Rick, who ducked almost into Marianne's lap.

"You get a lot of tourists otherwise?" He looked around the bar as he asked, noting the uncomfortable couple sitting at a table next to the bandstand, nursing a couple of beers. They looked as if they knew they stood out but couldn't figure out why their disguises weren't working. The man, puffy and balding, wore a new straw cowboy hat with a fan of feathers; his wife, a hennaed redhead, was bedecked with turquoise and silver jewelry that spoke of a recent trip through Santa Fe, New Mexico.

Others in the bar were obviously locals, addressing the tolerant Lisa with uproarious familiarity; but an anachronistic hippie-looking pair, obvious newcomers, clad in denim vests and flowered shirts, were sitting at a booth not far away, sneaking glances up at the iron plows, spurs and wicked-looking bits, branding irons, blacksmith's hammers, miner's hats, picks, kettles, and other Old West memorabilia hanging from walls and ceiling. They looked as if they wondered how they'd landed in the middle of the Old West when they were trying to set their time machine for Woodstock.

The band began a quieter song, something Willie Nelson had made famous, David thought, but couldn't recall the name.

"Oh, there's always some. We get people left over from Jim Butler Days in Tonopah, and there's always a few strangers in town to talk to Dr. White." Rick's Adam's apple moved up and down as he drained his mug. "Lees! More here!"

"Who's Dr. White?"

"He's the drilling site Project Manager, the guy in charge," Gil said quietly. "He runs the show out there."

"Dr. White lives in town?" Maybe he could interview him too.

"Nah, they set up their own little town out there. Trailers and stuff. They only come into town to get supplies once a month or so. They don't like to mix with us common types."

"They just pay us." There was an implied rebuke in Gil's tone. Rick shrugged. Esher found his attitude interesting, and filed it away for further contemplation. Rick didn't like Kostner; he didn't have a lot of respect for the scientists at the site; but he respected Gil. Perhaps Gil was Rick's boss, though neither man acted like it.

"Would *you* work in the mine if it opened again?" Esher asked Gil.

The quiet man turned his mug in a steady circle, studying the wet ring it made. "Nope," he said quietly. "Won't go under the ground."

Hmmmm, he thought. Gil was very definite. He wondered why. Perhaps he just didn't like the idea of working with a pick and shovel. But the man's hands were scarred and callused, had obviously seen hard use.

"Are you from Nintucca too?"

Gil shook his head. "Pennsylvania," he said, to Esher's surprise. He was certain, based on accent as much as anything else, that the man was a Westerner. He had an Indian or Hispanic look about him. Gil didn't seem disposed to elaborate further.

"And I'm from Wisconsin," Rick added. "Marianne's from Vegas, though, so she's practically a native."

Mikey seemed to object to that idea, leading to a great dispute about the merits or lack of them of the state's largest population center. Gil and Esher both listened, amused. After a while Gil got up, stretched, and threw a five-dollar bill on the table.

"Got the early shift tomorrow," he said, and stalked away.

Esher watched him go, wondering again about the decisiveness of his remark about working underground. "What about you, Rick? Would you go to work in the mines if they opened up again?"

The young man laughed, a deep, relaxed laugh. "My daddy was a badger man in Wisconsin, and he made me promise I'd never work in a mine. Besides, I don't want to work for good ol' Harry. I do okay out at the site."

"Badger man?"

"That's what we call miners up there. 'Cause they dig like badgers in the dirt. It's not for me." A few couples were dancing now, and Rick glanced at his girlfriend. She shook her head and leaned back against the bench, watching Esher.

"I'd rather he worked out at the site too," she said unexpectedly.

The site.

"Any possibility I could go look at that site? It isn't secret or anything, is it?"

Rick sobered at once and traded an uneasy glance with Mikey. "Nope, it isn't. But Dr. White, he runs the place, he doesn't like people poking around. Don't think you better try."

"You could show him around some of the old mines, though," Marianne suggested. "You know, like where that old car is, and stuff?"

David thought it over, took another sip of ginger ale. That could be another slant for the article. He could get pictures, "Mining Then and Now in Nevada." "Yeah, I'd like to see some of the old mines. That sounds pretty interesting. Can I get a map out there? Where are they?"

"All over the place. There's lots of little mines. Kostner family owns the rights to them now. Guys used to come out and stake claims and dig out their own mines, and then they all lost them," Mikey said. The big mild man sounded a little bitter. "Kostner won't like you poking around there either, Dave."

It was enough to challenge Rick, who sat up, dislodging Marianne, who shot him a fond but exasperated look which he missed completely. "Hey, yeah. I could take you out there tomorrow. Show you the way they used to do stuff before they put in the big mine. Maybe run some horses. I need to get out there anyway, see if I can find that herd of antelope. Wanna come?"

Esher hesitated. "Yeah, I'd like to do that. I could use a guide around here—I don't imagine the roads are that great?" Laughter greeted this suggestion. "In fact, I could pay you something too. You'd be a research assistant. The money won't be much, five bucks an hour, but you'll be mentioned in the article—"

"Ah, hell, I'd do it for the fun of it," Rick started. Marianne elbowed him. He shot her a guilty glance. "On the other hand, the cash would be pretty handy, but I could only do it in my spare time."

"Hey, that's great. I don't know about tomorrow, though. I've got some appointments, need to get some background stuff. How about Tuesday—would that be okay?"

"You're down for a search party," Marianne reminded her boyfriend before he could answer.

"I could go tomorrow instead, couldn't I? I'll trade off with somebody. They'll have found Tessy by day after tomorrow anyway."

"Mr. Kostner isn't going to like it, you going around those old places . . . " Mikey said, anxiety knitting his sandy eyebrows.

Esher snorted. "I'm here to write articles, not to answer to him. Besides, it's research. He can't object to that."

"Yeah," Rick agreed. "It's research."

"It's a deal," Esher said, getting to his feet and trying not to yawn. "Look, I'm sorry to break this up, but I've still got jet lag. I'll see you Tuesday, okay?"

Rick nodded, eyes dancing. The band picked up the strains of "Brother Love's Traveling Salvation Show," playing with more enthusiasm than accuracy. Esher had to raise his voice again.

"And I hope you find the little girl," he told Marianne. She smiled and held out her hand in an unconsciously royal gesture. He took it with pleasure.

He left the bar with a great deal of satisfaction and hardly any thirst at all. This assignment would be interesting. He could do it. He could succeed.

For the first time in years, David Esher was feeling confident about something.

# 4

"Kostner's got a writer man in town," the woman's voice on the telephone said. A burst of static followed the words. "I saw him in the bar with some of the guys from the drill site."

"A writer? What the hell does Harry want a writer for?"

"I don't know. Lisa says he's working for some magazine back in Ohio. Says they're opening up mines back there. He's going to compare them."

A silence followed this. More static crumbled along the lines. "You still there?" the woman said at last. "You hear me?"

"Yeah, I heard you, Helen." The man's voice was impatient, almost angry. "I'm thinking. I was just wondering what this guy is really here for. Maybe we should talk to him, show him a little different point of view."

"He's working for Kostner!" the caller protested. "He's just going to be interested in the mine opening up again!"

The man's answer was thoughtful. "Maybe. Maybe not. We can't miss the chance. We can use this guy. Maybe those guys will show him things at the site. Maybe we can find out from *him* what's happening. Get him to publicize it. Bring us some national attention."

"Like what?"

The man's voice shrugged. "I don't know. Something. Anything can happen, you know."

A silence as the woman considered this. "We need to tell Wanda. Anything that has to do with the mine, she should hear about it. That was our agreement, Jerry."

"Since when are we taking orders from Wanda? She's just our local contact!"

The other shivered. "I don't know. I don't know. This guy—"

"Oh, forget it." Jerry's voice dripped scorn. "Just forget the whole thing."

"Hey, you just *said* maybe we could use him!"

"And maybe we should just give up this whole project and move out!" The words snapped with frustration and anger, and fingers holding the receiver whitened. "If you're so chicken about it—"

"Can't you feel it?" There was a strain now in Helen's every word, a suggestion of fear. "I looked at the cards, and something terrible's going to happen. And it all points to a stranger, and this writer is the only one who might—"

"Oh, God, are you getting mystical on me again? Look, you promised me you'd put away the crystals on this trip!"

Silence. Then, with offended dignity, "Yeah, yeah, okay. But—did you have any luck tonight?"

"Oh, yeah, they're gonna love it. But—" A pause, as Jerry reconsidered what he had been about to say.

"What?"

"Never mind, tell you when I get in. Goodbye." Jerry replaced the handset in the box nailed to the telephone pole and listened. A wonderful thing, the desert. There was no silence like it, and the stars in the sky looked like snow fallen upside down. Around him, the decayed and abandoned buildings, assayer's office, processing building, all the others, were only shadows in the moonlight. It was so quiet. So peaceful.

But if you listened hard enough, you could hear things moving.

# MONDAY

# One

## 1

The sun was just coming up, peeking though the venetian blinds covering the windows in the sheriff's office. It wasn't hot yet, which made it a good time to come in and get some work done when the air-conditioning broke down. Which was most of the time.

Laura Bailey sighed and pushed back from her desk, picking up the photograph to study it one more time. Bailey was a stocky woman in her early forties, with broad solid shoulders, short graying curly hair, weary dark gray eyes. She wore careful, low-key makeup; her only jewelry was a small pair of gold loop earrings, and a gold band on the ring finger of her left hand.

And, she was sometimes heard to joke, the handcuffs that hung from the back of her leather belt. Laura Bailey had once been a cop in Las Vegas. After her husband, also a cop, was killed in a high-speed chase in the middle of the road to L.A., she quit and came to Nintucca, looking for a decent place to raise a kid. A few years later she ran for sheriff. She'd been unopposed ever since. Even the old-timers got used to having a female sheriff after a while.

Truth to tell, it had been pretty quiet. More drugs now than there used to be, but still not nearly what they got in the cities.

It was hard for a stranger to come into the tiny Nevada towns and set up as a dealer; there was no anonymity in a place like Nintucca.

Just as the child in the photograph was not anonymous. Laura Bailey knew Tessy Marie Kozlowski by sight, even though the family had only moved in a few months ago. One of Kostner's outsiders, Jim Kozlowski was, brought in from out of state to analyze the profitability of the mine and supervise its rebuilding. Not local folks, but nice people for all that. They'd never fit in, of course. Bailey smiled humorlessly. *She'd* been living in the same house for fifteen years, a block off the main drag, and the old-timers still called her "that new city policewoman."

But Tessy and her brother Jeremy had provided a bit of sparkle to the drab schoolyard, their pale blond heads standing out in the sea of dark-haired ones, drawing the eye at once. They were polite around adults. Gave their teachers no problems. Obeyed their parents.

And five nights ago Tessy Marie had disappeared from her own home, and no one had seen her since.

Bailey rubbed her eyes, trying to think of what else she could have done. There was no nonsense in Nintucca about waiting twenty-four hours before looking for a missing child. From the time Jim and Elga had come in, frantic but steady-voiced, and reported the girl gone, Bailey had been looking. She'd talked to all the neighbors, all the friends. She'd organized search parties for all the likely places.

Trouble was, there were too many likely places, too many holes. She didn't believe the girl had been kidnaped; that might happen all too often in Las Vegas or Reno, where there were enough people that sickos could hide themselves, but in a town of twenty-five hundred people, where the most interesting thing to do was stick your nose in your neighbor's business, it was highly unlikely. They weren't going to find Tessy's body in somebody's shed. And the only new people in town in the past few days were a few tourists, the latest environmentalists, and that reporter of Kostner's. And all had arrived after the girl had vanished.

The little girl's bicycle was gone. Bailey would bet five to two the kid had gone exploring and fallen down an old mine shaft, but that didn't explain the missing bike. She was sure that the little girl's brother Jeremy knew something about it, too; the boy had guilty knowledge written all over him, but he was afraid to tell, and the parents wouldn't let her talk to him alone.

Placing the photo back on the scuffed and battered metal desk, she riffled through the stack of reports. Volunteers had called from all over, talking about a truck that had gone through town that night, asking if she'd looked in the old Heartbreak hole, suggesting a runaway, reporting negative results of an unauthorized search of a neighbor's foaling shed.

She'd keep looking. She would never entirely stop looking for Tessy, but she was beginning to think they'd never find her. The truck looked like a lead for a little while, but then they located the drivers in Wichita Falls—a newlywed husband-and-wife team who barely remembered passing through. No reason to suspect them of anything except hauling too heavy a load too fast.

The phone rang. Standing, she picked it up and stretched, tucking the receiver under her chin as she did side bends, loosening up.

"Bailey? Kostner. Why aren't you out looking for that kid?" The voice across the phone was low, almost intimate. Bailey despised it. The first year she'd been in office she caught her own voice lowering too, and she despised that even more. As a result, she tended to shout over the phone now.

"We've got people looking, Mr. Kostner. Is there something I can do for you?" She kept her words formal and deliberate.

"You find that little girl now real soon, you hear?"

"We're doing our best on that, Mr. Kostner." What the hell do you want this time? she thought irritably. Why are you wasting my time now?

"You find out who tore up Evans' wall last night?"

"Not yet, Mr. Kostner." Jesus Christ, man, I haven't even seen a report on that yet. If it weren't for that gossipmongering waitress at the café, I wouldn't even know what you were talking about. Give me a break!

As if aware of her thoughts, the voice on the other end became harsh. "And what about my equipment? My people tell me that half my equipment was dumped over during the night, that dynamite and fuse was scattered all over. It's those damn demonstrators again, you know it as well as I do. This is the third time this month. What the hell are you doing about it?"

"We're conducting an investigation, Mr. Kostner." Bailey mentally counted to twenty in Basque, a technique she'd picked up at a festival in Reno years ago.

"Hell, woman, you can't do anything right, can you? We're gonna have to find ourselves a new sheriff if you don't get on the ball here. Got to show some assertiveness." There was a malicious chuckle in the back of the man's voice. "Look, Bailey, you're running out of chances. I want to know who's doing this. Or you're not going to get re-elected, and jobs are gonna be kind of hard to find, know what I mean? You know this writer fella I got in from back East?"

Bailey sighed to herself, knowing the man was trying to throw her off balance by the change of subject. It was an old ploy that had stopped working on her years ago. "Yeah, Mr. Kostner, I heard about him. What about it?"

"Little sharpish there, aren't we, Bailey? Did I hit you at the wrong time of the month maybe?"

"Was there something you wanted me to know about Esher?" she snapped, not trying to soften her tone.

"Now, now, just a joke, let's not get all huffy. I've got Esher doing interviews for these stories he's gonna write. I want to make sure he sees the right stuff. I want to make sure he knows this is a real law-abiding community, you know what I mean? So I want you to make sure it is. And keep that damn boyfriend of your girl's out of trouble. I think he's the one who messed up that wall."

"If you have some evidence, Mr. Kostner, I'd sure be interested in seeing it. Far as I'm concerned, Rick Zimmermann is a good kid.

"Now, unless you have something more specific, Mr. Kostner, I have a job to do here."

"Like finding out who's been wrecking my equipment? Or who did that wall?"

"Hell, Mr. Kostner, so far as I know at this time, we can't even figure out *how* it was done, much less who did it. Frankly,

I've got other things on my mind. Evans' insurance will take care of it."

"Hell they will, I'm taking care of it out of my own pocket. So you can see I'm real interested in not having it happen again."

"I'm a sheriff, not a miracle worker, Mr. Kostner. We don't have the budget—"

"Yeah, well, we got the budget for a sheriff. You keep on your toes and I'll make sure the commission keeps that budget. You just remember who pays most of the taxes in this county."

It was hard not to be reminded of that as she looked around the office. The Sheriff's Office was an annex of the Courthouse, and prominent on the wall was a photograph of Harry Kostner at the ribbon-cutting ceremony, sharing the scissors with the Governor.

"I want to make sure Esher writes the right thing," Kostner went on. "And I want you to help. So you keep an eye on him, you hear?"

"I hear you, Mr. Kostner." The disconnect buzzed in her ear. She set her receiver down gently, clicking it into its cradle and staring at it. She wasn't sure what the hell Kostner wanted her to do, but whatever it was better happen. Two county commissioners were relatives of his by marriage, and the other three either worked for him or had family members who did.

She felt a little sorry for Esher.

And a lot sorry for herself.

Sighing, she turned back to the file. The photograph had slipped to the floor, and she leaned down to pick it up and put it back. As she was about to close the file she stopped, frowning.

The image of the little blonde girl, smiling into the camera, was fading.

# 2

In daylight, most of Nintucca seemed to be trailers, kept with varying degrees of neatness. Esher left the motel early to walk to his appointment with Harry Kostner. Kostner lived "across town"; that meant a mile and a half farther down the highway that served for a main road.

The relative coolness of early morning burned off quickly as the sun rose high in the sky, sending the temperature soaring. Esher observed the town as he walked along, making mental notes, trying on opening lines to fit. "Nintucca, Nevada, doesn't look like a coal town in Ohio."

Trite but true. There was one large hotel, five stories, closed now; the cornerstone was dated 1911. The courthouse was faded red brick. A plain, boxlike affair, it looked like an afterthought, designed by an architect's least talented drafts-man; Esher smiled about this until he started considering how much it must have cost to import the brick. A few small businesses—a café, a launderette, a couple of churches, a dress shop—lined the road. One or two even had neon tubing.

There were no movie theatres in Nintucca. No national-chain fast-food restaurants. Two gas stations, each selling gas for half a dollar more per gallon than Esher paid in Las Vegas. One grocery store, with bread on sale for two dollars a loaf. One corner drugstore, with fading posters in the window. A video store, surprisingly large and modern-looking. A medical clinic that shared space with the one-garage fire station.

Dirt-lane turnoffs, twisting off erratically from the main road, were lined with painfully neat bare dirt yards. Some of the ranch-style houses were frame and stucco, some cinder-block. All were tiny and huddled together compared to houses in residential areas of the East.

By contrast, the mobile-home park out past the "business district" represented a substantial step up, with awnings and porches and more recent paint jobs; there were some double-wides, once even a triple-wide with bravely blossoming red and yellow flowers in a planter at the foot of the steps. Scattered between the mobiles were trailers, tethered to elec-tricity hookups like farm wagons at a hitching post. Children's toys lay abandoned in the dust; some yards had rusting swing sets.

There were so few people in sight that it took him a few minutes to realize he was missing them. A blond boy about twelve peered at him from the porch of a double-wide, not responding to his wave. Two or three people on the street nodded to him. There had been, he recalled, three diehards in the casino grimly pumping quarters into the video poker machines at seven-thirty in the morning. But the town gave the impression of emptiness, of waiting for one more good wind to sweep it away and leave nothing behind.

The road dipped down, then rose again toward the pass. Here there were nicer homes, yards with lawns, even trees. Some houses had late-model cars parked in their driveways.

He checked the map he had sketched out, turned two more corners to follow a twisting lane rising along the side of the hill. The house at the end, built of fieldstone and brick, had a freshly painted white fence defining a clipped lawn. A yard-man turned on the sprinkler. The bright glitter and distinct smell of water startled him; he could sense its presence on his skin from fifteen feet away, a cool heaviness in the increasing heat. He licked his lips, thinking for the first time that this was how a desert *felt*. More than the bare soil, more than the scrub vegetation—the desert had a smell, the smell of water or lack of water that he had never consciously noticed before.

The address was right. He rang the bell and looked around as he waited; the house overlooked the town and had a magnificent view of the bare yellow-brown rock and hills beyond it.

The door opened, and a petite, sharp-featured redheaded woman in her forties stared at him through the screen. "Can I he'p you?"

Her flinty brown eyes did not promise her willingness to "he'p" anyone, much less a stranger on her porch early in the morning. Esher put on his best smile.

"I have an appointment to see Mr. Kostner. My name's David Esher. I'm from *Town Life Magazine*."

Her lips thinned, and then without a word she swung the door open. He followed her in, wondering what he had done to upset her, through a large living room done in cool ivories and cream, furnished in buttery white leather and light oak, with glass-topped tables and standing lamps. It had a curiously uninhabited feel to it, like a decorator's model.

The woman paused at a half-open door across the room and spoke to someone on the other side.

"Your magazine man's here."

An unintelligible answer came from within the room. She stood to one side and waved Esher in. He nodded to her pleasantly as he passed. Charm failed; the faintly lined skin around her eyes tightened as if in anger, and she stalked away. Was it something I said, he wondered, or maybe just low blood sugar?

Esher turned with relief to the man waiting for him.

Harry Kostner was sitting behind a massive walnut desk and did not rise to greet him, though he did at least extend a hand and wave Esher into a chair. He was a bull-bodied man, with massive shoulders and hair beginning to recede, small square hands with no adornments. His forehead came in two shades, lighter on top where a regularly worn hat protected him and very dark beneath. Heavy-rimmed glasses emphasized a brow like a hawk's, with hard, dark golden eyes that made the red-haired woman seem as cheerful as Mary Poppins. He was wearing a cotton shirt, open at the neck to expose part of an angry sunburn on skin not used to exposure.

The study was beautifully appointed. The desk held a matched malachite desk set; the pen stand supported an eighteen-karat gold pen and pencil. Expensive Southwestern prints alternated with framed photographs, plaques, and degrees to line the wall between the glassed-in bookshelves and built-in bar. There was nothing out of place, not even, he saw, paper in the wastebasket. He had the feeling that there was something different about the wall behind him but couldn't tell what it was without turning his back on the other man.

"Well, Esher! Glad you could make it. Understand you want to write some articles about us here."

Esher raised a mental eyebrow at Kostner's tone. He sounded as if he, Kostner, was in some doubt about whether to give Esher permission. "Yes, I've got an assignment—"

"Yeah, I told Steve Migliori to put a good guy on this. You good, Esher? What kind of qualifications do you boys have to have to write magazine articles?" He got to his feet and stepped over to the bar. "A little early for the good stuff. Get you a cup of coffee?"

"Yeah, thanks." Esher watched the other man move, quick on his feet like a boxer, the top half of his body far too large for the bowlegged bottom half. "Just black, thanks."

"That's the way I like it," Kostner approved. "So tell me about your work, Esher. What've you done? Who've you written for? How long have you been in the business? How many articles have you sold and what were they about? I talked a little bit to Migliori about who he was sending me, but I'd like to hear what you have to say."

Esher sipped at his coffee and tried to hide a sudden annoyance. The man was giving him a job interview! "I'm here to do a series of stories for *Town Life*," he said finally. "I'd like to talk to you about the mines, about what you see as the role of the mines in the life of your town, what changes opening them up again could make. I'll be talking to a lot of other people too, of course.

"Then I'll be doing a similar series on some mine re-openings in Pennsylvania and Ohio. Comparing the East to the West."

Kostner grinned. "A-huh. But that ain't exactly what I asked you."

"When I do interviews, normally I do the asking," Esher responded evenly.

Kostner's smile did not change, but the temperature in the room dropped a degree or two. After a moment Kostner put down his cup and walked over to a table that stretched the length of the far wall. David rose to follow him.

He had been right—the other side of the room was different. Occupying the center of the wall opposite the walnut desk was a dull gray metal circle two feet across, pierced by jagged cracks or scars. The circle was surrounded by old photographs in oval mattes and good frames. The portraits showed a distinct family resemblance to his host.

Under them, spread across the table, was a miniature of the town.

"See this?" he said, waving his hand over the model as if the movement were creating it. "I own this. All of it. My granddaddy built it, and he left it to my daddy, and *he* left it to me. It belongs to me."

He wasn't talking about the model, Esher knew, but the model was amazing all by itself. He leaned over to study it more closely. It was accurate to the smallest detail; not only houses and hills, but there was a tiny hitching post in front of the hotel, and the garbage bins in the alley behind the businesses overflowed with model garbage. Tiny model cars were parked in front of model trailers. Tiny people walked along the main street where Esher had walked to come to this house. Carved wooden horses browsed on needlelike scraps of real hay in the model corrals. In front of Kostner's home, a tiny brown man pushed a shiny lawn mower over an impeccably green lawn four inches on a side.

"Pretty neat, huh?"

Esher nodded, intrigued despite himself. "You do this yourself? Can I get a picture of it to go with one of the stories?"

"I can get you all the pictures you need. You need anything in this town and you ask me. Anything.

"Now—" he was leaning against the wall, arms crossed over that barrel chest, one boot heel resting against the wall, his head tilted in such a way that, momentarily, Esher felt that Kostner was looking down at him, even though Esher had to be at least six inches taller—"you want to know about the 'role of the mines' in this town? Just look at the model there. Hundred years ago this was desert. All we had 'round here was Paiutes and Basques and damn sheep, all dying for lack of water.

"We didn't have a Jim Butler like Tonopah did. You ever hear that story? Ol' Jim, he was lookin' for a donk. Donk kicks a rock and damn if it isn't silver. Tonopah used to be the biggest damn city in the whole state, eighty years ago. Then Goldfield was."

Esher listened, wishing he had his tape recorder running. From the amused gleam in Kostner's eyes, Kostner knew it. But Esher'd been warned by Steve before he came that the man would stop talking if he started taking notes. He wasn't talking for publication, he was talking to impress just one man—David Esher.

"See, that's the way it is in Nevada." He flattened the middle "a" worse than a Boston Brahmin, Esher thought irrelevantly. Nevaaaaaaaada. "You got nothing. Then somebody finds silver, or gold, or copper, and there's a rush. Go from zero population to a couple hundred thousand in a week, in one damn week. I can show you the records.

"Then the ledges peter out, and they can't find any more, and they all leave. Go to the next strike. Or if they're smart they get out entirely. Unless they get the fever in them. Then they stay. There's always a few that stay." He pointed to a crumbling shack on the model, barely an inch high, falling to pieces and carefully, deliberately charred, on the other side of the model hills from the rest of the town. "My granddaddy, he had the fever. My daddy was born in that little house. They didn't have the tools, you know, but they did pretty well for themselves while they could. My granddaddy knew there was more silver in those mines. And he kept his hands on what he got." He pointed to tiny squared-off holes in the sides of the hills. "Those mines.

"People left, let their claims lapse, and my granddaddy, he picked 'em right up. People used to say he had more worthless mining claims than anybody in Nevada. But he knew. The stuff is still in there.

"He got the grazing rights too. Ran cattle when he couldn't dig, hired men to dig when the cattle died, watched 'em all freeze to death in the winter or die of thirst in the summer. He always got just enough to get by, just enough to keep the town going.

"Then they found the new ledge in Heartbreak. Vein of pure silver, his notebook said. He went down to look at it, and the mine caved in on him." There was a curious lack of feeling in Kostner's voice, as if he were reciting ancient history instead of the death of a near relative, events far away instead of one hill over.

"M'daddy, he didn't want any part of it. He stuck to cattle, got to be sheriff of the whole damn county. Not that there was anybody around to be sheriff of. Maybe a thousand folks, if you count the Indians. But it was his county. He was happy with things just the way they were. His cattle, his empty mines.

"But it's mine now. And I'm damn well gonna make something of it."

Esher nodded, the skin prickling at the back of his neck. The look Kostner gave the model was the look of an imperial duke for his duchy, where every tree and house and human soul was his own personal possession.

"Are you, uh, sheriff now?"

Kostner looked up from his reverie and laughed, a harsh cry

like the shriek of a hawk. "Me? Sheriff? Hell, no, I got better things to do. Let somebody else run for office." His tone clearly said that any office you had to run for wasn't worth having. "I spend too much time building up this town. New school. Library. Roads. Apartments. Stuff to make people want to come here and work the mines. That's what you're here for too, don't forget. But sheriff—I make my political donations. Let somebody else do the political scutwork."

That's what I hire them for, echoed unspoken in the room.

Esher leaned over and traced the thin line of road to one of the holes in the hill. "Is this road still good?" he said. "I'd like to go out there and look around."

"Well, *we* think it's a good road," Kostner said, crossing back to the desk and finishing his coffee in one long slurp. "I wouldn't advise you to go out there by yourself. This isn't soft country like you got back East. Tell you what, I'll give you a personal guided tour of the mines around here. I can show you the Heartbreak, my big one, this afternoon. The rest—well, I'm kind of busy the rest of the week. Got a big investors' meeting Friday. They're coming from all over to put money into this, back East, California, even Japan. But I'll get you a guide. Make sure you see all the good stuff."

"That's okay, I'm sure I can find somebody." Esher straightened and turned to look at the other man, squinting to see him against the light from the window. He was nothing more than a shadow, a darkness against the sunlight.

"You mean that Zimmermann boy? Hell, you really do think you can do this all by yourself, don't you?"

Esher glanced up sharply. Kostner chuckled. "Nothin' goes on in this town I don't know about sooner or later, Mr. Esher. You go ahead. I'll show you Heartbreak this afternoon, and then you go your own way. You run out of use for Rick Zimmermann, you come back to me, and I'll give you the *real* story. Even check it over for you once it's done, make sure you get all the facts right."

Esher nodded, slowly. "That's very kind of you, Mr. Kostner. I'll certainly take that into account. But I take it I have your permission to talk to the people at the mines, whether you're there or not?"

"Sure, sure. Any little thing your heart desires. But just you remember, you'll come back here anytime you get stuck." His eyes glittered. "The final answers are all mine."

Esher left shortly after that, having agreed to return for a tour of the mine at two o'clock. He was eager to find clean air to breathe. He did not like Harry Kostner. The man was a cocky, arrogant, overbearing asshole.

But he was pouring a hell of a lot of the family money into Nintucca.

Building up the family estate, no doubt.

He walked down the driveway, down the twists and turns to the main street, mulling over the interview. So Kostner knew that he'd been talking to Rick Zimmermann. Not surprising, in a way, but at the same time it was almost funny. The Stranger comes into town, and the Town Boss's spies immediately run to tell him all about it. There must not be much to gossip about in Nintucca.

On the other hand, the front desk clerk was Kostner's daughter, wasn't she? Esher laughed at himself. Start spinning fantasies about the Old West and see how far he'd get. Waste of time.

Kostner was building a new school and library, was he? And apartments for all those willing workers from back East who'd come to work in his mines. Maybe he'd do his first story about that, then. The population of Nintucca, and the schools. That would be a good upbeat story. Schools always represented hope.

He had reached the main part of town when he realized that something was—off. He stopped a moment and listened, trying to determine what it was he had seen, or heard—but he heard nothing. No sounds or even smell of traffic. No children playing. No radio blaring from an open window. Nothing. Silence, in the middle of town.

Looking around, he realized he was the only living thing in sight. Even the air was dead.

Then, in front of him, a transparent stirring. He backed up a step.

The air itself rose up in front of him, carrying with it a wobbling column of dust. It paused as if indecisive, and then began to whirl, lazily at first, languid, long arms of dust moving in long sweeps around an invisible center. It danced closer to him and then away again, coquettish, flirting. And he stood and stared, his mouth hanging open, and abruptly the reeling dust picked up speed, an ice dancer with a body of dirt and twigs and stone with veils of wind pulling herself in, spinning hard and tight, towering over him, pursuing, the air dancing, shrieking in elemental fury. He stepped away again, and again, and the whirlwind seemed to lose him, darting back and forth across the road sightlessly until it paused too long and faded and collapsed, the only sign it had ever been the rattling of pebbles on asphalt like spots of oil in a hot griddle.

# Two

## 1

Government in Nintucca was nothing if not centralized. Town hall, County Clerk and Sheriff's offices, jail, everything in the one brick courthouse building. He paused at the bottom of the flight of stone steps, struck by the contrast of faded red brick against a vibrantly blue sky. If there were only some green, he thought, to set it off—He noticed the same jagged metal symbol in the stonework under the eaves of the Courthouse that Kostner had on the wall of his study. It looked like something had clawed at it. He started to wonder what it meant when someone spoke sharply to him.

"Hey you—"

Esher looked over, startled, to see a lump of black and brown unwind itself from the steps and stand up into the shape of a man. A small, bent, weatherbeaten man, with eyes as vividly blue as the sky itself. He was wrapped in a rusty black denim coat, torn at the pockets, and faded brown pants. His shoes were leather, cracked, lines of white showing at the splits, laces missing on the right shoe. He wore a faded red bandanna around his neck. Thin cracked lips worked against each other for the suppleness to make more words.

"Hello," Esher said. Town drunk, he thought.

"You that writer man?" An indefinable accent flavored the

words, subtly different from the voices Esher was getting used to hearing. "You come to write for Kostner?"

Esher stuck his hands in his pockets and sighed. Who knows, maybe there was even a story in the town drunk. As long as he didn't have to buy for him—Though there didn't seem to be any liquor on his breath.

"I'm a writer, yes. I don't work for Kostner, though. I'm writing for a magazine back East."

'Back East.' He made a mental note of how easily he fell into using the phrase, referring to that bland homogenous mass of humanity on the other side of—what? Texas, probably.

The old man came up close, peering into Esher's eyes, his breath warm against Esher's face. "You work for Kostner," he said. It was not a question. "You write for the mines. Do you have the Beast?"

"The what?" Esher found himself stepping away, trying to create space between himself and the old man. The man followed, still looking into his eyes.

"The Beast. Is the Beast in you?" The old man's brow cracked and furrowed. Then he stepped away, much to Esher's relief, and answered his own question. "No. There is no Beast."

"Well, thanks, I'm particularly glad to hear that." Esher edged around him and started up the courthouse stairs, still keeping an eye on the old man. "Thanks a lot."

Like a snake striking, one clawlike hand reached up to grab his sleeve. "You be careful of the Beast. You be careful, and you may live. The Beast is not in you, not yet!"

Cursing, Esher twisted out of the viselike grasp and hurried up the steps. He paused only briefly at the door to look back and make sure the crazy old coot wasn't following him.

But the steps were empty. The old man was gone.

# 2

It took a while to find anyone in the basement of the Courthouse. He went down a narrow stairway to a dry, dusty cave lit by fluorescent lights, to a counter that by the dust hadn't been staffed for years, and looked around. Hot-water pipes ran overhead, looking as if they would crack any minute and spray water all over the rows of old filing cabinets lined up in aisles behind the counter. The counter itself looked like government surplus from World War II, dusty and empty except for a calendar showing last Thursday's date.

"Anybody here?"

His words echoed from the back wall. He expected a little old cockroach of a man to skitter forth from a half-open drawer, peer at him from over rimless spectacles, and inquire in a testy, high-pitched voice what he wanted.

He got nothing. Nobody responded at all.

Shrugging, he lifted the divider and went behind the counter.

All the county records were there, filed away in old metal lockers painted Army green. One bank of cabinets was labeled "Births–Deaths–Marriages." Another, "Land Deeds, 1860–1900." Court records filled three more cabinets. He wandered around, reading the yellowing labels, occasionally trying the drawers; they were all locked. He sneezed once or twice as his footsteps raised soft puffs of dust from the hardwood floor.

As he went farther back among the files he realized that there were other rooms at the end of the one he was exploring. One was lit up, and clicking mechanical sounds came from it, along with a swearword or two.

"Hello? Anybody home?" he said, sticking his head in the door.

"*Shit!*" The young woman sitting at the desk jumped and nearly came out of her chair. "Where the hell did you—oh, Mr. Esher. Hi. What are you doing down here?"

It was Marianne Bailey, Rick's girlfriend. She was sitting in an office that had nothing to do with the rows upon rows of green cabinets. It was brightly lighted, with Kliban posters on the walls and plants on the bookcase, and there was not a speck of dust anywhere. And it was cool, too. He could hear the purr of air conditioner.

"I called, but nobody came," Esher explained. "I didn't know you worked here."

"Oh, yeah. Microfilming the records." With a wave of the hand, she indicated a stack of files perched precariously on the edge of her desk. The microfilming machine took up most of the rest of it. "They decided they wanted to use the basement for something else, I guess. With all the junk down here I could retire at this."

"Mind if I sit down? I thought you'd be out looking for that little girl."

"Huh? Oh, no. Mom has her search teams all figured out, and she decided I needed to go back to work. I'll be reporting in later. But right now, I could use the break. Were you looking for something in particular, Mr. Esher?" She looked the image of the young executive this morning, in a dark skirt skimming the bottom of her knees, dark blazer jacket, prim white blouse, and—thank heavens—a shocking pink tie. Her only makeup was lipstick and something about the eyes. It was quite a contrast to the jeans-and-flannel-clad, cowboy-booted young woman from the bar last night. Esher felt a stab of envy for Rick Zimmermann.

"Please, call me David. 'Mr. Esher' makes me feel even older than I am. Yeah, I thought I'd see if I could find something about the schools here. For an article."

"About our schools?" Marianne looked puzzled. "Why would anybody—well—sure—But I don't think you can just get the records, I mean, there's private stuff in there."

"Oh, I don't mean about people's grades. I was thinking about when the first school was built, and how it was funded, and who taught there, and how many students. That kind of thing." He smiled what he hoped was a winning smile.

The girl chewed on her lip. "Well, I guess I could show you some stuff. But you'd probably be better off going to the newspaper."

"I was going to do that too," he assured her, mentally kicking himself. Of course the local newspaper would have more human-interest angles. But the newspaper machines outside the Rowdytown Hotel had held only the Reno and Las Vegas papers, and it had never occurred to him that Nintucca might have a paper of its own. "But I thought I'd start here. Get the official side of the story first."

"Well, I'll see what I can find. I'll be back in just a minute."

Esher swung his legs aside to let her go by, then glanced at the pile of papers waiting to be microfilmed. They appeared to be old deeds. The name on the top one caught his eye immediately: Daniel Kostner. He studied it with interest.

Dated 1912, the deed was an instrument of conveyance of

mineral rights to the Little Kitten Mine from one Rafael Gallita to Daniel Kostner—Harry Kostner's grandfather, perhaps? Esher wondered if this was one of the claims that Kostner had meant in their conversation earlier. Without knowing what values were current at the time of sale, it was impossible to tell if the price was fair or not, but it didn't look like it. Twenty-five dollars for all grazing and mineral rights? It didn't look right.

He asked Marianne about it when she came back, brushing dust from her skirt and carrying more folders.

"Oh, that. That was old Jessie's daddy. You might have seen Jessie on the street today—a little old guy, wears a red neckerchief? He looks like a drunk, but he's not. His daddy sold out, and they couldn't do anything but run sheep. And had to pay Mr. Kostner for the privilege. Ol' Jessie's older'n God, just about, and they say he's got something wrong with his brain, that's why he staggers like that. But he's not a drunk." Something occurred to Marianne suddenly, and she glanced up and away, blushing.

Not like me, huh? he thought, with more sadness than anger. "Never said he was," he responded with false heartiness. "You say there's a lot of these deeds? Could I look at some more? Were these good prices for the time?"

Marianne dropped her voice. "Daniel Kostner *stole* those mines. Everybody in town knows it. And he was too damn cheap to put in enough supports when the Heartbreak needed them, and that's why the mine collapsed. Nobody will *say* anything, but it's the truth."

Taken aback by the suppressed fury in her voice, Esher asked, "How do you know? And why does it matter now?"

"Everybody in town knows. Everybody that had family here. Like Mikey. His grandpa died!" Her voice dropped, as if she were telling secrets.

"It's like Mikey told you, everybody wants the mines to open, it'll be good for the town. We all know that. But *I* think the place is spooky. Things have been disappearing, big things like ore carts and stuff. And then—" she glanced around the brightly lighted room as if expecting to see something looming over her—"last week, Mr. Evans, he's Mr. Kostner's foreman, he woke up one night hearing something. It scared him so bad he wouldn't even go out with a shotgun to see what it was. And last night—David, you should see the side of his house."

"Oh? What happened?"

She shook her head, eyes afraid with something that was not a made-up fear for the thrill of it. Esher felt a chill. "You go see. They just left it. We don't know where Mr. Evans is—his next-door neighbor saw him leaving last night to go somewhere. He's going to be furious when he sees it. Some people say it happened because he works for Mr. Kostner at the mine." She might have been an adolescent at summer camp, staying up late to tell ghost stories, leaning far forward, almost whispering, scaring hell out of herself for the fun of it. But like the adolescent, she was too young to be afraid for long, and too grown-up to keep up the pose. "He's going to be snowed on all winter if he's too cheap to get it fixed.

"And Harry Kostner is just as cheap. They say he's not putting the right supports in the mine. He says he's got another way, but nobody's seen it yet. You watch, there's gonna be another cave-in. But people act like they support him because they say it'll 'boost the economy.' All Harry Kostner wants is the money. And the power. Those mines open up again, he's gonna own this whole town."

David was taken aback by the abrupt flood of anger in her voice. "Except Gil and Rick, by the sound of things last night," he offered.

Marianne agreed reluctantly. "Yeah, Rick doesn't want to work for him. But once the mines open, he'll have to. The site's just temporary, and he's too smart to be just a guard all his life. He's got to work in the mine. Or he'll go away."

And you aren't quite ready to go away with him, are you? he asked silently, knowing the answer even as she turned away, abruptly busy with the old deeds. Like my Patricia, who thought she was almost all grown-up, but never quite made it to the outside world. And the world outside this little town is a lot bigger than it is from almost anyplace else at all. At least you have the chance. Don't throw away your chance, little girl.

"So if nobody trusts Kostner, then the mine might not open, after all," he suggested, watching her.

She started to answer, and then stopped, thinking about it. "No," she said. "I don't think they do. Not the oldtimers.

They're superstitious about it. But there are lots of newcomers to work there. They don't know what he's like."

Possible safety problems at the mine, he thought. But that could be only because of the memory of the disaster decades ago, which had obviously scarred the town and the lives of everyone in it. He thanked Marianne for her time, went over the rest of the deeds, making notes, and then left, glad to go up the steps into the sunlight, feeling obscurely sad and not sure why.

# 3

Lunch was a surprisingly good hamburger in the tiny café sandwiched between the Latter-Day Saints chapel and the town laundromat—the former looking more prosperous than the latter, with its six washing machines, three dryers. The laundromat and the café shared a connecting door, presumably for the convenience of the customers of both—lunch on the spin cycle? And up in the front of the café, next to the cashier, conveniently located to relieve the customers of their spare change, crouched a bank of three slot machines and three video poker machines.

At least the café was cool. One of the differences between heat back East and heat in the desert West, he decided, was that in the West, shade made a difference. The relative dimness of the back booths was a relief after the glare of sunlight on bleached-out buildings and white earth.

Esher poured out a pool of ketchup and dabbed massive ranch fries in it, going over his notes and trying to find a good lead. The waitress took his order, put the food and the check in front of him, and ignored him, sitting at the counter and dabbing color on her fingernails. He munched and scribbled, trying to concentrate, remembering a time when he would have three beers' worth of inspiration with his hamburger. This was better, he thought wryly. This way he'd be able to read his notes later.

He had just about decided that he'd better visit the newspaper office before doing any more outlining when the door from the laundromat swung open. He looked up with interest, noting the wash of humidity that spread over his face, to see the dark-haired, beehive-styled woman from the casino coming in with a large cosmetics sample box.

His waitress sat up immediately as the other woman swung the case up on the counter and opened it. Avon, he thought, or Mary Kay—no, some other company, one he'd never heard of. There was a ritual involved, he saw. The two women put their heads together and looked over the samples, rubbing colors on the heels of their thumbs and holding them up to the uncertain lighting, touching perfume to their wrists and sniffing judiciously. The beehive-haired woman never stopped talking, shoving one after another of her wares forward, until the waitress finally made her selections.

Conversation shifted then, and Esher was amused to see the beehive-haired woman hold up a small mirror, ostensibly to check her eye makeup, in perfect position to give him a once-over. Smothering a chuckle, he bent down to his notes again; she scribbled down the waitress's order and snapped her case shut, took her leave, and turned to go. A wave of floral perfume almost as powerful as the humidity hit him in the face.

She made quite a production of seeing Esher for the first time. Her kohl-lined eyes widened; if her hands hadn't been full with the sample case, he was sure one would have flown up to cover an "Oh!" of surprise.

"Oh!" she said, as predicted. "I didn't see you sitting there. Hope I didn't interfere with anything—Bobbi Jo doesn't usually have too many customers this time of day—"

At lunchtime? Esher wondered. The woman slid into the seat across from him, still talking. After a moment or two he decided the perfume wasn't so bad, after all. Or maybe the nerves in his nose had gone numb.

"I would never do that, you know, never take time away from her proper job or anything, so I hope you don't think that I'd just come in any old time, only when Bobbi Jo has slack time, you know, because that's when I can catch her, she's so busy all the rest of the time. And it's really not fair when somebody has customers waiting to take up their time, I really think that's so rude, though some people do it all the time, you know?"

She paused, possibly to take a breath, and Esher smiled politely. The silence stretched out for half a minute, and he realized that she was studying him, assessing the impact of the flow of words almost the same way that Gil had assessed him the night before, coolly measuring his response. It was an uncomfortable feeling.

"No—I mean, of course it is," he said at last. "But you weren't bothering me at all."

She nodded, quick, birdlike, satisfied. "Well, I didn't think so or I would never have come in, you know that, that's just not the kind of thing I do. By the way, my name's Wanda. Wanda Kostner. You must be that writer. Everyone's talking about you. Are you going to write about all the people in town and everything?" She stopped again, and Esher felt a vast unspoken pressure to agree, to say yes to whatever the torrent of words suggested.

In self-defense, he took another tack instead. "Wanda Kostner? I'm David Esher. Are you by any chance related—"

"To Harry?" The assessing look disappeared, replaced by a glimpse of fury. "Not any more I'm not. I'm his ex-wife." The prefix was heavily accented. Esher found it more interesting that she described her relationship to Kostner, instead of his to her; what would it have implied, he wondered briefly, if instead she'd said that *he* was *her* ex-husband? Divorced or not, Kostner apparently never gave up possession.

"Are you staying at the hotel? Of course you are, there isn't anyplace else to stay, is there, but Bobbi Jo thought you might be staying up at the big house. I told Bobbi Jo there wasn't any way that you'd stay there. Have you written a lot of things? Have I read anything you wrote?"

Abrupt stop again, assessing look back. It was an interesting technique, he realized; one had to fill up the silence when she stopped talking, and the easiest way was just to agree with whatever she said, supply whatever information she asked for. That ridiculous hairstyle disguised a very sharp brain indeed.

Unfortunately, she'd asked two of the four questions he hated most. Have you read *War and Peace*? he thought. *One Day in the Life of Ivan Denisovitch*? *Life on the Mississippi*? How the hell should I know if you've read anything I've written?

And yeah, I've written a bunch of stuff. Just not lately, but that's changing too.

"I write for magazines, mostly," he said at last. "Back

East." He took another bite of cold hamburger, half wishing she would go away, half fascinated by the sheer characterness of the woman. "You probably haven't read any of my stuff."

"Oh." Disappointment oozed from every pore. "I thought maybe you were one of those famous writers, you know, who get a billion bucks a book. But that's silly, isn't it, what would a really famous writer be doing in Nintucca, huh? They'd stay in Vegas. Or Reno. Do you know Jackie Collins? She's a writer. She writes the most wonderful books, and she gets a lot of money for them. I think she wrote a book where everything took place in Las Vegas, but maybe that was somebody else. I like Mary Higgins Clark, too. I read a lot. You probably don't believe me, but I do. Lots of people up here read, there's nothing else to do. Except gamble, of course. I could have gone to work at the casino, but I like to gamble, and you can't gamble there if you work there, they've got a rule. Well, listen, are you going to be taking pictures? I'll be in a picture for you if you want, but you've got to send me a copy of the article you write. Will we be getting copies?"

"I don't know." He finished his coffee and picked up the check, making a small production of looking it over. "I think you'd have to buy copies. That's up to the editor."

"Oh." She studied him a moment longer, then hopped to her feet. "Well, I really enjoyed talking to you and all, but I have to get my work done, can't spend any more time here. It was really nice to meet you and everything. If you want to ask me any more questions you can probably find me at the casino, they all know me. Especially—" she lowered her voice and bent over, so close that he pulled away—"if you want to know the *real* truth about Harry. *I* know things nobody else does, you betcha. I've lived in this town all my life, and I *know*. Ask anybody. Wanda Mirielle Kostner knows where the bodies are buried."

# Three

## 1

He would go back to the Rowdytown and start organizing his notes, he decided, get ready for his afternoon tour. One of the shops by the hotel should carry batteries for the recorder, too. He was pleased to find Mikey, Rick's friend, hovering behind the counter of the combination gift shop/drugstore.

Mikey remembered him too, and greeted him with the same cheerful smile. "Dave! Good to see you. What can we do for you?"

"I thought you worked out at the site," Esher said, looking around. The stock was much the same as one would find in any such store: cards, music boxes, Post-it notes with funny sayings. And a few things unique to Nevada: dice clocks; maps to "Recreational Nevada," showing the location of all the licensed brothels; ashtrays in the shape of roulette wheels; glasses with slightly off-color invitations to the state's specialized vices. In the back he could see a sheaf of poster hangers featuring teddy bears and tigers. It was a nice, pleasant, bland place.

Mikey looked uneasy, picking up a delicate blue china shepherdess figurine and polishing the glass underneath it with the side of his hand. The little ceramic was almost hidden in his huge hand. He replaced it on the glass almost tenderly.

"Oh, we had a little trouble out at the ranch, so I took the

65

day off. Turns out there's nothing to be done about it, so I'm just helping Kathy out. Kathy! Come on out here, here's Dave Esher I was telling you about." Mikey came out from behind the counter, moving with amazing lightness for such a big man.

"Nothing serious, I hope?"

Mikey's cornflower-blue eyes looked bleak. "Lost twenty head of cattle last night. Got to talk to insurance adjusters and stuff."

Twenty head? That was—David remembered Mikey saying his family had "a couple of hundred head." They'd just lost ten percent of their herd. "Any way they can tell who did it?"

"Oh, we know what did it all right." From the back of the shop a petite brunette came bustling out, making hand-washing gestures. She offered her hand and glanced almost anxiously from Esher to her husband and back again.

"Now, honey—" Mikey looked tired, as if this was part of a conversation that had been going on too long.

But Mikey's wife swallowed her bitterness to remember her manners. "Mr. Esher, is it? It's so nice to meet you. Mikey tells me you're going to write some articles about our town."

"Well, mostly about the mine that's going to open up." David smiled his best company smile in an effort to change the subject and get the other man off the hook, at least for a few minutes. "Mr. Kostner has offered to give me a personal tour this afternoon."

"Oh, no! You mustn't!" The outburst was followed by a small silence, and Esher looked at her questioningly.

"Now, honey," Mikey began again. David looked from one to the other, confused. Somehow his effort hadn't distracted Kathy at all, and Mikey was looking even more frayed around the edges.

"I don't care, he shouldn't go. Mr. Esher, that mine should never be opened up again. It's evil. You shouldn't help Mr. Kostner."

"Why not, Mrs.—" Esher suddenly realized that he'd never heard Mikey's last name. His killer-journalist instincts were definitely rusty, he thought wryly.

But Kathy didn't wait for amenities. "It's evil," she insisted. "People from around here know it. That mine shouldn't be disturbed. Bad things happen. We know that our own selves, don't we, Mikey? There's something terrible—"

"Now, Kathy, hush, you're being silly." Mikey was clearly embarrassed. He put one placating hand on her arm.

"I thought you were eager to see more trade," Esher said slowly. "If the mine opens up, there'll be more jobs, won't there? More money in the local economy?"

Kathy's lips tightened and she snapped away from her husband's grasp. "It would be wonderful to have more jobs and more money in Nintucca, Mr. Esher. I'm no fool. But we're getting that already with the people out at the site. We don't need the mine. People died there—Mikey's grandpa, my great-uncle. Jessie Gallita says the mine wants to be left alone, and he's right."

"The *mine* wants to be left alone?"

Mikey sighed. "It's just an old superstition around here. The miners used to give their mines names to go with the mines' personalities—the mines' personalities. My grandpa had a claim he called his Generous Lady. It was real good to him until he gambled it all away. The big mine, the one Kostner's opening up again, they called that the Heartbreak. I guess the old-timers spent so much time in them they took them real personal. But it doesn't *mean* anything."

"Yes it does, Mikey Denton. Yes it does. You mark my words, our cattle, Mr. Evans' wall—that's just the least of it. There's going to be more trouble if Mr. Kostner keeps on with his planning. And I'm not the only one around here who thinks so, and you know it. How come you think Harry Kostner had to bring so many outsiders in, in the first place? Nobody from around *here* will go under the ground. You don't tempt fate." Her voice was light and a little shrill, as if she was angry as well as frightened. Her skirt showed signs of having been wrung by sweating hands.

Mikey smiled again and shrugged, rolling his eyes helplessly to Esher as if to say, Women—what can you do about them? But Esher remembered that it had struck him at the time he had first met the other man that even though Mikey supported reopening of the mine, he'd talked about supplying meat to the workers—not about working in the mine himself.

There was something else that Kathy Denton's words reminded him of, too, if he could just catch hold of it . . . No, it was gone. "But do you think the site's a good thing, Mrs. Denton?"

Kathy took a deep breath to compose herself, perhaps a little taken aback at her own vehemence. "Well, of course it is. Pays Mikey real good. They bring in a lot of people, too. Construction and such. They're doing some kind of testing out there."

"Some kind of testing," but a sublime disinterest in *what* kind. He wondered if that was a general attitude in the state. Remembering the newspaper in Beatty, Esher probed. "What about demonstrators? Do you get a lot of them?"

Both Kathy and Mikey were transparently relieved to be talking about something else. "All the way out *here*?"

Mikey went on, "Well, we get a few. It's like traditional. Anywhere the government does anything there's got to be somebody out there holding up a sign to stop them."

"So they don't really cause trouble?" They wouldn't chop up twenty cows, for instance?

Mikey rubbed a thumb over a smear on the glass countertop by the cash register. "Well, we don't know for sure about that. We've had some trouble, things come missing and damaged and stuff. Had the sheriff out to the mine last week, they had some trouble over there too. But nobody can prove it was the demonstrators. There's only two of them at a time, after all. I think they're just harmless crazies, myself."

Crazies, Esher thought. Maybe I should talk to these crazies, find out what they're all about. He picked up some office supplies and set them down by the counter.

"What about Jessie Gallita?" he suggested. "Isn't he that old man I saw—"

But Jessie evidently wasn't considered a crazy, or at least was the acceptable, home-grown variety. The Dentons were happy to tell him about Jessie, whose family had herded sheep in the area long before there were any silver mines. Jessie was a Basque of pure blood, one of many in Nevada. He was also the town character, Esher gathered. He got the impression that Kathy was a little uneasy about her husband's flippant attitude toward the old man, and that interested him. He paid for the supplies and batteries and left, promising to look the Dentons up later, filled with ideas. It was going to be a good series. Steve would be pleased.

# 2

A line of people, men and women both, moved on foot and on horseback down the hill, at arm's length from each other. Their heads were down as they examined the ground in minute detail. They had the air of having done this before and expecting to have to do it again—efficient, careful, no wasted motion. Laura Bailey pulled up in a truck and stopped below the line.

As one, they turned at right angles until they had all arrived, crowding around as Bailey dispensed large cups of Gatorade and juice from six large coolers in the truck bed. The horsemen unloaded a shallow trough from the truck bed and filled it with water from a cask for the horses.

Without any special acknowledgment, Bailey handed a cup to Rick Zimmermann as he finished watering his horse. She and Rick had an agreement: he got no special privileges for dating her daughter, and he didn't push his luck. It worked well for them both.

"Find anything?" she asked as soon as everyone had had a drink. She knew they had not; they were equipped with walkie-talkies and would have contacted her long before if they had seen anything.

Shaking heads confirmed her assumption. Rick took a bandanna and soaked it in water from another cooler sitting in the passenger seat and wiped his face. "Nothing. But, Sheriff, you might do something about the kid." A jerk of his head indicated the slope the searchers had just left. "He's been following us all day."

"Jeremy?" Bailey asked.

"Yeah," one of the women said, sharing the sopping neckerchief. "He just ducks behind a rock when we turn around. We all pretend we can't see him, but he's going to get a real bad sunburn if he keeps it up."

"Poor little guy," murmured another.

"Don't want to have to go looking for him too," still another contributed.

Laura Bailey looked up the hill, shading her eyes against the afternoon sun. She could just glimpse a tow-headed child crouching behind a large boulder. "Tell you what. You get finished here and go back to it. I'll stick around a while and see if I can round him up."

The searchers nodded, and after a break went back onto their line, scanning every inch of ground. Bailey waited, watching for Jeremy to break cover to keep up.

But the child was aware of her, and afraid. After half an hour the searchers were over the rise out of sight, and she could see him creeping away, back toward town.

# 3

"White?" Kostner's voice was low, and he glanced at the open door of his office. No one was visibly eavesdropping, but he suspected his wife was around somewhere, listening. Kostner always suspected someone was listening. He was hunched over the desk blotter like a vulture, the phone tucked into the curve of his shoulder as he paged through an appointment book. "I have them coming in Friday. This Friday, got that? I want to do a full demo. Are you going to be ready?"

Static at the other end, sounds of protest.

"What the hell are you trying to pull on me? I've given you enough money to fill a dozen tankers, and I haven't seen anything for it yet."

More static. Kostner snapped the book shut and took a firm grip on the handset as if on the other man's throat.

"No, I'm not coming out there, are you crazy? Besides, I'm going to be showing somebody around the mine today. Yeah, my writer. He's going to give me some good publicity. I'll send copies to all my money men. They're going to like seeing themselves in a national magazine making like philanthropists, putting money in this town."

He paused and listened, his gaze drifting to the model of the town and the symbol above it. Despite his anger, the beginnings of a thin smile formed on his lips.

"I don't care about *your* problems. I care about *my* problems, and I have *my* problems all under control. Which is what you'd better do damn fast if you expect to see any more money out of me. Do we understand each other?"

He didn't bother to wait for an answer.

# 4

"That's where we processed the ore," Kostner said, pointing to a warehouse-sized building with weathered walls and three-fourths of a roof. "That little place next to it, that's the assayer's office. We'd bring in samples and find out how much richer we were that day."

Kostner spoke as if he personally had taken the chunks of silver-bearing quartz seventy years ago into the tiny office, not much better than a shed, set them down and watched as the assayer processed out the gold and silver, evaluated them, and calculated the answers.

Esher slid him a wary look as he unlimbered his camera and tested the light levels. Kostner didn't appear to notice. His clothes already had a patina of dust from walking across the deserted area. Ahead of them, a foot-long black snake glided under a grayish clump of sage.

"That over there, that's the headframe." He pointed to a hole gaping fifteen feet tall by twenty feet wide standing high on the side of a young mountain, framed by timbers eighteen inches thick. Railroad tracks led from the headframe to the processing building. "That's where we're going."

Around them, workers buzzed in a hive of activity, sawing, cutting, clanking, moving in steady streams in and out of the processing building, driving lift trucks and unloading huge timbers, steel plates, carrying rolls of engineering drawings at a half-run from one place to another. A newly graveled road led to a two-story warehouse half a mile away. Past it, just around the side of another hill, Esher could just glimpse Nintucca, farther away than it appeared to be in the clear desert air.

There were several other buildings as well, mostly of wood, all weathered and old, with gaping holes in the sides and doors hanging off their hinges. At least two dozen men swarmed over them, tearing down and constructing, cleaning away the tumbleweeds that towered up to the eaves of the windows in huge brown balls. They looked up at the two of them and nodded to Kostner. He waved back and forged forward to the gaping hole in the mountain, Esher following reluctantly behind.

"Here," Kostner said. "This is the Heartbreak. This leads to the main shaft."

Esher cleared his throat, glancing again at the state of disrepair of the buildings around them.

Kostner saw it and grinned. "Oh, it's safe. That's where I've been putting my money, in the mine itself. We're just starting to work on the processing building and cleaning up the other stuff."

A vagrant gust of wind whipped sand into their eyes, moaned through the jagged timbers. Glancing down at the hair on his arms, Esher could see them waver and rise as the temperature plummeted. He shook himself. Kostner didn't appear to notice anything unusual; in a moment or two the chill was gone and the desert sun glared hot again.

"In here." Kostner led the way through the frame, past a small group of men bent over a blueprint to a generator just inside, checked levels, and flipped switches. In minutes it had roared to life, a pounding that Esher could feel through the soles of his shoes. Another switch, and lights came on.

It was all Esher could do to keep from gasping. From the outside, it had looked like a hill identical to a thousand others. Inside, however, a room fifty feet long was filled with glaring spotlights and machinery. The two men were alone in the room. Esher could barely gather his wits together sufficiently to take more pictures, hoping the lighting wouldn't ruin them all.

A large frame that looked like an old-fashioned elevator cage, enclosed to hip height by wooden panels and open to the top, without even wire siding, occupied the center of the area. A stink of diesel fuel pervaded everything. His gaze followed the railroad tracks to the edge of the cage.

The shaft over which the cage hung was a couple of feet wider on one side, leaving a gap between cage and wall and room for a ladder bolted to the side of the shaft. Esher peered down, fascinated, at the ladder descending into nothingness. He could just make out the first tie that fastened the ladder to the rock; then it was swallowed by the dark. He stepped back involuntarily.

More machinery roared, and another light in the roof of the cage snapped on. Esher turned off his recorder, aware that it could pick up nothing useful over the roar.

"Come on," Kostner said. Shrieking metal set Esher's teeth on edge as the cage door opened.

It was surprisingly large; he estimated that it could hold six people in comfort, plus an ore cart in the middle of the floor. Kostner hit a red button on the inside of the door frame and the cage jolted and swayed. Esher gulped and groped behind himself for the railing as the cage began to descend, at first slowly and then with increasing speed.

He couldn't look up past the brilliance of the ceiling light; he couldn't see down through the wooden floor. All he could see was the dizzying passage of the ladder rungs two feet away from him, and the grin of contempt on Harry Kostner's face. The cage kept dropping. He found himself counting—not the rungs, they were passing too fast to count, but the endless seconds as they dropped farther into the earth. He had reached three hundred before he realized that Kostner was talking, and he reached into his pocket to turn on the recorder again. The roar of machinery above him had faded to a hum; only the squeaking of the pulleys interfered with recording now. He took three deep breaths to steady himself, was startled to smell heat and dampness deep in the earth.

"Used to be they used buckets in this shaft," Kostner was saying. "Still do, down on the lower ledges. Three, four men could climb right in and get lowered down. And if you didn't want to do that, well, there was always the ladders." He nodded at the wall.

"How—" Esher had to clear his throat to make the words come out right. "How far down are we going?"

"A hundred fifty feet. Down to the first big ledge. Almost there, in fact." Kostner leaned back, arms crossed against his chest. "Claustrophobic, are you?"

Esher swallowed. "I never thought so. No. No, it's not that—this is no worse than an elevator in a New York high rise. Brighter, though." Licking his lips, he tried again, without success, to peer up past the bare bulb.

He spoke the truth. It didn't feel closed in, not in the cage, not even thinking about the hundreds of feet of honeycombed earth hanging over him, not even breathing in the smell of wet earth and oil and—something else he couldn't identify. No, he could stretch out both arms and not touch the sides of the iron box he rode in, and it didn't feel as if it were shrinking in on him.

But he was bothered by something, something besides Kostner grinning at him and enjoying his discomfort. He knew there were only the two of them in the mine shaft; but his skin still crawled.

With a jerk, the cage's movement halted, and he had to catch himself to keep from falling as his sense of balance protested. Kostner chuckled and swung the door open, slapping a light switch on the frame. Lights strung along where walls met roof flashed on.

The room was thirty feet by thirty feet, with a floor of massive steel plates scarred by glittering scratches. The roof was webbed with rotting timbering. Tunnel mouths gaped in three directions. Off to one side another, smaller frame stood over a square hole in the floor five feet on a side.

"This is Level One, the first big bulge in the ledge," Kostner said. "Quartz carries the silver in ledges, and where it bulges, you get thick veins, if you're lucky. We're lucky. We mined three branches out of here. Loaded up the carts in the tunnels, brought 'em back here and up in the cage. That's what made all the marks on the floor. Over there—" he pointed to the square hole—"that's the shaft down to Level Two. Ladder or bucket, that's the only way. Want to take a peek?"

Esher shook his head, and Kostner laughed, the sound echoing weirdly down the tunnels.

"Those tunnels, they followed the quartz ledges. A ledge is the quartz outcropping that holds the veins of ore. You can see it in the walls, bands of pure silver ore two or three inches thick." His voice was low and caressing, and David shuddered despite himself. Kostner might have been talking about a woman he loved. "Sometimes they'd connect up with somebody else's mine. You never knew, when you followed the silver down from the surface, where the vein would take you. Used to be quite some excitement sometimes when two claims intersected a couple hundred feet down. Accidents happened."

Esher remembered the accounts in the newspapers and nodded grimly. Accidents. Of course.

"When they opened up Level Two, my granddaddy held a dance down here, lit it all up with candles, served a picnic supper, and had a dance band. It was a real nice party."

Esher, remembering the account in the local paper, nodded again. He hadn't realized, reading about it, that the festivities had been held a hundred and fifty feet under the earth. He swallowed. He wondered what the music had sounded like, violins and accordions echoing and re-echoing off the tunnel walls, the strains of music penetrating deep into the earth and disturbing whatever creatures lived there. If anything lived there . . .

"But we were still drilling, even then. And when the dynamite went off, all the candles were snuffed out by the concussion, and everybody was left in the dark—" And Kostner hit the switch, and the lights went out.

"Sure it's not claustrophobia, Esher?" Harry Kostner's voice rang out mockingly, echoing.

Esher stood very still.

Once, when he was five, he had taken a warm cookie from a plate in his grandmother's kitchen. And his grandmother, a stern righteous woman, had locked him in a closet for a day to teach him not to steal.

He used to think that closet was dark.

His eyes strained until they ached to adjust, to find some shape or substance to the dark, in vain. He could hear—the suffocating blackness was a blindfold on his eyes but did nothing to block his hearing—he could hear his own breathing and his own heartbeat. He held his breath, and could hear Kostner rasping. Blindly tilting his head back and forth, he found he could determine where the other man stood. He took one step toward the sounds.

And stopped. The cavern was not silent. There were—other sounds—whispering sounds—coming from his left. From far away. Scraping, like scales over steel. Clicking.

"Imagine all those people down here when the lights went out," Kostner said. His voice was loud and sudden in the dark, and Esher flinched. "Dressed up in their very best, clothes they had brought in from San Francisco by railroad, and when the railroad ran out, by mule team the last sixty miles." His voice was almost dreamy. "Quite a party. My granddaddy even had some of the little stakers in. They paid a silver dollar for water for a bath to clean up and dance with the respectable ladies. And all the lights went out, and the music stopped, and they counted the blasts, one, two, three, all the way to nine. Because if there weren't nine, somebody was going to have to find the dynamite still down here hanging fire, waiting to explode."

The temperature in the cavern was dropping steadily. Esher's skin crawled. He wished Kostner would shut up so he could hear better. He was almost sure that there was something else down there with the two of them. He could feel—something—brushing featherlight against his face.

"And if the dynamite exploded too late, why then it would set off the gas released by the other blasts, and the whole thing would go. Start a fire in the mine, down under the ground. Fire follows the galleys—the tunnels—the galleys and the shafts. They might feel the ground tremble, but the first they'd know they were dead was when the fire roared up from below, like a fountain of heat and—"

He hit the switch again. Esher gasped and staggered as the light hit his eyes, blinding, and Kostner laughed. "Pretty spooky, huh, Esher?"

The writer stood panting, blinking furiously against the glare, scrubbing the tickling feeling from his cheek. It took a few minutes for him to recover his composure. "Is that what happened to your grandfather?" he said at last, his voice strained and creaky with effort.

"Probably." Kostner didn't sound perturbed. "Nobody knows. Some of the oldtimers say he was cursed, but hell, you don't have to be cursed to die in a mine." He nodded at the winch frame. "Down there on Level Two, they had a stable and a blacksmith shop. Used mules to haul the carts from the galleys. Lowered them down in the bucket until they drilled out a side shaft.

"My granddaddy, he was on Level Four. They'd just opened it up. Found a new vein. A new bonanza. He came up and got more men. Told his investors. They went down with him to see the strike—he said it was the richest strike in Nevada, richer than Comstock, or Tonopah. That's what I'm going after, Esher."

"Maybe you'll find your grandfather's bones down there."

The thought amused Kostner. He laughed again, the sound

reverberating from wall to wall, almost obscuring his words. "Hey, maybe I will. He's been holding on to it for me all this time, after all." Esher forced himself to put one foot in front of the other, walk over to the elevator cage, put one hand firmly on the door, and not look at the other man.

"You're not going to do this alone. You're going to bring in labor—the unions—It's not going to be all yours, Kostner."

Kostner chuckled deep in his throat. "Yes it will."

"*How?*"

A smile slid across his face like a snake and was gone as quickly, and Esher thought about what Wanda had said about this man. "Some things just belong to you. Don't you know that? This mine—" he waved at the vault above them, the tunnels, the shaft—"we bought this with Kostner blood. We've got an *agreement* here. Nobody can take it away."

He stopped speaking, and in the following silence Esher thought, once again, that he heard something else. He looked up quickly at the tunnels, hoping to surprise a glimpse of whatever it was; but it was difficult to tell where the sound, if it really was a sound, was coming from. Rats, he thought. Or snakes. What would they find to eat down here?

"The tunnels," he began, trying to change the subject. "Do they connect all the mines around here?" He was remembering what Mikey had told him, about the network of tunnels extending all the way from one end of town to the other.

"Just about." Kostner didn't appear interested in following up. He slapped dust away from his jeans and scuffed at a shiny mark in the steel flooring. "You could probably go down one of those tunnels and see, if you wanted. Wouldn't advise it. The flooring doesn't go down there, and the timbering's pretty rotted by now."

"Are you going to shore them up?"

"Nope." The slapping sound was beginning to double back on itself, sound like thunder. "They cleaned out those ledges. I'm only interested in what's deep."

"How many people will it take?"

Kostner shrugged, glancing around as if estimating how many it had taken to carve out the smooth walls of the cavern. "Who knows? Depending on what we hit—a couple hundred, or even a thousand men. Mining engineers. Processors. I'll have my own processing facility, that'll employ a lot. Then the labor, the pick-and-shovel men. This mine will employ more people than live in this whole town right now."

"For how long?" He couldn't keep the skepticism from his voice.

Kostner looked amused. "As long as the strike lasts."

"So it could all collapse again. *Borrasca*." It was the word for the collapse of a silver strike, the opposite of "bonanza," that he'd picked up in his reading. Esher thought it might be a Basque word, since the Basque influence seemed to be so strong in the state. He made a mental note to check.

"You're learning the lingo, aren't you? Yeah, that could happen." But he sounded as if he didn't believe it. Confirming Esher's impression, he went on, "This land will support me and mine forever."

"You have an agreement, right?" Esher said wearily. Suddenly all he wanted was to get out, get to the surface, get away from the unimaginable tons of earth poised over his head. He stepped into the cage again.

"Damn right," Kostner said, and followed him.

# 5

The second bed in the hotel room made a good filing area. Esher spread papers around, stacked by subject: schools, land, history, economic development, crime statistics. The stacks made a semicircle around the photograph in the center of the bed.

The photograph showed the face of a man with glaring, obstinate eyes shaded by a hawk's brow and bushy eyebrows. Full sideburns framed his face. The photo was yellowed with age, but the streaks of gray in the sideburns still showed up clearly. The brim of a battered hat emphasized the hawk look even more.

It was another copy, only smaller, of the photograph that Harry Kostner had framed on the wall behind his tiny village. Esher stared at it speculatively.

Every official town document dated before 1912 had Daniel Kostner's name on it somewhere. Every land transaction bore his mark, either as buyer or as witness, never as seller. His name figured large on the tax rolls, and even more prominently in editorials to reduce those taxes.

After returning from his tour of the mine, Esher had spent the rest of the afternoon and into the early evening in the offices of the local newspaper, going through old issues, reading stories from microfilm and from the actual newspapers, now tattered with age. He had been looking for the story of Nintucca; what he was finding was the story of the Kostner family, grandfather, father, and son.

Daniel Kostner had arrived in Nintucca with the first wave of miners, somewhere around 1898. He had staked a claim—everyone had staked a claim, even children—but didn't seem interested, at first, in exploiting it. Instead, he opened the two businesses sure to make a profit in a mining camp: a saloon and a brothel.

Shortly thereafter he opened a general store. At about the same time, some enterprising newspaperman had started the *Nintucca News*. It held on for half a dozen weekly issues, supported by very little advertising, then folded, not to be revived for six years.

By that time the town had stabilized at a population of about twenty thousand—Esher checked the figures three times, but it seemed accurate. There were churches, a town hall, schools with three and four hundred students, an opera house. Ore refining facilities were being built. Nintucca was entering its period of bonanza. Esher counted references to at least twenty mines in the area, separate claims that were being worked and showing a profit. Among them he saw the Gallitas' Little Kitten Mine and Mikey Denton's Generous Lady.

Kostner had sold the brothel and was making a name for himself as a mining magnate at last. Over the next few years, he served on the town council and acquired mining claims. Esher was interested to see a definite sequence of events: the *News* would report a mining accident, a death, or some disaster at one of the claims; shortly thereafter, with a straight face, the paper reported that the town benefactor, Daniel Kostner, "a well-known and respected citizen of Nintucca," had made an offer, usually to the widow of the owner. Sometimes the paper would have to report another incident or two before the transaction would be reflected in the county clerk's records.

By 1912 all of the large competing claims had been shut

down, one by one, and it was clear that most of the miners in town had gone to work for Daniel Kostner at the Heartbreak Mine. The *News* offered speculation that the discovery of a new ledge was imminent, perhaps even a mother lode. Kostner was putting all of his energies, and all of his investment, into the Heartbreak Mine, driving miners to their limits to sink shafts ever deeper underneath the town itself. There was even a report of a small riot, apparently to do with hours and wages.

Then on Statehood Day, October 31, 1912, the accident.

The reporting issue of the *News* was bordered in black. It listed the names of two hundred and seventy-four men caught in a collapse deep in the Heartbreak Mine, and first among them was that of Daniel Kostner. Only a handful had escaped, and those had lost their senses at the horror of the tragedy, unable to explain what had happened deep within the earth. The mine was shut down, and with it, the ore refining and processing plant.

Nintucca began to die.

The few independent claims left began to peter out as well. The last issue of the *News,* published in April of 1914, confirmed that the town was now in a period of *borrasca*.

The population had melted away like summer snow; fewer than five thousand remained, and more were leaving every day. The schools and churches and opera house had closed. Only its position as the county seat, and the unflagging determination of the Widow Kostner to secure the heritage of her infant son, Thomas, kept what was left of the town alive. There was a tone of bitterness in the last editorial that had never shown in Daniel's lifetime, suggesting that haste to wrench riches from the earth and lack of expenditure for basic safety measures might have had a role in the disaster. The word "hubris" was used with a certain vindictive relish.

It was fifteen years before another newspaper appeared in the town, this time to take over the responsibility of posting legal notices relating to the Depression. The Kostner family was keeping a low profile, Esher noted, but survived the Crash well enough to extend its holdings into ranching. Publication was spotty for the next several years, but in 1939 a special issue came out to note the marriage of Thomas Kostner to Estelle Pandowski of Reno, Nevada. A year later, his son Harold was welcomed into the world.

World War II brought small industry to the town, mostly in support of government installations never directly referred to. Thomas Kostner served with distinction in the Pacific theatre, achieving the rank of Major, and then faded into the background, content to remain a rancher. He served two terms as Sheriff, and thereafter his son Harry was more prominent in the news than he was.

Harry Kostner dominated his high school class of twelve students, winning honors in sports and state speech tournaments. He had gone out of state to get a degree in mechanical engineering and mining technology, but unlike most sons of Nintucca, he had returned. He married two years after the death of his father in 1967, to one Wanda Mirielle Prinzchen, apparently his high school sweetheart. The marriage lasted fifteen years, producing no children. Harry made Kostner a name to conjure with in northern Nevada, serving on the Gaming Commission, Special Advisor to the Governor, winning a lawsuit or two against the Bureau of Land Management. But he never left Nintucca, and he never let go of the mines.

He had enough now. More than enough. He could start writing. Turn in a draft tomorrow.

The cursor blinked against the otherwise blank orange screen, waiting for him.

Esher shuffled papers, licked his lips, and wished for a drink.

A drink. Oh, God, the burning fire of good whiskey so smooth it had no taste until it hit his stomach and blossomed into warmth, hard liquor that made him feel light and powerful and capable and—

And nothing. Turning off the computer, he lay back on the bed and reached for his wallet, dug into the scraps of paper with scrawled telephone numbers, business cards, driver's license. One plastic card, for gasoline: all that was left of his credit. And the photos: two, small. One a school picture of a little girl, laughing into the camera, shining brown hair bound back by a red ribbon, eyes so green even the school camera picked up the color. The other a folded newspaper picture, creased until it was frayed at the folds, of a car wrapped around a tree. He laid the picture of the little girl on the bedspread beside him and opened the other, staring at it until his eyes blurred, studying the way the roof had caved in, the passenger side collapsed, the roots of the once-live oak, torn out of the earth by the impact, hung in the air. It took only a few minutes, this time, until he didn't want a drink any more.

# 6

"Hey, Dave? Steve. How's it going, big guy?" The voice at the other end of the phone was perhaps a touch too casual to be convincing. Esher allowed himself an ironic smile.

"Fine. Doing great. Met Kostner, looked at his mine. Got some background material." Shoving a neat stack of paper out of the way, he stretched out on the bed, wedging the telephone in the curve of his neck. "This is one strange little town."

"Oh yeah? Strange how?"

Esher could picture him, sitting in his Cleveland office overlooking the tree-lined bend in the river, twisting back and forth in the swivel chair, tapping a pen against his teeth. The walls papered in *Town Life* covers. The discreet little glass-fronted bookcase that held journalism awards instead of books. Dozens of awards, most of them won under Migliori's editorship.

Back in the old days, Steve Migliori never called him while he was on an assignment. Never felt the need to check up on him.

"It's a little town in the middle of nowhere—" For a moment, he was tempted to add, *I was talking to some locals in the bar last night,* but decided against it. Why worry the man? Why waste the energy? Steve was already nervous enough, risking expense money and a kill fee on a known drunk. Esher didn't need to get a rise out of him; he owed him too much. Financially and every other way. "I mean, there is *nothing* here. Maybe three thousand people, and it's the biggest town for two hundred miles."

"Is there a story?" *And are you getting it? Or are you getting drunk?*

Esher found himself hesitating, thinking about the questions his editor asked out loud rather than the ones between the lines. "Yeah, there's a story," he said slowly. "I'm not sure it's the one we thought it was. There's a lot going on here for a little nothing town."

"Is Kostner serious about opening up the mine?"

"Oh yeah, dead serious. Some people are pretty happy about it, too."

"But not everybody?"

*Where's the conflict?* It was Migliori's favorite question, his contention that the story was in the differences and not the similarities. Esher smiled again, genuinely this time. It was like the old days. And it felt terrific.

"Well, we've got your standard generic protesters, but I think they're more worried about some government testing going on outside town. Some of the oldtimers aren't too thrilled about opening up the mine—lots of superstition about it. There's a nice human-interest angle there." There was, too. He picked up a pencil and made a note to himself on a yellow legal pad.

"Are you following up?"

For a moment, a flash of professional irritation. *No, I'm not following up, I'm sitting here on my duff collecting expense money!* "Yeah," he said evenly. "I'll put a draft of the first article in the mail to you tomorrow if you want, Steve."

A silence on the other end, punctuated by the crackling of the long-distance connection. He could hear the tension, Steve trying to decide whether to say *Yes, send it on,* or *No, go ahead and do your job.* He felt a stab of sympathy for the man on the other end of the line.

"No, that's okay." Migliori had made up his mind. "I'll trust your judgment on this. Let me know how it's going, okay?"

*Report in so I'll know you haven't gone on a bender,* in other words. Still, it was more than anyone else would have done—a hell of a lot more. "Sure thing, man. It's going fine, really. And Steve—"

"Yeah?" Wariness. Unwillingness to acknowledge what was coming.

"I appreciate the chance." It had to be said, whether Migliori wanted to bring it out in the open or not. Sure enough, Esher could hear the other man clearing his throat in embarrassment. Fumbling, Migliori changed the subject, and after a few more minutes of small talk he ended the conversation.

Esher hung up and stared bemused at the phone. What the

hell could you do with a man who believed in you even when you didn't believe in yourself?

He washed the dust off his face and stared into the bathroom mirror, examining his eyes. Bloodshot, from all the endless dust and sand. They hadn't been this bloodshot since—

*Since the last time you got drunk,* he told himself. The hazel eyes closed at the memory:

Late, late night, or early morning it was; what you called it didn't matter. Rain lashing down like whips. Smell of gasoline, and the terrible numbness where his head had hit the frame of the car door. Something warm rushing over his left cheek. And his own eyes in the driver's-side mirror, bloodshot, glazed, confused. Seeing themselves and not recognizing themselves. Slowly declining whirring noise of a wheel suspended in midair and spinning to a stop.

His eyes had closed then too and not opened again until he was in the emergency room, to see interns and nurses and men in blue uniforms rushing back and forth across his vision, blocking out the fluorescent lights and acoustic tiles, saying anxious things and leaving again. He remembered trying twenty-seven times to count the holes in one of the tiles, and never managing once to finish it before someone else leaned over him and made him lose his place. He was cold. He couldn't move his arms. And his mouth was so terribly dry, and nobody would give him anything to drink.

*Damned if I will,* he thought to himself, and going back out to the bedroom he set up the laptop and booted it up, playing back the pocket recorder while he waited.

The blank screen still waited for him, the cursor patiently blinking in the upper left-hand corner.

What to say, what to say . . . He found himself remembering again, this time the bedroom in his apartment back in Columbus, staring at a blank sheet of paper in an old Selectric and wondering how the hell he could possibly fill it up. Wondering who he thought he was kidding. Not that there was anyone left to kid—his eyes filled with easy tears. He was alone in a ratty three-room apartment, rented furniture and a repo notice in yesterday's mail, no job, no income, no home, no *family*—no inspiration. Deadness where the words used to be.

Getting up and walking to the refrigerator with its posted

schedule of AA meetings and wondering if it was too late to get to one. It would be easier, he considered, to stand up in front of a group of total strangers and identify himself as an alcoholic than to fill up that empty sheet of paper . . . Opening the refrigerator, licking his lips and trying to see a bottle of beer where there was none, where there was nothing at all but a wilted head of lettuce. He had always hated lettuce. He couldn't remember why he'd bought it. Or when.

The apartment felt as if it were closing in on him. Constricting. He wanted out, away. He wanted to get away from the crummy living room/bedroom/kitchenette, out to a place where decent people lived and he could *do* things again. He wanted to have a party.

Big party. Lights and dancing and people, and liquor, lots of booze. Can't have a party without booze. Shut up, Katie, I'm feelin' fine. Feelin' real fine 'til you started in. Can't a man have a good time any more? Patty's crying? Shut her up too.

Then the dark. The road.

No money. And he didn't know anybody having a party. All his friends looked the other way when they saw him on the street.

Couldn't stand the soiled shirt, stained trousers, six-day beard, and the look in his eyes. He was sober and he hated it. He went back to the kitchen and began opening drawers, not sure what he was looking for, sure that there was something there that would make him feel better. The drawers were empty. He didn't have money to buy things with, things like pots and pans and forks and spoons and knives. Sharp knives.

The empty drawers went flying across the room, gouging chunks of plaster off the walls. The teakettle, iridescent with grease, followed, the top coming off and spraying water across the linoleum. It gave him an idea, a precious, original idea, and he turned the water on, hot, and stuck his hands in it.

The water came out red with rust, gurgled, howled in the pipes, and began to steam, and he left his hands under the water, watching them parch white, and he cried. He cried until he couldn't stand any more and slumped to the floor, water still thundering in the sink above him, and held his burned hands and wept.

There were days like that, he remembered. Many, many days like that.

Until the day the telephone rang.

It had startled him more than it should have; he didn't remember having a telephone, or, having one, paying the bill—what would he have paid a bill with?—and no one ever called him anyway. There was no reason for anyone to call him.

It rang again anyway.

"H-hello?"

"Hey, Dave?"

It was for him. It was a voice he remembered, even if he was temporarily blank on the name and face that went with it. *Blackouts, I didn't think I was having blackouts* . . .

"Dave Esher? Hello?"

"Yes." His voice was rusty and unused.

"Dave? This is Steve. Steve Migliori? *Town Life*, remember?"

He would always remember that day, that call—that summons to hell and salvation. He owed Steve Migliori a lot. Maybe even everything.

He began to write.

# 7

The bowling alley was up the hill, forty yards from the local brothel, just inside the town limits of Nintucca. It had six lanes and a snack bar that consisted of four vending machines for stale snacks, two for soft drinks, and—of course—a bank of video poker games. It had been built twenty years before, and painted twice since, the last time a bright yellow since faded to a delicate pastel. In the moonlight, it glowed pale, with no color at all.

"What time is it?" Marianne murmured, nestling under Rick's arm. Rick was six-two; Marianne nearly a foot shorter. It made for a nice fit. Rick thought about Marianne's mother's job, and answered, "Late."

She chuckled, reading his mind or the tension in his arms. "So, time to get home."

"Yeah." He nuzzled her hair and they stepped off the porch, arm in arm, and started down the hill. "Yours or mine?"

"I've already been over to your place twice this week. If Mom calls me one more time and I'm not at the apartment—"

"Do you really think she doesn't know what's going on?" He squeezed her close.

"Oh, she knows. But she doesn't *admit* it yet." Marianne looked up at him with love in her eyes, and he had to stop and acknowledge it until they were both breathless. Finally Marianne pulled away. "Come on. I have to go to work tomorrow."

He grunted and allowed her to walk on, keeping one arm around her just in case she changed her mind.

"You guys didn't find anything today, did you?" Having established who was in charge, she allowed herself to explore other topics.

"Nope. Did you think we would, and I wouldn't tell you?" He guided her around a pothole in the road, snatched a kiss to her cheek. "Maybe one of those environmentalist wackos got her."

"Rick Zimmermann, that's an awful thing to say!" She stopped in the middle of the road and glared up at him. "You take that back."

"Friends of yours, huh? I thought we had a few too many tourists in town." His teeth gleamed in the moonlight. "How do you know they didn't kidnap her and stash her away?"

"They're not that kind of people! They're just trying to protect the environment. They're good people. And they don't like Harry Kostner any more than you do."

She was really angry with him, and he found himself getting a little angry in turn. "And they're gonna get themselves shot if they keep sneaking around the site and ripping us off, or setting fires and turning over equipment around the mine.

"And now they're really crazy. You heard Kathy talking about those cattle. Who around here would do something like that? Somebody crazy like your demonstrators. Or those idiots down to the Test Site, hiking in to sit on Ground Zero. They ought to let them come right in and sit there and get blown to smithereens and save everybody a lot of trouble." At the look on her face he laughed.

"Come on, Marianne, you know they're nuts. They don't even know what's going on and they're dead set and determined to stop it. Somebody feeds them a line and they swallow it without ever bothering to find out what's what."

"And I suppose you know all about it." Spinning, she marched down the road.

"Marianne, at least got out of the middle of the road!" Swearing, he went after her. "Marianne, can't you hear—"

She stopped and looked back at him. "What?"

He stopped too, a puzzled look she couldn't see crossing his face. "I thought I heard a truck coming up the hill, but I guess I was wrong. It's gone now."

She snorted, uncertainly, listening to the dark. "There isn't anything out there."

# 8

*It was raining, great gouts of water sheeting across the windshield, the windshield wipers struggling against it without noticeable results. The darkness blanketed the car, smothered it. The accelerator pressed hard against the ball of his foot, resisting, and he pushed back, trying to drive out of the darkness.*

*Outside, shadows formed in the darkness, loomed, faded.*

*Inside, a child's whimper.*

*Inside, the thirst.*

*He was floating, the white lines on the highway blurring, shifting back and forth, doubling, tripling. He tried closing one eye, then the other. No. Both eyes. A shriek beside him, and he opened his eyes again in time to swerve away from the tree growing in the middle of the highway.*

*A voice beside him, high and staccato syllables without meaning, irritating. He shouted at it to be quiet, but his voice broke up too, slurring away. The child in the back seat sobbed.*

*Both feet on the accelerator now, pressing hard, but there was no light to drive toward. Around them hills, trees, shadows forming and sweeping in, the car cleaving through them and rushing onward and leaving him behind, tattered on the shivering road.*

*The woman's voice more hysterical now. He reached underneath the seat for the bottle and took a long swallow and for a moment all was clear: the road, the woman who was his wife, his daughter in the back seat crying. The liquor burned in his nostrils, slid down his throat, nestled warm in his stomach and tendriled out along his veins, down limbs to fingers and toes, making each one feel alive for just one moment, making the road before him steady and solidify; one moment, shorter than the blink of an eye, and then the burning rose to his brain and it all blurred again and the shadows moaned outside and came closer, whipping at the sides of the car, the scratching become part of the screaming, part of the sobbing until he was trying to get away from that too, sure that if he could only go fast enough he could get away from it all, from the shadows and noises in the dark, but the road was so blurry he reached for the bottle again . . .*

# TUESDAY

# One

## 1

Rick Zimmermann's eyes opened thirty minutes before the alarm clock was supposed to ring. He turned his head to the digital clock at his bedside to verify the time and stretched out, carefully, to turn off the alarm. His other arm encircled Marianne, who was pillowed on his chest making small grumbling noises as she slept.

The darkness was oppressive. Adjusting to the dimness, his gaze traveled from corner to corner of the bedroom, looking for whatever it was that might have awakened him. There was nothing.

He drew his arm back and rested one hand lightly on Marianne's hair, a blonde fan covering his stomach. The fine strands stirred under his fingertips in response to his own breathing.

Outside, the gray mare nickered uneasily.

Bending his head forward, he could brush his lips against her head. She murmured and hooked one possessive arm tighter around his waist, and he smiled to himself in the dark. It hadn't really taken all that much convincing to talk her into staying the night.

The gray mare nickered again, and he pulled himself up on one elbow to hear better. Muttering protest, Marianne came awake. "What is it?"

"Something bothering the old lady," he whispered. "Dog or something. Not important."

"Mmmmm." One hand slid suggestively down his body. "You aren't going out there right away, are you?"

"Hey, we both have to go to work, don't we?" he teased, but he was sliding back down, burying his face in the crook of her neck. "Ah God, lady—"

"Rick—" But it was difficult to shift his attention away from her body; after a few moments he stopped trying.

A while later he lay still, his face against her breast, listening to her heartbeat. "You were saying?" he murmured.

"I love you, Rick." Her hand rested lightly on his hair, stroking it.

He could feel himself tighten up at the words. Love. Marriage. Kids. He could see it all stretching in front of him like a life sentence—

"I love you too," he said. He was almost surprised at himself.

"I'm gonna go to school, you know." Her hand never stopped moving. "Out of state. Next year."

"I wasn't planning on staying here forever."

"Are you sure?" The words were wistful and uncertain, and he was filled with a sudden, wholly unfamiliar tenderness.

"I'm sure." He lifted his head and kissed her.

Outside, the horse neighed in alarm.

"*Damn* those dogs!" He threw himself out of the bed and went to the window, leaving her convulsed with laughter behind him.

He turned back to apologize, but she waved him away. "No, forget it. We have to get to work. Both of us. We need the money, remember? Go on! There's always tomorrow!"

# 2

The drill bit resting on the conference table looked like a giant ball three feet across, studded with dozens of black diamond shapes the size of a large man's fist. The diamond shapes were diamonds in fact. The three men examining it touched the corners and edges almost reverently, avoiding the jagged cracks that laid the diamonds open like wounds.

"What in the *hell* could do that?" one of them snapped. "Jon, I thought you said this was just ordinary tuff around here."

"It is." Jonathan White, Ph.D., studied the cracked diamonds with distrust. "I don't know what could do it. It has to be a flaw in the material. We'll have to replace it."

The other two men looked at each other uneasily. "Er, with *what*?" the sandy-haired one asked. "We don't have any more capital equipment money in the budget. We weren't planning on buying a new drill bit until next fiscal year, and you keep telling us we have trouble on the funding . . ."

White glared him into silence. He was a short man, bald except for a monk's fringe of graying hair, the fluorescent lights gleaming off the top of his skull and glittering in his glasses. Alone among the scientists at the site he insisted on wearing lab whites; the others joked behind his back that the day White actually went out in the field and got his precious lab coat dirty would mark the end of the world. He preferred to remain in his office, set up in the main administrative center some miles from the actual drill site, brooding over graphs and equations and crunching numbers on his desktop computer.

The other two, Perry Ruiz and Paul Northhampton, at least a dozen years younger, much preferred getting their hands dirty. They were dressed in jeans and long-sleeved cotton shirts and wore baseball caps with odd logos. Privately, they felt the project was more theirs than White's. The theoretical work was his; he would be senior author on any publications; but he would never, never get his soft pale hands actually dirty.

"This didn't happen downhole," White said now. "It didn't hit something and crack. Where's Santillanes? What does he know about this?"

"He was the one who reported it. He found it in a check this morning and told me about it." Perry shook his head. "I don't under—"

"Get him in here. I want to talk to him."

The younger men glanced at each other, and Paul shrugged. He walked around the desk, behind White, and made a small production out of picking up the base station microphone.

"Santillanes, Northhampton. Santillanes, report to Dr. White's office immediately."

"Ten-four." The acknowledgment crackled with static.

Northhampton replaced the microphone on his hook and looked down at White's gleaming pate. "He's coming in, sir."

White snorted. "I don't trust these security people. This is the third incident in as many weeks, and who else has been out here? I think they're being paid to sabotage us."

"I wouldn't say that too loudly," Perry cautioned. "We may have a couple of flakes, but these are good men. Gil Santillanes has excellent references—I called them myself. He's a professional. And if it is sabotage, we can't afford to have him walking off the job."

White looked pale and unhealthy in the fluorescent lighting. "He's replaceable. Nobody's indispensable, Ruiz. We can hire more—"

"Do you have any idea how hard it is to get people to come up here in the middle of hell's own nowhere to take a job sitting around for hours maybe in the middle of the night doing nothing but look out a car window in *case* something *might* happen?" Ruiz snapped as Northhampton came out from behind the chief scientist, frantically making useless shushing gestures. "And then we have to spend eighteen months getting them cleared! By that time they've gotten themselves a job somewhere they can get off work in time to see their families!"

"For what we pay them, it can't be too difficult," White responded imperturbably. "With the overtime they put in they're getting rich. We could use that money better—"

"Do *you* want to sit out here all night, night after night, day after day, with the horses and the coyotes, watching the damn drill rig? You bet *I'm* gonna ask for a raise!"

"That will be enough," White snapped. Perry had opened his mouth to answer when they heard the rumble of a truck pulling up on the gravel outside the metal building. A vehicle door slammed; moments later came a knock on the office door.

"Come in." White was still struggling with his temper. "I mean, come in, Mr. Santillanes. I understand that you were the one who discovered this latest—problem." He waved at the cracked bit on the table.

"Yes, sir."

"Well, dammit, tell me how it happened!"

Something sparked deep in Santillanes' flat brown eyes and was shuttered away. He shifted his weight, balanced evenly on both feet, and clasped his hands behind his back. The holstered .38 at his side seemed a part of him, and the other men in the room took on an uneasy insignificance. "I can't say how it happened, sir. I was making a routine check this morning at oh-six-thirty over at the drill site, Hole Sixteen, and found this bit lying outside the equipment shed. Upon examination I found that it was cracked. I contacted Mr. Ruiz and informed him of the problem. He came to the site and took possession of the bit. That's all. Sir," he added as an afterthought.

The two younger scientists glanced at each other and swallowed grins.

"Did you look around any further? Was the equipment shed open? Were there any tracks? Any other damage?" White was looking for a flaw in procedure more than he was seeking information, and the man before him recognized the fact.

"I took pictures of the scene," Santillanes said, without smiling, as he reached into a pocket of his khaki shirt and produced a sheaf of Polaroids. "As you can see, the bit was lying a few feet outside the door. The door was padlocked and the lock did not appear to have been disturbed.

"Nothing else at the site seemed to be out of place.

"There may be tracks in the dirt there," he added, pointing to the flat-packed desert sand shown around the bit, "but if so, I can't find them. Sir." He resumed his parade rest, and the other men stared at each other.

"Did you check the other holes?" White was still trying to re-establish his superiority and was having difficulty doing it. "The chemical storage shed? The rig?"

"Yes sir." All of the items named were on the regular checklist, and all four men knew it.

"When was this bit added to the inventory?" White demanded. Santillanes remained mute, staring into space a few inches over the Project Manager's gray-fringed head.

Northhampton cleared his throat. "That's, er, that would be in the receiving report," he said. "They wouldn't have those records in Security. I can go find that out."

White stared at Santillanes a minute more. Santillanes remained unaffected.

"I suppose we'll have to report this to the sheriff too," Ruiz

said, breaking the silence. "Maybe it's those demonstrators. Or
that old man who's been hanging around."

Santillanes almost spoke, then decided against it. The others
watched him, the two younger men with interest, their boss
with irritation. Then, with a grunt, White waved the three men
before him away. "Let me know what you find out," he said as
they filed through the door. "Report it. Maybe the law can
solve this mess."

"Shit," Perry said as the door swung shut behind them.
"Sorry about that, Gil. You know his problem."

Outside White's office, Santillanes' resemblance to a tin
soldier evaporated. "Hey, no sweat. He's a paranoid little shit.
I can deal with that."

"Yeah, by driving him nuts with that parade ground act,"
Paul said.

Gil grinned, transforming his expression for just a moment
into that of a relaxed, rather cheerful person. "But it's so *easy,*
man. How could I resist?"

The three men were still laughing as they left the building
and got into a pair of pickup trucks, Perry and Paul in one and
Gil in the other. They pulled away from the temporary building
in a cloud of dust and gravel.

The "road" to the drill site was a badly bladed path with
well-defined ruts; the pickups jounced and bumped from one to
the other, slamming spines and skulls. They passed a small
herd of horses, scrubby hammerheaded bays, and a pair of
coyotes trotting alongside the road on some private business of
their own. A flock of ravens called raucously overhead.

The drill rig stood beside three medium-sized, weatherbeaten sheds two miles from the administration building. Gil
came to a stop in front of the nearest, the other truck pulling in
behind him. Perry and Paul slid out and walked over.

"This is where the bit was," Gil said. "You can see nobody's
done anything to the lock on the shed. I didn't open it up before
I called you."

"Mmmmph." Perry examined the shed door, and Paul
walked fifty feet or so over to the rig. The drill shaft had been
unshipped from the drilling frame and lay beside it, curiously
forlorn. A couple of discolored, empty fifty-five-gallon drums
lay on their sides beside the drill hole. Nothing seemed out of

place. Paul walked back by way of the other sheds, checking them as he went.

"But you know, there's something else," Gil was saying to Perry. "I didn't want to tell White. But one of the boys was on long patrol, down by the old site, and he found something a little weird."

"Whaddaya mean, a little weird?" Perry pulled out a cigarette and twirled it between his fingers like a mini baton. "What kind of weird?"

Gil shook his head. "I don't think I can explain it. I think you guys better come look."

"All the way down to the old site?" Paul protested, overhearing. "Hell, I don't have any kidneys left just from coming out this far. And somebody has to check the receiving reports or White'll hang us all out to dry."

"*And* we've got to pour in that new mix," Perry added. "So why don't you just go ahead and take care of all that, and I'll go see what has our chief security honcho here all spooked up."

"Thank God," Paul said, and got into the truck.

Gil and Perry waited for him to pull out before getting in, Perry still twirling his cigarette. "So what's the big deal?" Perry asked again as the plume of dust settled.

Gil shook his head enigmatically. "Nope. I want you to see this."

"O-kay, let's go." They got into Gil's vehicle and took off.

"This stuff you're pouring down the holes," Gil said minutes later, slowing to avoid a massive pothole in the road. "What are all these chemicals supposed to do?"

Perry laughed. "What are they supposed to do? Stabilize the drill hole. Turn the walls into instant plastic. No more holes collapsing. And incidentally, make our Dr. White a million-aire. Imagine what drillers and miners would pay not to have to shore up walls and holes."

"Hmmmmmm." Gil chewed over that thought. "Just what are these chemicals?"

"Now *that* is the magic question. What they are, and how they're mixed. Or how they ought to be mixed. White's still working on the fine details for this stuff."

"Mmmmmph."

Paul studied him curiously. "You don't like it."

"Just wondering about your environmental impact statement, that's all." Gil kept his eyes on the road.

"Oh, come on! Don't tell me you sympathize with our tame protesters!"

"I'm not telling you anything." He shifted gears and the truck came over the crest of a hill to the old drilling site, where White had started drilling operations eighteen months before. The site had been abandoned without explanation shortly thereafter. Now all that was left was a pattern of roads where the desert flora had been ripped away by construction equipment and automobiles, breaking the thin shell of soil that prevented erosion. Perry looked over the raw gouges in the desert skin and shook his head; Gil pulled up and got out of the truck, expressionless again. "It's over here."

"Over here" was beside a slight dip in the ground that defined where a storage shed had once stood. The ground was discolored with red circles of rust where steel drums had been. The two men walked over.

"Oh, man." Dismay was thick in Perry's voice. In the center of the depression lay a small body, a bloated hill of flesh with four slender legs sticking up awkwardly. Flies and the odor of death smogged the air.

The colt couldn't have been more than three days old, or more than two days dead; the coyotes hadn't gotten to it yet. It was bloated, but the part of the hide visible was intact, except for the eyes. Unlike most of the wild horses in Nevada, this one showed signs of elegance and breeding—probably the get of a stallion run away from a local rancher. Perry liked horses. He caught a lot of hell about it from the locals, whose opinion of the wild horses was less than edifying. "Poor little guy."

"A-huh." Gil walked over to the pathetic corpse. "C'mere."

"Huh? Why?" Perry was sympathetic, but he had no desire to examine the foal more closely.

Gil squatted down next to the tiny head. Crows had already picked out the exposed eye, and ants crawled in and out of the empty socket. "Well, are you coming to look or not?"

"Look at what? It's a dead horse." But he walked over, a sick feeling in the base of his stomach. "What's wrong with it?"

"This," Gil said. He pulled his .38 out of the holster, slid the barrel underneath the white-striped muzzle, and flicked his wrist to one side. The little head twisted over completely, exposing the other side, which had been resting against the desert sand, protected.

Perry gagged.

The other side of the foal's head was nothing but a skull; and the bones, which should have been clean and delicate, were melted together like wax.

# 3

Helen Vanderhaas sat cross-legged on the bed, rumpling the beige spread underneath her as she tucked her legs up tighter to give herself more working room. The tip of her tongue protruded between buck teeth as she leaned over the poster-board, stenciling in words in black Marks-a-Lot on the yellow background. It was going to take some more layers; social research showed that the easiest combination of colors to read was black on yellow. But it had to be really *black,* not faded-out gray. She wished there was enough money in the budget for real poster paint. This was going to take hours.

DON'T RAPE THE EARTH, the sign said. The words were nicely centered, lots of margin to balance things. Two more signs on the floor said CHEMICALS ARE POISONOUS and US GOVT POISONING MOTHER EARTH. That one hadn't worked out very well; the last word was crammed in and it looked junky. Oh, well, there were only two of them to carry the signs anyway. She'd make more tomorrow night.

Her glasses slid down her nose again. She pushed them up, using the same gesture to tuck her bangs behind one ear, and kept scrubbing black ink into the paper.

She and Jerry were the third team the Friends of Dirt, Grass and Trees (Inc.) had sent up here. The last pair had told Helen and Jerry the rules: Stay on the other side of the fence, don't block the road. Don't yell. Be polite. And always remember, the guards carry guns.

The guards were pretty nice most of the time. Marti, who'd been on the last shift up here, said one of the guys at the gate had even offered her a cup of coffee last spring. But when they tried to get pictures of what was going on, the site guards had called the sheriff and had them arrested.

Arrested. That would be exciting. Helen contemplated it for a moment: herself, limp in the arms of some massive brown-shirted security guard, being dragged away to jail, never revealing the presence of the incriminating roll of film hidden in her bra . . .  Where would Jerry be?

Beating the ape across the back with a protest sign, probably.

And then she'd stand up in front of the judge and make an impassioned speech about the environment, about the evils of abusing the earth, and everyone would be so impressed that the judge would actually be crying real tears as he condemned her to prison, because he'd have to, after all she *did* break the law, and it was one of the rules of civil disobedience that you had to suffer the civil penalties, but he'd fling off his black robe and pick up the sign from the floor and march off to take her place in the long line of protesters and people who knew what was Really Going On.

Maybe this very sign. If they used it for evidence. They might. So it was especially important that it look right. She couldn't use the US GOVT one at all.

Finally the letters were black enough to pass inspection. Stretching, she unwound from her almost full lotus and checked her watch. Jerry should be back by now. Maybe they could catch a quick dinner and see if they could do a night reconnoiter. The Friends weren't exactly sure what Dr. White was doing out at his site, though they knew it involved chemicals and drilling—anybody could figure that out from the trucks going in—and it was important that they get hard evidence. Dead animals. Poisoned water holes. Then they'd plaster it all over the newspapers. The people had a right to know what their taxes were paying for, after all. These security guards, why, their very existence was illegal. It was a free country, wasn't it? Government of the people? So how could they keep the people out?

Their jobs were illegal, she amended. One flexing foot knocked the Marks-a-Lot off the bed. The guards as *people* weren't illegal, of course. She supposed they could be pretty nice, if they didn't have such ugly jobs. Marti said they were.

It was a shame that the Friends could only afford to have two people at a time up here. She stood up and began to do yoga exercises, breathing deep and trying to balance into the Crane position. After the third stagger, she gave up and started touching her toes in time to the muffled blare from the band down in the bar. At first she'd been upset to find that this room didn't have a television or even a radio, but at six o'clock, when the band came on, she'd understood why—you got all the music you wanted through the thin walls. Lucky she liked country-western.

The hotel put them in this room on purpose, of course. The clerks knew right away they were with an environmentalist group—probably because nobody else checked in with poster-board under their arms. It worked out all right with the hotel, because who else would want a room right over the bar? and it worked out fine for the Friends, because they didn't spend too much time in the room anyway. Except for planning sessions, and making signs, of course. And even some of their planning sessions they had somewhere else. They weren't alone in this town, not by a long shot.

The door opened as she was in her third set of deep knee bends. Jerry was sneezing, his eyes were watering, and he was covered with dust—Helen really had to admire his commitment to the cause; anyone with allergies that bad really shouldn't be walking a picket line out in the open desert. He dropped his knapsack on the low bureau and lurched into the bathroom, coughing so hard he gagged.

"Jerry? Are you okay?"

Her answer was more coughing and the sound of running water. She straightened up and followed him into the bathroom to find him splashing water on his face and beard.

"Wow, you look awful. Hey, don't drink that water! It looked kind of green this morning, remember?" Helen didn't feel she deserved the look he gave her between hacks; he really did look awful. His eyes were all red where they weren't brown, and the water running into his dusty beard was making rivulets of mud. "Do you have some medicine or something?"

Jerry shook his head. His breathing was getting a little easier, though. "Do you mind?" he asked. "I'd like a little privacy here."

"Huh? *Oh*." Blushing, she ducked out again. It would be nice if the Friends could afford two hotel rooms, she thought.

Of course, it wasn't possible on the existing budget. They'd had to sit through a long lecture before the Friends let them come up here, about how they had to uphold the moral principles of the organization and not do anything to injure the reputation of the cause. They always had to get two double beds when persons of opposite sex went on a crusade. And, the director had reminded them, sign in as Mr. and Mrs. Just in case.

She hadn't been too sure about the idea at first, but Jerry had been a perfect gentleman. So far.

Resolutely ignoring the sounds coming from the bathroom, she continued with her exercises, long brown hair arcing through the air as she twisted from side to side, hands on waist. A healthy mind in a healthy body, she reminded herself.

"Fuck," Jerry said, entering the room. He was stripped to the waist, scrubbing at his head and neck with a towel and flinging his discarded shirt on his knapsack. "Do you know how hot it was out there today?"

"Ninety-six," Helen said, not pausing. "They said it was cooler than usual."

"And you believe that?"

"Well, isn't it?"

"I hope you used something besides crayon on those new posters." He held up for her inspection one of the ones he'd carried in: LOVE THE EARRRHTRHH. Or something. The last few letters seemed to have melted.

# 4

Wanda Kostner was singing along with the country-western band on the radio as she jounced along a few miles outside of Nintucca, on a side road leading to one of the local ranches, her latest delivery wedged into the seat beside her, when a spray of tiny purple flowers against the edge of the road, where rain gathered the few times it rained, caught her eye.

The road had been paved twenty years before, but now was deteriorated so badly that it was barely wide enough to accommodate her car; she had to check in the rearview mirror to make sure she wasn't going to block the way for someone behind her before she stopped. If she pulled the huge old Cadillac off the road entirely, she'd get stuck in the soft shoulder and never get out of it without a tow truck. Satisfied, she got out, leaving the engine running and the radio blaring, and teetering on her high heels, she stalked back to examine the flowers more closely.

They were pretty, and they matched her purple pantsuit.

Glancing around, she saw that no one was around to see except a curious cow fifteen feet away, swishing its tail and munching its cud. Cows never bothered her, though she liked them better as steaks. Carefully she crouched down, not quite on one knee, and placed the palm of one hand against the earth. Her lilac-tinted nails pressed into the dirt, leaving tiny semicircles. A good thing the polish was dry, she thought, or she'd have sandcast fingernails like those old candles she used to make years ago.

What she was about to do would have made her feel silly if most anybody was watching, but it was important nonetheless, and she'd been brought up to do it right. It was tradition, after all, and it went all the way back to the Indians. Wanda Mirielle was a strong believer in tradition, and in the bad luck that followed if you didn't do it just right.

"Spirit of the earth, you know me. I am your child. Share your beauty. Let me wear these flowers in your honor."

She paused and watched and waited for the omens, as her mother had taught her to do.

She could hear the breathing of the cow, deep and hollow like bellows working, its contented, steady chewing; the whisper of a breeze in the scrub; k.d. lang yowling on the radio. Smell the delicate scent of the flowers, the animal smell of the cow. Feel the grains of sand against her fingertips, the heat of the sun on her back.

The sun stayed bright.

She reached for the flowers, pulled them. The tough stems resisted. She had to brace herself and yank hard.

The roots came loose quite suddenly, tearing free from the earth and bringing up clods of dirt, releasing a stench so thick it could almost be cut with a knife, an odor of rot and death and decay.

Wanda fell backward, throwing the flowers as far away as

possible. The cow threw up its head, caught a whiff of the odor, snorted, and wheeled clumsily and galloped away.

Wanda scrambled to her feet, scrubbing her hands frantically against her pantsuit, backing unsteadily toward the car as a mist rose from the hole where the flowers had been. It rose up, and up, twenty feet over her head, and began to take a shape that looked almost human.

One heel caught in a creosote bush, and she went sprawling as the translucent misty figure reached out one stinking, dripping hand to her, and a sound came from somewhere, a moan, a cry.

Screaming, Wanda yanked free of the bush and lunged for the car, throwing herself in the open door and turning up the radio as loud as possible, trying not to look at the Shape in the air behind her.

The Cadillac peeled rubber as it had not done in fifteen years as Wanda tore away, refusing to look in the rearview mirror, refusing to see the gigantic image of a little girl picking up the discarded flowers and holding them out to her, pleading.

# 5

And far away, in a well-lighted room in a finely appointed house on the other side of town, someone else stared into the empty space between himself and a symbol on the opposite wall. His lips moved soundlessly. His hands drifted above the detailed model of the town, reaching and pushing against the air as if shaping it, pulling on it, trying to draw something to himself. One square, small-fingered hand clenched suddenly, so hard the knuckles went white. The other caressed a model hill, flowed over it to investigate the holes in its side, set a fallen building back upon its foundation. And all the time his lips moved in silent chant and his eyes continued to stare, unfocused.

The air he stared into began to thicken, darken. He did not see. The open hand drew a line from a hole in the hill to a toy of ruined buildings, barely making a mark in the sand of the model; the index finger nudged a truck out of the way, rolling it an inch or two and continuing to mark a path.

"Give me your bones," he whispered. "Show me your bones. Show me silver. Show me. By my blood I *order* you—"

An angry subsonic mutter came out of the thickened air.

His hand rose and hovered over the sculpted hills.

The other hand, his left hand, trembled.

The mutter increased. Behind him, a whiskey glass on the liquor cabinet jittered on the walnut surface, the liquid it contained crashing and foaming. He began to pull in harsh breaths, as if struggling. The skin around his unseeing eyes tightened.

The air before him began to take a shape.

Morning recess, and the smaller children gathered at one end of the schoolyard around an old man with blue eyes and a red bandanna, an old man who scooped up a fistful of dirt and rocks and showed it to them, talking low; and they listened soberly, nodding, reaching down to pat the ground reassuringly. This was the earth, and they were its friends, and the old man taught them as he had taught some of their parents before him, as old men have always taught young children, by telling stories.

# Two

## 1

The pickup threw up a half-grown rooster tail of dust as it pulled into a parking place on one side of the Courthouse, in between two green and white patrol cars with blue flashers in place. They needed washing, Gil thought; mud was caked on the side panels. Mud from the puddles that formed on dirt roads when it rained. And when was the last time it rained, anyway?

The thin, balding deputy sergeant on the desk looked up at him as he entered and then back to his desk, stuffing last month's issue of *Playboy* into a bottom drawer and ostentatiously flipping through a stack of papers, opening a drawer and pulling out a file, scribbling a note and placing it in the top drawer of the desk. He was making a fine show of being busy, and it was all for Gil's benefit, and both of them knew it.

Gil waited, leaning on the wooden dividing rail beside the counter, rocking back and forth and letting it squeak. He counted out three minutes before his patience ran out. "Okay, cut it out, O'Malley. These are your tax dollars speaking. Where's your boss?"

O'Malley looked up at last, a little too wide-eyed and innocent. "Oh. Mr. Santillanes. Sorry, didn't see you."

"Bullshit. Where's your boss?"

O'Malley's gaze narrowed. "There's no reason for abuse, Mr. Santillanes. Is there something I can help you with?"

"No," Gil said bluntly. "Where's Bailey? For the third time."

"Sheriff Bailey is not available at this point in time. If you have a problem, you'll have to deal with me." A gleam of triumph crossed his face. Considering it, Gil figured that the balding deputy was probably telling the truth. This time, anyway.

"When's she going to be back?"

"Sorry, that information is not available. If you have a report to make, you can tell me, and I'll give it the attention it deserves." Meaning: None at all.

Which meant that he didn't know where Bailey was—she'd left without telling him, and he was pissed off about it. Gil considered, staring at the other man until a red flush began creeping up from O'Malley's collarbone. He knew what would happen if he made a vandalism report to O'Malley; it would be round-filed before he got back into his truck. Besides, he wanted to talk to Bailey.

Meanwhile, there was O'Malley, whose whole world was central Nevada, and who had trouble grasping a vision any larger. Gil shrugged mentally. He had time to kill.

"Where'd you go to high school, O'Malley?" he asked gently.

"Nintucca County High. Who wants to know?"

"Just curious, that's all." Gil picked up a stub of pencil lying on the counter and tapped it, drumstick fashion, on the Formica top. "College in Reno, I s'pose."

The deputy didn't answer, but the flush deepened. He had never gone to college.

"Seems like everybody around here, mostly, went to Nintucca High. You have a good team?"

"Good enough."

Gil, who knew that for most years the local high school had never fielded a football team and never had a basketball team at all, smiled to himself. O'Malley leaned back, trying to figure out what he was getting at.

"Lots of people at your reunion?"

"Just about everybody. 'Cept a couple who got killed in a highway accident a few years back."

"That's pretty good, that is. My high school reunion, we were lucky to get sixty percent of the class. Scattered all over to hell and gone. Still, we had over seven hundred. Quite a party."

A snort of disbelief escaped O'Malley, whose senior class had numbered twenty-two. Gil affected not to notice.

"Hard to know everybody, a crowd that big. Did you know everybody at yours?" The pencil rattled into a drumroll.

"Yeah. What about it?"

"Nothin', man. Just making conversation, that's all." He shifted his weight, held the pencil upright and dropped it through his fingers onto the brown Formica divider top, catching it before it fell and dropping it again. "I guess your family came from around here."

"Lived here for ninety years." There was a naïve pride in O'Malley's voice, and he leaned back his chair onto the two back legs and waved a hand expansively. "My great-grandpa bought railroad ties for ol' Daniel Kostner himself."

Gil shook his head in awe. "Ninety years. Imagine that." His own family held a land grant in New Mexico signed by the Viceroy of Carlos I. "I'll bet you know everybody in town. Miz Bailey must appreciate all the help you give her."

The chair thumped back into place. "Miz Bailey got her own ways of doin' things."

As he spoke, the outer office door opened, and Laura Bailey came in, dust-coated and weary. Five or six men crowded behind her, all talking at once, their voices raised in dispute over something. Gil caught her eye and she nodded, indicating the crowd and silently asking him to wait. He settled back against the divider as she led the men into her office and shut the door.

O'Malley went back to his paper shuffling, dimly realizing that his visitor had shown him up somehow but not sure how. Gil had lost interest in the game and stood, not thinking about much, waiting for whatever came. He was good at waiting.

Hoarse voices were raised in the office, unintelligible demands or threats. He couldn't hear Bailey's answer, if any. After ten loud minutes the crowd came out again, still disgruntled, casting angry glances back toward the open office door.

A minute after that Bailey yelled, "Santillanes? You waiting for an invitation?"

Gil grinned and pushed open the swinging divider door.

Laura Bailey was seating herself behind her desk as he came in, her hands wrapped around a chunky ceramic mug whose contents steamed gently. "You want coffee, it's over there," she grunted, pointing chinwise at the table in the corner. "So what did you lose this time? Or did you just come in to make my so-called deputy's life miserable, not that he doesn't deserve it?"

Gil fixed himself a cup of coffee, carefully adding two gray lumps of sugar, and stirred it with a pink plastic spoon as he came back and seated himself on the cracked-leather couch parallel to the desk. "Who says we lost anything?"

"I did ask if you had any other good reasons for being here." Bailey sipped and made a face. "Swear to God that little asshole puts chicory in my coffee cans."

Tasting his own, Gil was inclined to agree. He set the coffee cup aside. "Well, maybe just to see your sweet face."

Bailey rolled her eyes. "Give me a break, Santillanes. I've had a rough day and I don't need any more shit, okay?" Her eyes were bloodshot, and sweat drew thin lines down her face. "What's the mad scientist bitching about this time?"

"Damaged equipment." He decided to dispense with the small talk and get to the point, allowing for the other's evident weariness. "He thinks the demonstrators are doing it, or maybe old man Gallita."

"Did you tell him he's a damn fool?"

"Nope."

"So what else has been going on out there?"

Gil sighed. "This latest thing is a damaged drill bit. Cracked clean across, like somebody took a two-million-pound sledge-hammer to it." He started ticking items off on his fingers. "Huge holes in the roads. White thinks somebody—naming no names—is setting off grenades, never mind that nobody ever hears anything. Whole damn shed full of rig disappears like the earth swallowed it up. Couple boys go out hunting and can't find any deer or any damn thing else—now that *really* got them spooked—"

The two of them looked at each other.

"And what do you expect me to do about it?"

Gil shrugged. "Take the report on the drill bit. If you could run something about these two new peaceniks from Las Vegas, I'd appreciate it. I don't think they have the brains to get on the site, much less do the kind of damage we're talking about, but somebody's doing it."

"But you won't let me on your precious site to do an investigation."

Gil cocked his head. "Nobody to arrest yet, Sheriff."

"You think Gallita's responsible?" she challenged.

"Sure, and pigs fly." He paused. "He *has* been coming around. Some of the boys don't like to chase him off—they're local, and he's one of the original oldtimers, I guess. We found him a few days ago at four in the morning sleeping it off in his truck in the middle of what we thought was a protected area."

The sheriff nodded to herself, rocking back and forth in her swivel chair and pinching the bridge of her nose. "Yeah. That old man. He doesn't really cause any trouble, but he keeps showing up in the wrong place at the wrong time and nobody wants to do a damn thing. They take care of him like he's everybody's oldest uncle."

"Well, White won't." He set his mug down on the wrought-iron plant stand next to the couch and leaned back, arms stretched out against the back of the couch.

Bailey smiled grimly. "White's not from around here. Neither are you, and neither am I. I'd just as soon put him in the tank and let him dry out with the rest of them, but the one time I tried it . . ." She shook her head. "Harry himself was on the phone, breathing fire.

"You ever run into this kind of shit before?"

Gil stared at the water-marked ceiling, deliberately misunderstanding her. "Kind of hard to argue with government regulations. You can even jail the parish priest if you want. Makes things easier."

But Bailey persisted. "I mean the Fine Old Families syndrome. You were in law enforcement, I can tell. C'mon, 'fess up. I'll even buy you a beer."

A rare, engaging smile crossed the other's olive-tan countenance. "Oh, hell yes. You get the assholes everywhere. Company commanders and site bosses who think that every poor schmuck of a guard should carry their pictures around so the guard will know who he shouldn't be searching. But they raise hell when the inspection report shows their security stinks. They all think they're above it all. Too good or too important to obey the same rules as everybody else."

"Where'd you serve? You were in the military?"

"Military, civilian. Civilian in Pennsylvania, my last job. Air Force for a while down South and in 'Nam." His last words were reluctant, and Bailey gave his tone due consideration and shifted the subject.

"So why the hell would these folks protect Jessie Gallita?"

He rolled his shoulders in a horizontal shrug. "Fond of him, I guess. I don't care. If I find him out on the site again I'm gonna bust his ass."

Bailey smiled and drank her coffee. The silence between the two was not uncomfortable. Gil was looking around the office, noting the framed certificates on the wall, photos on the desk, the lush potted plant in the corner situated to hide the place where a six-inch chunk of plaster had come off the wall. It all seemed refreshingly normal.

Bailey followed his gaze and his thoughts. It was a down-home kind of office, and she liked it. But thinking of down home reminded her of something else, less pleasant.

"While you're here, I've got something I want to show you," she said, putting down her cup and scrabbling in her desk drawer for a manila folder. "Ever seen anything like this?" She handed a photo over to the man.

He examined it curiously, hunching forward and holding it up to the light.

"What am I supposed to see?" he said at last. "It's picture of the Kozlowskis and their kid—what's his name, Jerry, Jeremy. What about it?"

"That's all you see?"

"That's all that's there." His tone was confident but curious. The casual manner had disappeared, replaced by a sharp professional interest. "But you expect me to see something else. What?"

"Tessy."

"Not present and accounted for, ma'am." He placed the picture face up on the desk corner between them. "She's not in that picture."

Bailey picked it up again, holding it by the edges, as if she didn't like the feel. "No, she isn't." She replaced the photograph in the file and shoved it back in the drawer, slamming the drawer shut as if to trap something.

"You think the parents did something to her?" Gil's brows

were knit. It was clear to him that Bailey wasn't giving him the full story, and it bothered him, and he didn't mind that it showed.

"It's been known to happen," she said slowly, "but I don't think it did this time. I wish to hell I knew what happened to that little girl."

"Yeah." Gil was still leaning forward, resting his forearms on his legs. "We had one like that once, when I was in the Air Force. Sergeant, he was. He used to baby-sit for some of the families in base housing. Everybody liked him. Then one day a little girl, two years old, a Major's daughter, came up missing. Nobody thought of this guy, he hadn't been taking care of her that day. We turned that base upside down, had the FBI in, the local cops, everybody.

"They found her body crammed under his kitchen sink." He let loose a long breath, releasing the strain in his voice. "I was on the General Court. The guy got life at hard labor. I would have put him up against the wall and shot him."

He looked at the woman. "I had my people looking for Tessy, out at the site. Didn't find anything. Doubt she ever got that far, but I figured it couldn't hurt."

Bailey nodded gratefully. "I was going to ask you if you would. I appreciate it."

He waved it away. "Hey, it's a kid. It's worth putting in some overtime for." He found himself thinking of the dead foal, and flashed on an image of Tessy Marie Kozlowski's bones, melting, and shook himself. He didn't want to think like that.

Bailey studied him. "How come you stay, Santillanes?"

Straightening, he looked her in the eye. "The pay is good."

It was a lie, and they both knew it was a lie. But Gil couldn't tell Laura Bailey—not yet—why he stayed in a place that made his flesh crawl in the daytime and twisted and squirmed in his dreams at night. He wasn't sure he had it figured out himself. He got up and brushed at his khaki pants, effectively ending the conversation.

" 'Preciate it if you'd let White know I did my duty," he said sardonically. "Otherwise I'm going to find that fine paycheck a little short next week if he decides I came into town to goof off."

"Hey, no problem. Let me know if you find out anything

about your little mysteries out there. I have a few mysteries of my own I'd like to solve. Maybe they're the same thing."

Bailey was up, holding out her large square ringless hand.

Gil took it and shook it, in the firm grasp of a respected colleague. "Same here. Nice talking to you, Sheriff." He glanced down at the drawer into which Bailey had shoved the photograph. "Let me know about that someday too, huh?"

Bailey smiled grimly. "If I ever figure it out myself."

# 2

The high piping sound of children's voices poured across the playground like birdsong, swooping and trilling into the four corners and filling them up, rebounding and echoing against the red brick walls of the school, clustering into themes and counterpoint as the cliques and clubs re-formed and re-acknowledged themselves in their free time.

One child, intensely fair-haired, clad in blue jeans and a red-and-white-striped shirt, walked down the steps alone. He approached a group of boys, veered away as they looked up at him and turned away, sniggering. He wandered aimlessly by the fence for a few minutes, kicking at nothing, oblivious to the playground monitor who kept an anxious eye on him. After ten minutes or so the monitor directed her attention to the kindergarteners, and he approached another gang of boys huddled under a stunted cottonwood tree, monopolizing the only shade and making catcalls to the sixth-grade girls by the steps, thirty feet away.

A bigger boy, dark-haired like all the others on the playground, came out of the center of the group to confront him. "You told yet, Jer'my?"

"No," Jeremy said. "I didn't tell." His voice was wretched, low. "I don't break my promises."

"You better not!" the bigger boy said, glancing back at his friends for support. They grumbled encouragement.

"Are you gonna let me in?" Jeremy said. He hunched deeper into his shirt.

"What'sa matter, you gonna cry? We don't want no cry-babies in our gang."

"Crybaby! Crybaby!" The boys, ranging in age from about nine to twelve years, took up the cry.

"I did everything you said! I wasn't scared!"

"But you're cryin' now!"

"I bet he wants his little sister to come save him!"

"Yeah, but he dumped her down the well!"

"Badger took her!"

A silence fell suddenly, and the boys glanced about them nervously until one said too loudly, "Badger took Tessy down the well!"

"Down the well, Jer'my! Down the well!" Ragged at first, the chorus grew until they were all shouting it. The boys circled Jeremy, chanting in chorus, darting in to push at him and away again before he could respond. "Tessy's down the we-ell, Tessy's down the we-ell—"

Swallowing his tears, Jeremy broke loose and fled.

# 3

"Why is it important to you?" Esher asked. The microcassette recorder whirred silently on the bedspread, wedged in the maroon folds rucked up by Helen Vanderhaas' lotus-folded legs.

"Well, look at the ozone layer. Look at the rain forests. We're just destroying everything, and we have no right. We have no right to destroy everything."

For a moment, looking at her, David Esher felt a sense of déjà vu. More than twenty years ago he had sat cross-legged on a blanket talking to a woman with long braids and a beaded headband, a painted love symbol on her cheek, and between them a large clunky tape recorder took down almost identical words. Helen Vanderhaas could have been that woman; probably was her daughter.

And on the other bed sprawled Jerry something or other, his arms crossed over his eyes to hide what Esher was sure was a snicker.

"Why are *you* here?" He raised his voice to direct it to the other man, challenging him. Jerry's arm lifted from his face long enough to send him an incredulous look and fell back again. "Do you believe that the work out at the site is a danger to the environment?"

"Sure it is." Jerry's voice was muffled in flannel. He twisted up into a sitting position, leaned forward to paw under the bed and come up with a beer. The top popped off and the smell of hops and malt filled the air. Esher could feel his nostrils flare to take it up.

"Jerry's really committed," Helen said hastily, trying to make up for her partner's lack of enthusiasm. "He's been out there all day, talking to the people going into the site, trying to get them to see what they're doing is wrong. But he's tired now."

"Do you take turns?"

"Oh yes. Tomorrow I'll go out. Then we'll got out together. Sometimes they stop to talk to us on their way in."

Esher winced inside. He had heard the kind of "talking" that defense installation workers did to demonstrators at the gates of laboratories and military bases. They rarely listened.

"I think some of them really agree with us, but they just don't know how to say so," Helen went on gamely. "Some of them, you can tell they have a real feeling for it. That's because they're outside a lot, I think. If you're shut away inside a plastic cocoon, how can you get in touch with the real world? But if you're outside, it's different. It's as if the planet has its own heart and you can feel it beating. I can, anyway." Pushing up her glasses on her nose again, she glanced up shyly. "You probably think I'm crazy."

"No," he heard himself answering.

From the other bed came an ambiguous grunt.

"And you know," Helen went on, obviously choosing to be selective about the responses she heard, "I think the planet knows too, you know? I think it knows what we're doing to it. Like that earthquake in San Francisco—"

"God wanted a turn at bat, that's all," Jerry said, sitting up. "Come on, you know what the Friends told us. No New Age stuff. Stick to the science."

Esher studied him a moment, surprised. He hadn't figured out why Jerry was involved—other than to share a hotel room with Helen—but it sounded for a moment there as if he really did care.

"Don't you feel pretty isolated, doing this all by yourselves up here?" he asked at last.

"Oh, we're not alone. We have some local—"

"Shut *up*," Jerry interrupted her harshly. "That's enough."

"You have some local support?" David talked over him, hoping Helen's urge to talk would overcome her companion's orders. "There are local people who feel the way you do about the earth?"

"Yes there are," Helen said, shooting Jerry a defiant glance. "They think the earth is important, and the drilling's bad. They even think the mining's bad. Important people in this town, too."

Important? The only important person in the town that David had heard of so far was Harry Kostner, and he would crush these two like cockroaches if they got in his way. But he filed the idea away and kept asking questions, getting background, coaxing names out of her while Jerry glowered and drank, trying not to compose the sidebar he would write about the Friends of Dirt, Grass and Trees (Inc.) until he had more information.

After a little while he excused himself to use the bathroom, a duplicate of the one in his own room, chipped porcelain fixtures and tile with the grout missing, a plastic shower curtain with half the support hooks torn out. He washed his face and tried to get the scent of beer out of his nostrils. The two of them weren't very good housekeepers, he noticed automatically, leaving hair in the sink and a litter of cosmetics on top of the toilet tank.

Cosmetics.

He examined the eyeliner and lipstick more closely. It was an odd brand, one he'd seen only once before, when Wanda Kostner had taken similar items out of a sample case to show Bobbi Jo in the café by the laundromat. Removing the cap from the eyeliner pencil, he tested the tip. It was still sharp. The pencil was new.

And they'd only been in town a couple of days.

The killer-journalist instincts weren't so rusty, after all. David smiled.

# 4

"Becky! Billy! Dinner!" Jan Henderson pulled the kitchen window shut, moving the African violets back into place. The kids were ignoring her, Billy still climbing up the steps to the new slide, Becky pumping away determinedly on the swing, her white socks flashing in the sunlight as she arced higher and higher.

I'll have to warn her about that, Jan thought. She'll swing so high she'll flip herself right over the top bar. Her own mother had told her about a little girl who had done that. But Becky enjoyed it so much, and she didn't want to make her daughter a coward. Like me? she thought, amused.

Smiling, she shifted the pieces of chicken from frying pan to platter, put the potatoes into a dish. The flowered dish her Aunt Emma had given her, telling her she'd need something pretty in the godforsaken hole she was letting that husband of hers take her to—

Broccoli. Billy hated broccoli. Not because he'd ever given it a try, but somebody at school had convinced him it tasted awful. And if he kept it up he'd convince Becky in turn and then she'd have to battle both of them.

Well, she was still Mom, still bigger than both of them—as long as they stayed ages six and four, she ought to be able to give the orders.

That was the theory anyway. "Becky! Billy! Right now! Get in here and wash your hands for *dinner*!"

"Do you have to yell at them, honey?" Matt Henderson was a big man, six four and 220 pounds, fair and blond and with a perpetual expression of sleepy good humor in his blue eyes. He was twenty-nine, and Jan loved him "more than is good for her," she'd overheard Emma say once. Not, however, in Jan's opinion. Marrying Matt was the first thing she'd done against the advice of her relatives, and she'd never regretted it for a moment.

Matt glanced out the window, reaching for a drumstick as he did so. Jan slapped his wrist smartly and moved the platter out of reach onto the kitchen table.

"Wait 'til everybody gets in," she scolded. "Maybe you should call them. They sure aren't listening to *me*."

"Aw, they got a new toy. They just don't want to leave it." Matt pulled a big bowl of salad out of the refrigerator and took four wooden bowls down from the top shelf of a cabinet. That was one of the things that Emma couldn't stand and that Jan loved about him: he never had to be asked to do little things in the kitchen; he just dived in and did them. He'd grown up in a family with three older sisters and he could cook and sew and iron his own shirts, and Jan's mother and Aunt Emma were horrified.

Jan set the table as he tossed the salad and divided out the portions. "I know," she said. "But they still have to eat dinner. It's not going to go away. Call them in, Matt."

"Okay." Cranking the window over the sink open again, he bellowed, "Boy and girl! In the house! Now!"

The children looked up reluctantly. Matt waved them in, and Becky started slowing her arc, scraping her heels in the dirt. Billy took two more steps to the top of the ladder and pushed himself down the slide, holding on to the sides so he came down inch by inch, dragging the moment out as long as he could.

"I'm not gonna tell you twice!"

Finally convinced he meant it, the two hopped off the play set and ran to the house, crowding in the door.

"Chicken! All right!"

"Chickun," Becky agreed. She reached for the same drumstick her father had tried to filch, and got the same response from Jan, albeit more gently.

"No, you don't, young lady. You both go get your hands washed before you sit down at this table. Clean all the way past your wrists, and clean fingernails too. Scoot!"

By the time the two came back and exhibited their hands, back and front, for a perfunctory inspection, Jan and Matt had already seated themselves. Jan passed out napkins and bowed her head while Matt said a short Grace Before Meals, adding her own prayer of thanks not only for the food but for the health of her family as well. Two years before, the Hendersons had been struggling to make ends meet, while Matt finished his doctorate, and she was working in a Los Angeles law office with the salary of a secretary and the duties of a paralegal. A year ago, he'd been considering a job in Germany, and she'd been praying for the right decision, terrified of a move to a foreign country with two small children, ears filled with stories of terrorists and strange foods, the one as bad as the other, according to her mother.

And now, a home, a good job, a secure future. Well, perhaps Nintucca didn't have very many amenities—Matt had had to travel almost three hundred miles to get the playground set for the kids. But they didn't have to lock their doors when they drove to the market, either. And the Kozlowskis across the street had been talking, last week—before Tessy disappeared— about renting a small refrigerated truck and going to Ely or Reno or Vegas and stocking up on milk, meats, and frozen foods because it would be so much cheaper. They'd asked if the Hendersons wanted to share the cost.

Well, Tessy *had* disappeared. Jan studied the two children surreptitiously. That was another reason to get the play set, to keep the kids at home in their own yard. She felt sure, personally, that Tessy had wandered out and fallen into a chute or winze, a slanted ventilation shaft. Nobody in Nintucca would kidnap a child.

It had been comforting to think that, when they first came to the little town in the middle of the desert; comforting to believe that even with no McDonald's, no movie theatres, no malls, and no really nice restaurants, at least their children would be safe. And then Tessy had—dropped off the face of the earth.

Shaking herself, she turned her attention back to her own children, now squabbling over the last drumstick. "Now cut that out," she said firmly. "If you're going to fight over it, neither one of you can have it."

Becky burst into tears. "But I promised it to Badger!"

"To *who*?" Matt said.

"Whom," Jan corrected automatically. "Who's Badger, honey, and why are you promising him drumsticks?"

The little girl's lips pressed tight together and she shook her head, soft brown hair whipping through the air.

"Now, Becky, your mother asked you a question. . . ."

"Promised I wouldn't tell." The pink lower lip jutted. Jan sighed. Wild horses couldn't get anything out of her daughter in this mood; she took after Matt's side of the family. They might be easygoing, but they were also stubborn as Missouri mules.

"Is Badger a friend of yours?" she probed.

Billy snickered, and Becky looked uncertain. Then she nodded, slowly.

Jan thought of Tessy Koslowski, and her blood turned cold. "Do you know anything about this Badger, Billy?"

The boy snorted. "Oh, that's the spirit game. He's just pretend."

"Is *not*," Becky burst out. "Badger lives in the ground and . . ." Suddenly realizing her promise was chipping around the edges, she shut up.

"Hey," Matt interrupted, "I hope she's not talking about the real thing—is your friend Badger a real badger, honey? Did you see him out in the desert?"

Hair whipped back and forth again. "Badger's *bigger* than that."

Jan was puzzled. "Do you mean she might have made a pet of a real animal, Matt? Are there badgers out there?"

He nodded. "Badgers, sometimes wolverines, though they're damned—er, very rare. Billy, is your sister talking about a real animal?"

"Nope," Billy said. "He's just 'magination. Jessie's been telling her stories."

"About a—" Jan began, but Matt exploded.

"Listen to me, young lady. I don't know what Jessie told you, but you are going to stay away from anything that looks like a badger, do you hear me? If I catch you trying to feed one of those things, I'll spank you good. Understand? No badgers. Tell Jessie your daddy said so."

Becky's eyes filled with tears. Looking to her mother for permission, she pushed away from the table and ran to her room, crying.

"Billy, if you're finished, go wash your hands again." Jan waited until the boy was out of the room, and then said, "Wasn't that a little harsh, Matt?"

Matt picked up the drumstick of contention and bit into it, chewing the mouthful thoroughly and swallowing it before he answered. "Honey, back in the bad old days of the mine camps, one of the things they did for entertainment was dog fights. And when they could, they'd catch a badger and put the dogs up against it. I've seen records of badgers tearing pit bulls to pieces. If that old man is trying to teach my baby girl that it's okay to feed a wild animal like that, I'll make him think *he* ran into a badger."

"But they're little," Jan protested.

"You read *Wind in the Willows* when you were a kid, right? Trust me, badgers are not like that. They're first cousins to weasels, and they're just as vicious and just as bloodthirsty. Wolverines are even worse, because they're bigger. But you'd find those up in forests rather than down here."

A shadow passed over the sun coming through the window, plunging the room into long moments of gloom as Matt finished his food. Jan shook her head. "If you say so, dear." It was her stock phrase, the one she used when she didn't really understand her husband's point of view but didn't see any harm in letting him have his way. She still thought in terms of Toad and Mole, and if Becky had found an invisible friend like Badger, it couldn't be all bad. However, feeding invisible friends from her table would have to stop. They could eat invisible food like all the rest of the invisible world.

The ground shuddered beneath them.

"My goodness, what was that?"

Matt checked his watch. "Drill test, I imagine. A little late in the day, though." He got up and walked to the front of the house, lifting the shade beside the door. "No dust. Maybe a big one down at the Test Site."

"Oh, come on, we couldn't feel that clear up here."

Billy came running out of the bathroom, hands dripping. "Daddy Daddy Daddy, what was the noise?"

"Don't know," his father said, catching him under the arms and swinging him in the air. "What do you think it was, boy?"

"I think it was a train!" Billy screamed with laughter.

"I think it was a boat!" Matt responded, swinging him again until Billy's heels scraped the ceiling.

"I think it was a plane!" Billy came back, red-faced.

"I think it was Superman!" they said in chorus.

Jan smiled and ducked past them, going into the back bedroom to find Becky curled up on her bed, pink teddy bear tucked up under her arm. Teddy had one button eye missing; Jan had tried to fix it once, but Becky had thrown a fit, insisting that her mommy wasn't a doctor and shouldn't be working on her bear. She wanted a real doctor. Jan had surrendered, and Teddy waited half blind until a real doctor

could be persuaded to operate. Jan entertained thoughts of
kidnapping Teddy and sending him to the Mayo Clinic first,
but Becky wouldn't sleep without him.

"Honey, are you okay?" She smoothed back the hair across
the flawless forehead, checking for fever, mother-instinctive.

Becky shook her head and curled up tighter.

"What's wrong?"

"Daddy's mean."

"Oh, honey, no." Jan resisted the temptation to gather her
little girl up in her arms. Becky didn't want comfort; she was
mad, and she was going to stay mad until she decided not to be
mad any more. Even at four, Becky was a very decided little
girl. "Daddy isn't being mean. He's trying to take care of you.
He loves you very much."

"Daddy's mean." Judge, jury, executioner.

Her mother sighed again and folded her hands into her lap.
"Well, maybe he is, honey, but he made a rule, and you know
what that means. You have to do what your daddy tells you."

Becky sat up, rumpling the quilted bedspread further in the
process. "I know." But her lower lip still jutted, and Jan
studied her suspiciously.

But she knew she would get nothing further out of her
daughter, so she said, "Why don't you go wash your hands and
then you can play on the swing some more, okay? And let me
put your hair up with a pretty bow."

Becky decided to allow this. As Jan brushed the silky hair,
watching her reflection in the bathroom mirror, and listened to
the roughhousing in the living room, she wondered what it was
that her little girl had fixed on this time. Becky wouldn't give
it up; like the idea of Teddy's eye, her imaginary friends were
sacrosanct. At least Jan was fairly sure she would obey her
father and not try to adopt any wild animals out in the desert.

"Okay, honey. You go play."

Becky burst out of the bathroom and collected Billy, racing
him to the back door. Matt's and Jan's eyes met, ruefully, as
their children battled over who would open the door.

Neither parent was prepared for the scream that came next.

They lunged to the door and clutched at son and daughter,
staring in disbelief at their back yard.

Where an hour before Becky and Billy had played on a
brand-new factory-guaranteed playground swing set, with two

swings, teeter-totter and slide; where Jan had started a rock garden and planted marigolds, and set a careful rounded fence to keep children at play away, there was nothing. Nothing but a yawning, gaping abyss.

"Badger's mad," Becky said, smiling softly. "Told you he was hungry."

# 5

Roy Evans got back home late in the afternoon, driving too fast into the shadow cast by the setting sun against his back. He had a check in his pocket and an empty burlap sack behind the driver's seat, and found his next-door neighbor standing on his front porch waiting for him. He had forgotten about his haste to leave. The sooner he'd got the stuff assayed, the better—it only made sense to do it at once, before Harry got suspicious—

"What the hell is going on here, Evans?" His neighbor was a new man, moved to Nintucca thirteen years before to do a little hunting in his retirement. "How come you took out of here so fast? And why didn't you report this to the Sheriff?"

"Report what?" Nobody could know. The man hadn't got a real good look at him through the window, couldn't know anyway what was in the sack.

His neighbor looked at him like he was crazy. "Your house, man. Didn't you know?"

Evans just glared at him and went inside, slamming the door behind him. A beer, that was the thing. But time to take a leak first.

There was something funny about the wall in his bedroom. He was in too much of a hurry to examine it closely. After he was through, giving himself a final shake and tucking away, zipping up, he went back and looked again.

Grooves in the damn wall. Deep, parallel gouges that tore through the stucco and into the drywall, notched deep into the cinderblock foundation. Like giant claw marks.

He went outside again and circled the house. Came to the back. Stopped.

No one had removed the pieces of the dog.

# WEDNESDAY

# One

## 1

Sunlight touched the drill rig, glared off the steel polished by blowing sand. The bit churned deep in the earth beneath the crew, chewing a shaft straight down into what had been, millions of years before, thick green swampland, now compressed by the weight of time and sediment into solid rock. The roar of the drill was muffled by its depth under the ground.

A hundred yards away two men, one in uniform and one in blue jeans and a polo shirt, sat in a battered brown pickup truck, sipping from water bottles and watching the drilling crew mantled in dust.

"They're gonna run out of slurry," Gil predicted. "Bet they use more of your secret gunk."

Perry Ruiz flung his arms out as wide as he could in the constricted area of the truck cab. "What's so damn secret about it? That guy visiting from Albuquerque, Willie, he's been telling everybody in town. He can't keep his mouth shut on anything. I heard him last night in the Rowdytown telling the change girl about how the stuff makes green bubbles when they shoot it into the hole. Trying to impress her."

Gil grunted agreement. "Good luck to him. Linda don't impress."

His partner grinned. "You tried?"

Gil shrugged. Perry was as close to a friend as any of the

drilling staff, but Gil wasn't the type to exchange stories of conquest with anybody. He might have tried, but his success or failure was his own business. He allowed himself to remember what was, in fact, pretty much of a dead-loss effort. Then, after a moment: "Yep, there they go."

As they watched, members of the drilling crew got out white pullovers and wrestled their way into them, completely covering themselves from head to foot in a shiny, tough-looking material. Cowled headgear with glass faceplates went over their heads and thick gloves on their hands. Thus prepared, they trudged awkwardly over to a pair of fifty-five-gallon barrels and wrestled them onto a handcart.

"God, they must be cooking in there."

"Yeah. White asked me if I wanted to be on the crew one time, when I first started out here. I told him I could think of better ways to kill myself than wear that shit in a hundred and fifteen degrees. Last month six guys passed out." The two men continued to watch as the handcart was maneuvered into place beside the hole.

The suited-up members of the crew fiddled with the rig, hooking up a clear six-inch-thick hose from one of the barrels to the drill shaft, setting up a pump attached to the hose, running wires back to a truck parked some distance away. After some time all was arranged to their satisfaction, and they moved off to another tanker truck. Pulling the headgear off, the driver hosed the workers down with water as they peeled out of the suits.

"Pretty bad if they mixed up the tanks, put the water down the hole and hosed'em with the fixer," Perry snickered.

As the last driller stripped, Perry Ruiz stepped out of the distant truck and waved his hand, guiding the crew back. Once they had retreated to his satisfaction, he pulled a switch. Thick yellow-green fluid pumped from the barrel into the shaft.

"They ready?" Gil asked.

"Here they go," Perry answered. He and Gil slipped yellow spongelike pellets into their ears.

Willie had told Linda about the green bubbles. But he hadn't mentioned the noise. It started low, rumbling, and ascended to a deafening, wailing shriek that went on and on and on and then, abruptly, ended.

"Sounds like they're gassing foxes down there," Gil said.

"Goddamn big foxes if they are."

"What makes that noise anyway?"

His companion shrugged. "That's one of those little details White doesn't quite have worked out yet. But it works, I guess. Makes the drill shaft wall solid. Or at least," he amended thoughtfully, "none of them have collapsed on us yet. Not from *this* batch."

"Hell with that shit. Give me open sky."

"Yeah, well, you know, I think I agree with you. But White thinks he's gonna make his fucking fortune, and I guess he's right."

"Unless Willie shoots off his mouth to the wrong person."

"Well, there is that."

"They ever try stuff like this in those mines you worked back East?" Perry asked as Gil put the truck in gear.

"They never got that far," Gil said obscurely. He refused to elaborate.

# 2

The rough-hewn boardwalk outside the Rowdytown Casino was knotted and uneven, filled with traps for the unwary, the drunk, or the old, ready to catch and trip at uncertain feet. It seemed miraculous that Jessie Gallita could stagger from railing to wall and back again and never once sprawl full length with his face full of pine slivers.

Certainly Roy Evans and the other men standing outside the card shop thought so. They nudged each other and laughed and gestured with hands holding cans of beer, and Roy stepped forward to come face-to-face with the old man. He caught Jessie by the shoulders, slopping most of his beer across the faded black denim jacket in the process. "Hey, where you goin', Jessie? You look like you're having a little trouble there." He laughed and looked back to the others, inviting them to laugh too. "I've been looking for you, old man. Want to talk to you about a wall!"

Jessie quivered and tried to pull himself up straight. "Let me go, Roy Evans."

"Let you go?" Evans turned back to his cronies and winked

broadly. "Let you *go*? Why sure, Jessie." He released the other man abruptly, pushing him at the same time into a whittling bench set up for the convenience of tourists, passersby, and other slackers. "Oops. Got to watch your balance, boy."

The old man glared at him, but made no attempt to move.

Evans offered him a hand. "C'mon, boy, let me help you up there."

Jessie turned deliberately and spat, his saliva forming dusty bubbles on the planking.

"Why you—" Evans lunged for him, grabbing the jacket. Jessie bobbed up again, unresisting and unafraid. Behind Evans, the onlookers stirred uneasily, muttering to each other. The entertainment was taking an unexpected and not entirely welcome turn.

"Your father would have known better than to lay hands on a Gallita." The words came out in jerks as Evans shook him, terrierlike. "Your father kept tradition."

One of the onlookers stepped forward in alarm, laid a hand on Evans' arm. "Hey, Roy, let the old geezer go."

Evans snarled. "Don't tell me you buy that shit too. Have you heard this old bastard? He had his way he'd shut down the mine before we ever got it open again, and we'd all be out of a job. And now he's wrecking my house—"

"He's just an old man," the other persisted. "Let him go."

Someone else said something about bad luck.

Evans paused to redirect his anger at his former ally. "Don't tell me you believe this shit about spirits too."

To agree would be to subject himself to Evans' condemnation, and that the man was not prepared to do. "Hell, no, I don't believe. But he's just a superstitious old man, what can he do? So he shoots his mouth off. It's a free country."

"Bullshit," Evans said as Jessie slid down onto the bench again. "He's a troublemaker. He fucked up my house. Killed my dog. We know how to deal with troublemakers. Don't we, boys?" The other men looked as if they didn't believe what they were hearing, but they couldn't afford to disagree with Kostner's mine foreman. At the reluctant nods of agreement he swung back to his victim. "You keep your damn mouth shut about that mine, you hear? Nobody wants to hear what you have to say, nobody."

Jessie looked up at him, serene. "I do not have to speak. The mine showed once what it could do; if you disturb it, it will happen again, and you have only yourselves to blame. That which feeds on evil is itself evil."

Evans drew back one booted foot to kick, then realized that half lying on the bench, Jessie presented no convenient target. "Shut up, old man."

Jessie merely smiled.

# 3

"Christ Almighty, is it always this hot?" Esher wiped his forehead, replaced his borrowed hat, and squinted at the hill in front of him. Loose rubble, made up of white and yellow rocks of varying sizes ranging from fist to sand, covered the surface, reflecting the glare of the noonday sun. Rick Zimmermann, halfway to the top, grinned down at him.

"Hey, this ain't nothin'. This is springtime. Come summer, now, it really gets *hot*."

Esher grimaced and started climbing, placing his feet carefully. It took him nearly three times as long to make the climb as it had taken Rick, who leaped from one invisible foothold to the next like a two-legged mountain goat. He caught his breath, panting, as Rick swept out his arm like Satan on the mountaintop showing all the kingdoms of the earth. "There you go. That's Nevada. Well," he corrected himself, "that's this chunk anyway."

The terrain unrolled from the hilltop beneath their feet onward for miles, the colors changing from yellow and white to gray, to blue, to haze, and then to sky, the horizon marked by mountains hundreds of miles away. It looked like a giant mud flat millennia old had been left to dry out under the pitiless sun, leaving cracks and shallows where salt had settled into white pools miles across. Black dots of vegetation were sprinkled across the landscape like ants in a sugar bowl. A blur of movement caught Esher's eye, and he held his breath to see a pair of coyotes following the ruts cut into the ground, crisscrossing each other while they sniffed casually for game, sometimes leaping at each other in play. Then one stopped, staring at the hill—staring at him, Esher realized—and a moment later the two vanished as if they had never been.

The truck, parked at the bottom of the hill, looked absurd, out of place.

"So, where's this mine you were going to show me?" Esher said, wiping sweat out of his eyes.

"Over here." Rick crested the hill and disappeared over the edge. "C'mon."

Esher paused on the top of the hill, looked down at actual signs of human habitation. Built into the side of a bump in the hill, blackened wood defined a tiny shack, a circle that must have been a corral. Bright green grass sprouted against one of the rotting posts, shocking against the pale desert sand. Not far away, at the base of the hill he stood on, the shell of an old Model A Ford rusted peacefully.

"Hey, this is great!" Esher shouted with exhilaration. He had spent most of the day before in the hotel, looking over his notes or adding to his collection of interviews. The midmorning sun, warm but not yet blazing, and the fresh air seemed to pump great gouts of life itself into him. He went leaping out of control down the hill. "God, let me set up the camera! This is great—"

"Hey, watch it!" One long lean arm reached out and grabbed him as he was about to touch the fence post. "You've got to be careful around here. There's snakes and stuff. Don't get in such a damned hurry."

"Oh." Abashed, Esher pulled away. Zimmermann handed him a long stick, and he poked experimentally at the green grass.

The stick sank an inch or two into the dampness of a spring. As he pushed the greenery aside, a long shadow hissed at him.

Zimmermann laughed as he leaped back. "Hey, don't sweat it. That's just a king snake. He won't hurt you. He just doesn't like being waked up, that's all."

A yard-long dusty black snake slid out of the grass and away from the two men, heading for the rotting hulk of the car. Esher stared after it, still paralyzed with shock. He had never seen a snake that big, that close; it was terrifying and beautiful too, flowing hypnotically across the earth to shade and shelter and safety. He was glad it was nonpoisonous; he was suddenly more aware of the film of sweat across his face, sweat from fear instead of heat, sweat that chilled in a vagrant wisp of desert breeze.

"More scared of you than you are of him," Rick said cheerfully. "At least it guaran-damn-tees there aren't any rattlers nearby."

Esher doubted both those bits of conventional wisdom, but once the snake was out of sight he took a cautious step back toward the corral.

"What else is around here?" he said, suddenly disinclined to go poke around inside the shed.

"Well, there's the mine."

"What mine?" Esher looked around, expecting Zimmermann to laugh at him again. He saw the shed, the corral, the old car, and nothing else. No assayer's office. No processing building. Nothing that indicated mining.

"Up there. We passed it coming down. See that hole?"

Esher shaded his eyes to look back up the hill. Sure enough, he had galloped right past a dark hole in the side of the hill. "You're kidding."

"Nope. C'mon." Up the hill again went Zimmermann, with Esher following more slowly. Zimmermann paused outside the hole, waiting for him.

It was clearly man-made, not natural; he saw that now that he was standing before it. The dirt edges were squared off on a hole about eighteen inches wide and five feet high about three-quarters of the way up the side of the hill. Sunlight illuminated the interior for less than a yard. Beyond that was blackness.

"That's a *mine*?"

"Yep. This is the Generous Lady. Used to belong to Mikey's folks. That car belonged to Mikey's grandpa."

"You're shittin' me—" Esher looked from the other man back to the hole in the hill, comparing it to the sophistication of the Heartbreak. They might have been two different universes. Blowing out a bemused breath, he tried to figure out how far back the hole went. Grinning, Rick handed him a flashlight.

The beam lanced into the darkness—and faded. Esher stepped forward, following the light, until he bumped his head against the low overhang of the entrance.

"Run it along the floor," Rick suggested from behind him.

Esher did so, noting small black creatures skittering away from the beam of light, a pair of yellow scorpions with tails arched high fleeing from the intruders in their desert world. The floor changed from smooth path to crumbled, eroded dirt within a few feet of the entrance; then the beam lost power, unable to pierce the darkness.

Esher played the light along the sides and roof of the hole, edging just inside from the heat of the sun to the sudden chill of shadow, keeping one hand on the rim of the hole. Blackened logs supported the sides and roof, spaced at wider and wider intervals as the tunnel plunged deeper into the side of the hill. Within six feet of the entrance the tunnel sloped downward and widened out; it looked large enough for a medium-sized man to stand comfortably. Esher took another step inside, hunching down to fit.

"Wouldn't do that if I were you," said Rick.

The remark, echoing into the blackness, startled him, and he tried to turn back. A shower of dirt fell into his eyes, and he raised his hand to wipe it away. His elbow hit the side of the tunnel and the flashlight went flying, the light going out as it hit the floor and rolled away. The log supports above his head groaned. Something shifted.

He backed out hastily, shaking his head against the dirt and the glaring sunlight. "Good God," he muttered. "That's unreal. I guess I dropped your flashlight," he added after a moment. "Pardon me if I don't go in after it. I'll get you another one."

"Yep, you will that," Rick agreed. "Good thing you didn't try to go much farther. There's a drop-away hole about twenty feet in on this one."

"You've been in there?" Esher finally got the last bit of dust out of his eyes and sat on a huge boulder by the side of the hole, reaching into his pocket and turning on the tape recorder.

"Sure. Been in a lot of'em. Wore a miner's hat, with a carbide lamp, though. The light's better." The young man hunkered down next to the rock and tossed a chip of quartz into the hole. "It's like we told you that first night you were here: you can go from one end of town to the other underground if you know how. Mikey's done it. So's Marianne. All these holes, they connect up sooner or later. They all hook up to the Heartbreak in the long run.

"All those hills in town, those little rises and things? Those are piles of mine tailings. Like this stuff. Junk they took out of the hole so they could dig deeper." He picked up another, larger rock, rubbed his thumb over it. "See that gray streak? That's silver."

"Just lying on the ground out here? Why doesn't somebody pick it up?"

"High-grade it?" At Esher's knit brow, Rick explained, "That's what they called it when the miners tried to smuggle out pieces of rich ore from the big mines."

"Why don't people come out here and pick the place clean?"

"Because Harry Kostner will sue your ass, that's why. He owns all this. See, when Mikey's grandpa first staked this claim, first dug the hole, he couldn't recover enough metal from the tailings to make it worth his while. But Harry figures he can use modern techniques and grub out every penny. He figures if he owns the mine, he owns the tailings. So you better not let him catch you picking over his tail." He held the rock out to Esher. "Here. Have a sample."

Grinning, Esher accepted the rock and slid it into his pocket. "So is Harry going to dig up the whole town?"

Rick came back to his feet in one lithe movement. "Prob'ly. I hear he's been talking to his lawyers about how to get his hands on the land the hotel's built on, for one thing. Should be interesting to see how it works out."

"Yeah." Esher turned off the recorder and scanned the area around the mine once more, trying to imagine what it was like for the man who had come to Nevada so long ago to dig this hole, live in that shack, drive that car. He, Mikey's grandfather, had lit his way with candles into the earth, used pick and shovel and his bare hands to dig out the ore. He had stayed months, years perhaps, but in the end he had left it all behind, not even taking his car. It might have been a romantic picture. David Esher found it profoundly sad. •

"So are those government guys using holes like this?" he asked. "What kind of work are they doing?"

Rick shook his head, too quickly. "Don't know. Really." He stretched. "They dig their own holes. Hey, didn't you say you had another appointment with Kostner this afternoon? I can take you by one more mine on the way back." Rick was clearly uncomfortable, eager to change the subject. He looked like a man caught between trying to please and knowing he couldn't.

"Hey, what is this site, secret or something?" Esher asked. "You sure don't like talking about it much."

"Nope. Just that Dr. White's near as big an asshole as Harry, and like Gil says, Dr. White pays me."

"Don't bite the hand that feeds you?"

"Something like that." Rick started up the crest of the hill. The reporter looked after him thoughtfully.

"How'd you come out here anyway?" Esher said, thumbing on the recorder and lurching after him. "I mean, what would bring you to Nintucca? You said you came from Wisconsin originally."

Rick waited to answer until they were back in the truck, backing around to head out again over the ruts to the road. "I was heading for California, and I ran out of gas and money at the same time. Mrs. Bailey said I could either go to jail or get a job, and White was hiring."

"So was Kostner, wasn't he?"

Grimacing, Rick nodded. "But he kind of assumed too much. Thought I'd be real grateful for the opportunity. So I went ahead and applied at the site. Mrs. Bailey loaned me the money for gas to get out there. Harry doesn't know that," he added, sparing Esher a quick glance as they jounced from one hummock of salt grass to another.

"I hear you. Bailey doesn't like Kostner either?"

"Mrs. Bailey's a good sheriff." Rick shut up then, ostentatiously concentrating on his driving, going a few miles per hour faster than the terrain allowed for. Esher grinned.

"Mrs. Bailey's daughter wouldn't have anything to do with it, would she?"

Rick shrugged, a major accomplishment in the jolting vehicle, but the look on his face didn't deny it.

"Gonna get married?"

Rick smiled to himself.

# Two

## 1

Helen Vanderhaas skipped into the Good Times café next to the LDS chapel, feeling very pleased with herself. She refused to notice the ostentatious way the waitress turned her back on her. The sun was shining, the sky was clear, and David Esher certainly was cute. Catching sight of Marianne Bailey seated in a booth at the back, she dashed over and slid into the bench opposite, not waiting for an invitation.

Marianne's eyebrows rose high, but she couldn't repress a smile. "Hello to you too," she said, spearing some more lettuce.

"Well, you know darn well they won't serve me unless I'm sitting with somebody. Guess what!"

Marianne shook her head, still chewing. They made a strange pair, with Helen's soft boots, long denim skirt, tie-dyed man's shirt, and headband in sharp contrast to her own neat business suit and three-inch heels. That was what she liked about Helen, she reflected, probing among the remains of the salad for another bit of tomato. Helen could appear in public in clothes thirty years out of date and nobody minded.

Well, they *minded,* she corrected herself, smiling again as the other woman twisted around in her seat and waved frantically at the waitress. But they didn't *expect* anything else. With herself, now—And how could you keep up with the ever-escalating standards of appearance and behavior in a small town?

Helen swung back, the waitress having been embarrassed into starting over with a menu in her hands. The other customers in the small café whispered to each other and stared pointedly anywhere else but at the back booth.

"You didn't guess." Helen's eyes danced.

"You hired Paul Laxalt to be your spokesperson."

The suggestion took Helen aback. Then she started chewing her lower lip, and Marianne realized to her horror that the other woman was seriously considering the possibility of enlisting Nevada's senior Republican senator emeritus to be a spokesman for the Friends of Dirt, Grass and Trees. She cast about frantically for an alternative. "Or, they're shutting down the site."

It was enough of a distraction. "Well, no, not yet. Or wait, have you heard something? *Are* they really?" She took the menu and laid it down unread before her, running the laminated edge under her fingernails.

"No," Marianne said shortly. "It was just a guess." The waitress, Bobbi Jo, had a boyfriend out at the site. She sighed in relief and started to turn away.

Helen caught at her arm, letting it go again immediately as she received a killing glare. "Wait, I haven't ordered yet. I want—" She skimmed the menu, as if it might have changed sometime in the past few days. Marianne, who knew from personal experience that it hadn't changed in the last dozen years, watched in amusement. "I want the vegetarian plate, please."

Bobbi Jo sighed again, took the menu, and trudged away.

"Okay, I guessed. So what are you all excited about?" Finishing her salad, Marianne folded her napkin beside her plate and leaned back to listen.

"We got an *interview*," Helen whispered dramatically, leaning over the table. Customers more than three tables away couldn't have heard her. "That man from back East, David Esher, he *interviewed* us. He's going to write an *article* about the Friends!"

"So?" Marianne was feeling unreasonable. "You've had stories written about you before."

"But this is for a *national* magazine. It's *important*. It'll tell *everybody* what's going on!"

"How can *Town Life* tell everybody what's going on at the drill site, when nobody *knows* what's going on out there? Besides, the articles are supposed to be about the mine, not the site. And anyway you told me yourself you didn't find anything but a bunch of equipment you didn't even recognize."

"Rick knows. And Rick's showing the guy around." Helen's lower lip jutted out stubbornly.

"Rick's showing him around the old mines. He's not taking him out to the site, and you'd better not say he is, because he could lose his job!" There was real anger in Marianne's voice, and Helen set back with a bump. As she did so, the waitress slid the "vegetarian plate" in front of her and slouched off again.

"Well, gee, you don't have to get so mad." Short stubby fingers plucked nervously at napkin and silverware, and Helen tried to defuse the moment by stuffing a forkful of sliced cucumber into her mouth. "It's secret, isn't it?" she said indistinctly. "And that means they're doing stuff they don't want regular people to know about. They're hiding something, that's all."

"Every government site in Nevada is hiding something," Marianne retorted, exasperated. "It doesn't mean they're doing anything wrong."

"Then why are they hiding it?" Satisfied with this irrefutable logic, Helen dug into her meal. "Jerry says he thinks they're using dangerous chemicals. He saw a bunch of tanker trucks go in there yesterday."

Over Helen's shoulder, Marianne could see the sudden movement of another customer raising his head to listen better. But Helen would not be hushed.

"Do you know how much damage chemicals do? They get right in the water table and contaminate the water, they poison all the plants and animals. Why, I wouldn't drink that stuff—" she indicated the glass of ice water with her fork—"for any amount of money. You'd probably fall over dead. Jerry and I, we've seen whole patches of nothing but sand out there. Nothing will grow."

"Those are playas, dummy. Nothing ever grows in a playa. It's a salt flat, a dried-out lake bed."

Helen shook her head. "No sir, not these. These are new. You know, if I were the Earth, I'd have myself a good earthquake and get rid of all those folks out there."

There was a sudden silence in the café, which Helen did not appear to notice. But the customer behind her got up abruptly and marched to the register to pay his bill and leave.

It was Harry Kostner.

# 2

Evans swirled a vial of liquid, watching the sediment in the light from his carbide lamp. The reflection glinted, making it that much harder to see the chemical reaction. "Damn," he muttered softly to himself.

DAMN DAMN DAMN the word echoed down the shaft at his feet. DAMN damn damn. He kicked a loose rock in after it. The rock made no sound as it fell.

He was standing in a large cavern, beside the rusting skeleton of a winch. A massive rope, stiff with decades of dirt, hung down the shaft. Pegs stuck in the cavern wall still supported a tangle of leather harness. As he turned, the light from his hard hat picked out a crumbling stack of wood, an ore car tilting crazily off rotted tracks, an ancient tin can gleaming in the dust, the bottom of the ladder leading up to the next level of the mine. He was supremely unconcerned about being three hundred feet deep in the earth. There were more important things to think about.

The rusty ore cart was still half full. Stepping carefully away from the edge of the shaft, he walked over to inspect the contents, large gray chunks of earth ripped out by pick and dynamite. Spitting on one, he wiped away the dirt and whistled softly.

The whistle echoed too, long shrill moments until it faded with the settling dust. Evans rubbed sweat from the beginnings of a graying beard.

"My God," he murmured. "Pure." The words didn't echo this time. He didn't notice. "Hey, babe, Harry know about you?"

Dropping the sample into his pocket, he leaned over and

began brushing decades of dust away from the rest of the contents of the cart. Fully loaded, it would carry more than half a ton of rock from the tunnel to the shaft, where the ore would be loaded into the massive ore bucket and raised from level to level to the surface of the mine. There it would be loaded into another ore cart and travel the tracks out of the mine to the crushing mill.

Or it could have if there were any tracks. Old Daniel Kostner used steel carts, but they were pulled from tunnel to tunnel by mules raised deep in the mine, animals who saw even less of the light of day than the men who cared for them. It was cheaper than paying men to lay track. Those men would do better to blast the mine deeper, follow the silver-bearing ledge farther.

Old man Kostner had his miners searched to the skin at the end of every shift to make sure that none of them dared slip a piece of ore into a pocket.

"Paid'em a fair wage, you did, old man. Just like your bloodsucking grandson. Not fuckin' likely—" He reached into the cart for another rock.

A sound echoed in the old mine, a whisper of a sound.

Evans jerked his head up to listen, not breathing for a moment. Times like this a man remembered how many tons of earth arced over his head, ready to shiver and collapse if the wrong support gave way. A man remembered how old those supports were.

Remembered that two hundred and seventy-four men lay smothered, only one level down, one tunnel over.

The darkness felt thick and hot.

"Probably a damn rat," he whispered for confidence. "That's all." He listened again, and heard nothing.

Turning back to the ore cart, more eager now to find good pieces, he scrabbled through them as if denying that anything had pulled his attention away, even for a moment.

His pockets bulging, he filled his hands, dropping specimens and picking up others to replace them. "Shoulda brought a damn bag," he said.

The sound again. Deep within the shaft, a mumble or a mutter of air shoved out of place by earth settling itself. He tilted his head, sending the beam of light at a crazy angle across the chamber, trying to listen harder. Roy Evans had worked in the bowels of the earth since he was sixteen. He thought he knew all the noises a man could hear—the hissing of lit fuses, the *chunk-chunk* of a pick, the soundless hammerblow of dynamite exploding, the scream of metal against metal. He knew the smells too. Dry mine like dust, make a man sneeze all the time. Wet mine like mud, give a man bad lungs after a year. Hot metal. That's what this smelled like: hot copper, so thick it curdled the tongue.

Something in the shaft of the mine.

He took one more step away from the old cart and stopped, leaning toward the shaft, rocking back toward the ladder. The sound increased to just below the level of audibility, still more a disturbance in the hairs on the back of his neck than a real sound a man could put a name to. But it was coming from the shaft, definitely from the shaft.

Evans' head moved back and forth, denying, searching for the noise.

He saw the vibration in the winch rope before he felt it coming through his feet. The massive cable, six inches thick, trembled and swayed. Evans dropped the mineral in his hands and ran for the ladder going up.

His hand was on the first ring when the ancient winch shrieked in protest and began turning, drawing up the rope. The sound grew louder, into a moan. A shower of dust erupted from the shaft.

Evans whimpered and heaved himself up onto the ladder, lurching upward. The moan beneath him grumbled, grew louder. Particles of dust got into his eyes and he could not stop to wipe them clear. Sweat made the ladder rungs slippery.

It was a hundred feet up to the next level of the mine, sixty-some rungs of the ladder. Roy Evans was in fairly good shape for a man of forty. He leaped from the top of the hole over the next ladder and paused to look over his shoulder.

The rungs of the ladder he had just climbed were creaking. The grumble was now a muted roar. Dragging air into his lungs, he swarmed up the next ladder to Level Two of the Heartbreak.

He could feel the pressure behind him. He risked one glance downward, letting the lamp on his hat illuminate the hole beneath him, and could see nothing. But it was there. He could hear snuffling in the roar now, angry grunting. He climbed faster, hands and feet barely touching the rungs before they reached for the next rung and the next and the next. One more level up and there was a ground tunnel, a way to the open air.

The thing below him wailed.

He did not pause on Level Two. His pulse pounded so hard he couldn't see anything but red flashes as the blood bulged in his capillaries. He ran for the next ladder, finding it more by memory than by sight, and pulled himself up.

A rung snapped in his hand.

Behind him a rush of air and dirt told him that something huge had emerged from the shaft.

Evans screamed, a thin scream that was all the air his laboring lungs could spare, and leaped for the next rung. His fingers caught it. He pulled himself up, hand over hand, until his feet could get purchase on a solid rung, and he climbed, feeling the hot, moist breath of his pursuer dampening his legs. He scrambled onward, sobbing for air, unable to hear past his own heartbeat. There were fifty rungs to Level One.

Forty.

Thirty-five.

A rotten piece of oak gave way under his foot and he hung by his hands. Beneath him something grunted.

He screamed again, silently, and clawed for the next good rung, boosting himself higher, his elbows touching the sides of the hole, the ore in his pockets bruising his hips as he lost his equilibrium and used it to push himself up, up, up, away from the thing beneath him, to the top, over the lip of the shaft, gasping, stumbling. Falling.

Falling over the abandoned bicycle.

He rolled, scrambling on his back toward the beam of light from the ground tunnel, his breath tearing out of him. Then a shadow moved at the top of the shaft, and a bellow louder than Roy Evans' heartbeat shuddered in the air.

# 3

Rick was whistling between his teeth as he drove, a thin bodiless sound that set Esher's teeth on edge. He pulled in a deep breath and stared out the passenger-side window, trying to ignore the sound by concentrating on the passing scenery. Unfortunately, there wasn't much to concentrate on, since the land was beginning to look all the same to him by now. Maybe that would make a good lead to his first article:

The land never changes—only the men who plunder it do. No, too obvious.

He wanted something that conveyed the sense of the land, though—something that would evoke in his readers, who'd never left their green and comfortable homes back in Pennsylvania, what that rusting Model A had evoked for him. It was a different universe, dry and pitiless and aloof, and men could invade and tear out the bones of the earth to get at the silver in its marrow, but eventually they would go away and the earth would remain, changed perhaps on the surface but remaining, nonetheless.

God, he was getting mystical, he thought, chuckling.

Rick glanced at him and asked, "What's so funny?"

"Oh, nothing. Just a thought."

"Gotta watch that, it's catching." The truck turned onto a nearly invisible dirt road.

Grabbing at the dashboard to steady himself, Esher asked, "Where are we going now?"

"The Heartbreak. Thought you'd like to see where that old disaster happened."

"That's the mine that Kostner's opening up again." It was also the mine that Kostner had guided him through the day before. It would be interesting to see it from someone else's perspective, he thought. Though he wondered how Rick proposed to get past all the workmen swarming over the mine.

"A-huh, that's the one. Though he wants to open up the whole network. He's already got a bunch of people working for him in tunnels on some of the upper levels. Hey—"

"Now what the hell is going on?" Rick muttered, slowing the truck. Esher shrugged, following his gaze.

Some fifty feet below the mainframe of the mine, a riot was in its first stages. Several trucks and an ambulance were parked at odd angles around a mass of almost a hundred men. Esher could hear curses and shouts of defiance.

"Let's go find out, shall we?" he said, and got out without waiting for an answer.

The crowd parted to make way for a sheriff's sedan, and

Esher could see that there was another hole in the side of the hill, evidently a second entrance to the mine. Most of the men wore miner's hard hats and were dressed in overalls. Esher clambered up to them and tried to move around, closer to the sedan.

"Hey hey, it's the Man," Rick muttered in his ear. "Looks like you wouldn't have had that appointment anyway."

Esher nodded, scanning the crowd. He could see several people familiar from the streets of Nintucca, from the bar in the Rowdytown. They ignored him, talking among themselves in low, ugly voices tainted with fear.

Kostner was standing beside the portal on a rise formed by a small pile of tailings, talking to Laura Bailey and a man in a brown uniform with sergeant's stripes. The uniformed man stepped away and spoke into a walkie-talkie, glancing back at the ground at something Esher couldn't see.

"What the hell is going on here?" he asked of nobody in particular. The man next to him swung around as if he were going to hit Esher, then stopped short.

"Oh, it's you. You're that writer fella Kostner hired, ain't you? You wanna see what's goin' on? C'mon, I'll show you!" With that, he grabbed Esher by the arm and dragged him through the crowd to the space just before the portal. "You want to see what's going on? Look!"

Esher looked.

He saw a body, a man's body, lying on its face, knees drawn up and arms stretched out, hands clutching at a clump of salt grass as if to pull himself farther away from the mine. He could see no signs of violence on the man's back. He stepped forward, toward the body, toward Kostner.

Sheriff Bailey came over and pushed him back.

"My God, what's going on here? Who is that? What happened?" The questions spilled out of Esher without his even being aware he was asking.

"Nothing here for you to see, Esher. Nothing here for anybody." Laura Bailey lowered her tone and increased her volume. The crowd shuffled back. "Nothing here for anybody! Go back to work! Go home!"

"It is the Beast!" A man's voice, shrill with age, interrupted the sheriff's attempted brushoff. "He has been taken by the Beast! Look at him!"

It was the old man who'd stopped Esher on the steps of the courthouse building. He was still wearing the red bandanna, now with torn blue jeans and plaid shirt. He pushed past Bailey and knelt beside the body. "Look!"

Before Bailey could stop him, he had taken the corpse by the shoulders and turned it over.

Someone next to Esher retched. Esher looked and looked away, trying not to believe what he had seen.

"The Beast has taken him. Look, his pockets are filled with ore from the mine—it is the Beast—"

Kostner cursed and swept out at the old man with a fist, knocking him away from the body. Bailey glared at Kostner but made no attempt to stop him or go to the old man's aid. Waving up the ambulance attendants, she positioned herself between the body and the crowd, tapping a stick into the palm of one hand. "You people have no business here. Now go home."

"The old man's right! There's something in that mine!" one voice answered her. "That's Roy Evans! You tell us, Sheriff, what killed him, and then we'll go home!"

"The man had a heart attack. It happens. That's all. Go home."

Someone else shouted something Esher couldn't hear, but by that time the ambulance attendants had the body loaded and were driving down the incline in a cloud of dust. Once the body was gone the crowd began to break up, encouraged by Bailey and her deputy. Esher and Zimmermann moved around behind them to where the old man sprawled in the dust.

"Hey, Jessie, hey, guy. You okay?" Rick supported the victim, using an edge of the bandanna to wipe away the blood welling from his temple.

The old man's eyes snapped open and he stared at the two of them. "It is the Beast!"

"Yeah, Jessie, right, the Beast. Come on now, let's get up on our feet and we'll take you into town, get that cut looked at." Rick looked up to see Kostner staring down at them from downslope and mouthed an obscenity. "Come on, Jessie. You know they can't keep a good Basque down."

Esher helped bring him to an unsteady standing position. The old man kept pushing away their hands, insisting he could do it himself. "You do not believe me, but I tell you it is the

Beast. This place is cursed for men like you. The Beast killed Evans."

"Like hell." It was Kostner, his thumbs hooked into his back pockets and his elbows stuck out at angles. Esher almost expected him to start scratching at the earth like a fighting cock ready to fly into battle. "It was a heart attack. Roy Evans had a heart attack, and I'd better not hear you saying anything else, Gallita."

The old man stared him down, until Kostner, surprisingly, turned away and strutted down the hill as if he'd won the confrontation.

Rick dashed over to his truck to bring it up closer, so Esher was the only one left to hear Gallita's muttered remark. "It has him already. The Beast has eaten his soul."

"What's that mean, Jessie? Giant radiated bogeymen living in the mine?" Esher was trying to lighten the moment as he maneuvered the old man down the slope toward the truck. He could tell as soon as the words left his mouth that he'd made a mistake. Still, he kept trying. "He was probably running from a cave-in or something and just burst his heart. Everybody around here's been telling me how dangerous these old mines are."

"You do not understand," the old man said, and would not speak again to either Esher or Zimmermann, not during the trip back to Nintucca, not while they stood by as the nurse at the clinic cleaned and stitched the cut on his forehead, not while they drove him home.

Subconsciously, Esher was expecting Rick to pull up to one of the trailers making up most of Nintucca's housing. Failing that, as they drove past the clusters of mobile homes, he expected to see an older house, perhaps crumbling stone or a wooden shack. But Rick skidded to a stop in the gravel driveway of a neat ranch-style tract home, built by the looks of it in the late fifties or early sixties, with a flower bed riotous with marigolds and four-o'clocks, divided from the dust by much-straightened wire fencing.

"He lives here?" Esher blurted.

Jessie turned and looked at him deliberately, brilliant blue eyes sharp with contempt. "You do not know what you do not know," he said.

Ashamed, Esher hopped out of the truck and offered his

hand; Jessie disdained to take it, wobbling down to the ground by himself. Rick slammed the door on the other side and stood by, not offering any help but ready to provide it if needed. Taking the cue, Esher hung back a step or two as Jessie wavered to his front door.

Somewhat to Esher's surprise, the door was unlocked. Neither Jessie nor Rick seemed to find that unusual. As the old man started to close the door behind him, Rick spoke up at last.

"Anything we can get for you?"

Jessie paused without turning. "No."

"You're sure?" Esher insisted, surprising himself. The old man was obviously independent, wanting no one's charity. Back home, Esher would have left him strictly alone, following the credo that said, "Don't get emotionally involved"—here he had been dragged into involvement. Somehow the sight of him staggering unsurely across the dust of his front yard, into an empty house, woke an image he wanted desperately to banish.

Perhaps Jessie could hear it in his voice. Steadying himself on the doorknob, he turned to the two younger men.

"You are good men," he said, the thickness beginning to leave his voice. "I thank you for your help. May the Earth give you what you most desire, and keep the Beast far from you."

With that he stepped inside and shut the door firmly behind him.

"What the hell?" Esher said.

Rick shrugged and got back into the truck. "Ol' Jessie's a little weird," he commented unnecessarily as he backed the truck away. "But he's okay. Gonna be interesting to see what people have to say about Kostner treating him like that."

"I thought he was the town drunk," Esher muttered, baffled.

"Well, he is. Except nobody's ever seen him drinking. See, he's a Gallita, from one of the old Basque families. His people were here long before the miners came. His daddy owned a mine for a while, but never did diddly with it. Wouldn't dig, just picked up from the ground. That stuff about the Beast, Marianne says he's been raving about it for years. According to ol' Jessie, if the Beast gets you, you're gone, man. Eats you alive. He used to baby-sit for the little kids until the parents found out he was telling them beast stories and giving them nightmares. Since then he just kind of ambles around town and scares the shit out of tourists."

"And gets slugged by good ol' Harry Kostner." Esher shook his head. "Well, I guess I can consider my appointment canceled."

"I take it you're in no big hurry to get over to the Man's office?" Rick flipped his sunglasses down onto his nose and paused with his hand on the handle.

"No." Esher could hear the loathing in his own voice and took a deep breath before going on. "No. I don't think I want to have anything to do with Mr. Kostner for a little while. Are you sure you can't take me out to that site of yours?"

"Not can't, won't." Rick studied him a moment, thoughtful. "I guess I could show you where they used to drill. Not that it'll do you any good. There's nothing out there to see."

"Yeah, why don't we do that." Esher slid back into the truck and slammed the door. "And I'll send Dr. White a formal request for an interview and see if that gets me anywhere."

Rick snorted. "Good luck."

# 4

Neither man noticed a curtain fall back into place at a window as they pulled away. Jessie Gallita shuffled away from the window to the back of his house, shaking his head to himself.

In a back room, originally a bedroom, all the windows were blocked off, providing no light at all. He moved through the darkness with a certainty marred only by his injuries until his fingertips brushed against the edge of a table.

With effort, he lowered himself to his knees, fumbled in his pocket for a lighter. After one or two tries it snapped alight, revealing a small room with odd things hung from hooks in the ceiling, ancient musty handwoven blankets in faded brown and grey draped irregularly on the walls. Stacked on the table were earthen dishes, some pinched out of raw clay, others shaped and formed and fired and elegant, but all ceramic. They surrounded a four-foot-long pelt, gray and yellow and white patterns of long, stiff guard hairs and rough fur, paws tipped with massive claws. Jessie lit a candle with trembling hands and carefully put the lighter back in his pocket. Taking one of the cruder pots, which had been used for the purpose many times before, he dripped wax from the candle into it and screwed the taper down. Shadows leaped and shuddered across the wall as the flame danced. He took the pelt in his hands.

"I am of the Earth," he murmured. "I am part of the soul of the Earth, and nothing of the Earth is strange to me. What I take from the Earth I return to the Earth. Spirit of Earth, hear me."

Silence answered him.

The old man stroked the fur, crooning. "Spirit of the Earth, hear me. I am a part of the Earth, a protector of the Earth. Hear me. Listen to me. Be not angry with me."

He stopped again, listening, but there was nothing, nothing but the faintest hissing of the candle flame consuming some stray dust mote. The gnarled fingers clenched deep. The claws clicked together. There was no response.

"I tried to warn them," he whispered, the flame dancing in his breath. "I told them. They did not listen, none of them. They do not believe. They cannot see you, they cannot see the Earth they walk upon, the trees. The running water, Antelope, Coyote, Badger." His fingers brushed the pelt fondly. "They do not know you are watching them. Spirit of Earth, will you show them? Will you teach them again what they should not have forgotten? Must more of them die?"

One of the dishes rattled on the table.

"They tear out your bones, sink poison into your veins. They are possessed of a beast as greedy as the wolverine . . ."

A flame tore loose from the candle, extinguished itself. The room was plunged into darkness, and out of darkness the old man's voice rose, pleading. "They are still your sons and daughters. They are still of the Earth. Let Earth itself teach them what they should have learned . . ."

Far away, a rumble, like a growl of agreement.

# 5

Rick and David hadn't made it twenty yards down the road before the radio mounted in the dash rattled to life, an unintelligible voice scrambled by static.

Rick reached for the handset and turned it on. "Zimmermann."

The voice on the other end came a little clearer. "Site Six here. What's your 40?"

The truck slowed. "East end of town. What's up?"

"Need an extra out here. Jase came down real sick. Can you come in for a few hours? Double time?"

Rick glanced over at Esher. "Wait one." Then, his thumb off the transmission switch, he said, "Hey, would you mind if we look at that site tomorrow?"

"No problem. In fact, if you could drop me off at the café, I could pick up on something else that's been bugging me." As a matter of fact, David wasn't sure what his next step was going to be; but there was an odd thread in the story of Nintucca, and he'd met at least one person he thought might enjoy telling him all about it. In fact, he expected that his only real problem would be getting a word in edgewise. Wanda Kostner *had* said she knew where all the bodies were buried.

And as long as he didn't think about Roy Evans' body, he was starving.

"That's fine." He switched the handset on again. "That's a big 10-4, Six. Be out there in forty minutes or so."

"Don't hit any cows on your way. Six out."

"Zimmermann out." The handset was back on its hook and the truck speeded up again. " 'Preciate that."

"Hey, no problem," the writer said, unconsciously echoing him. "Give me a call later and let me know when you're free again, okay?"

The truck stopped at the Good Times café next to the LDS chapel. "Listen," Esher said as he reached for the door handle, "I need to figure how much I owe you, and I haven't been keeping good track of the hours. What do you figure it's been?"

Rick stared out the windshield, chewing his lip. "Ought to have Marianne figure it, she's good at that kind of stuff. I dunno. Got to get out there, though. How about I tell you next time when I pick you up?" Esher nodded and got out, and the truck peeled out, coating him with a layer of white dry dust.

Shaking his head and brushing at his clothes, Esher stepped into the café and settled into the same booth he'd had before. Nothing had changed, except perhaps the wad of bubble gum in the waitress's mouth. Bobbi Jo, that was her name.

"Menu?"

"No, just a burger and fries and—"

"Anna ginger ale," she finished for him, snapping her gum vigorously. "Right?"

"Yeah, right." He was going to be immortalized as the guy who ordered ginger ale, he realized.

He sat back and wondered about why he was so hungry of a sudden. Even the sight of the greasy hamburger, the fatty smell of the fried meat didn't take the edge off his appetite. It still tasted surprisingly good.

He munched, considering what he'd seen so far. He did need to talk to Kostner again, even though the thought tasted worse than the re-warmed fries. He had an angle for his articles now, but he didn't think Migliori back at *Town Life* was going to buy it. Steve wanted something upbeat, positive.

And he wanted it good; and he wanted it soon.

And there was positive stuff here, after all. New jobs. Increased opportunity. More people. More money in the town. How could all this be bad? Why didn't the longtime residents want to work in the mine? They seemed to think that the disappearance of the little girl Tessy, the cattle mutilations, the death of Evans—even the earth collapsing under the Hendersons' swing set, for God's sake—was all because Kostner was opening up the mine again. Gallita had as much as said so before he clammed up on them. Was Kostner really wrong in his single-mindedness?

He finished eating and stood up; Bobbi Jo ambled over with the check. "S'cuse me," he said. "Can you tell me where I can find Mrs. Kostner?"

She shoved her gum into her cheek and stared at him suspiciously. "Miz Kostner? And which one might that be?"

Somehow he hadn't visualized Harry as a 'til-death-do-us-part man anyway. "Wanda? You know, she was in here with the cosmetics . . . ?"

The gum almost disappeared down her throat in the snort of laughter that greeted this. "Wanda? This time of day? She's doin' her rounds. But you could catch her—" a quick glance at the clock over the grill—"innabout three hours, at the casino. She eats dinner there ever' night. Whatcha want with Wanda?"

"Well, whatever works." He would have felt ashamed of this, but she didn't get it. The fringeless brown eyes narrowed even more. "She suggested I talk to her, that's all." He doled out eight dollars for the meal and the tip, hoping that Steve wouln't blow his stack at the expense account. Maybe he should append a copy of the menu, but it looked like they only had one. "Thanks."

# Three

## 1

The turnoff to the site was several miles past the mine road, marked by an aluminum statue of a drill rig and a sign, pocked by shotgun pellets, reading "U.S. GOVERNMENT RE-STRICTED AREA." Rick negotiated the turn and waved at the hippie with the sign sitting under his umbrella beside a green station wagon. The hippie glared at him and didn't wave back. Rick chuckled to himself and kept going. Only in Nevada did they still call them hippies. His big sister, who had abandoned New Age beliefs to get married and drive a BMW, would have been appalled at the attitudes in the small towns dotting the Great Basin. Personally, he liked them. Didn't agree with them, but he found them different. Refreshing.

Another five miles down the road he came to the Administrative Area, a collection of beige-painted metal temporary buildings surrounded by a fence with three strands of barbed wire on top, slanting inward to the compound. The barbed wire was supposed to slant outward, to make it more difficult to climb, but someone had put it in backward and had never bothered to correct the error. It made no difference as far as Rick could see; he'd never heard of anything classified going on, and nobody had ever conducted a security audit of the place. Dr. White was just paranoid about anyone finding out what he was doing.

He waved to the guard at the compound gate as he drove past and pulled up at the security building. It wasn't all that unusual to be called in to cover for someone, but he found himself wondering what had happened so late in the day. Entering the building, he greeted the secretary and headed for the locker room to change into his uniform.

"Gil wants to see you," the secretary said as he came out again ten minutes later.

"Put me on the clock, will you?"

"You're on." She nodded to the closed door of the office in the corner and he went in without knocking.

Gil was staring at the dirty window behind his desk as if enough effort on his part could make the grime-encrusted glass transparent again. A pair of dying spider plants framed his view. On the walls beside the eraserboard, framed sharpshooter certificates from the NRA alternated with pictures of small-arms teams and Sierra Club landscapes. Tucked into a corner, half hidden by a coatrack, was a diploma from the FBI Law Enforcement Training Academy.

Rick threw himself into one of the green chairs and propped one foot up on the desk. "So what's the big deal?"

Gil continued staring out the window. "Got a problem," he said at last.

Rick waited, curious. He'd been working for Gil for a couple of years now, and he had never seen him like this. When the other man finally turned away from the window and sat down, Rick was truly startled. Gil was almost pale, and lines of strain were etched in the corners of his mouth.

"You know about that horse," he said without preliminary. Rick nodded. Rumor spread among the guards even faster than it did in the town of Nintucca, and every one of the force had found occasion to swing by and see the corpse of the foal dissolving away on the sand. Rick had seen it too, surrounded by dead ants. Not even the vultures would touch it, but it was shrinking away every hour.

"And you've seen them do the tests."

Rick nodded again, mystified.

"You see any connection?"

Rick opened his mouth to deny any such thing, then closed it again. "I don't know," he said cautiously.

"Jenks, the guy I called you in to replace, got stuck in the sand over by the old well. He got himself dug in pretty deep. I went over to pull him out and I found out I couldn't. His truck was buried up to the axles, and when we hooked it up to mine we found out he didn't have any tires any more. It was sitting in a pool of green goo and the stuff had eaten everything away. Tires, wheels, the works. That truck was dissolving the same way that horse is. Only faster."

Rick sat, waiting.

"They're telling us this stuff is safe to be around, and they're pumping it into the ground. I asked Northhampton specifically and he told me our guys weren't in any danger." Gil's dark brown eyes were unreadable, but Rick knew the expression. Gil was furious, and the younger man was very glad that anger wasn't directed at himself.

"Did you ask Ruiz? Northhampton says what White tells him to say. Perry's pretty straight with us, I thought."

Gil shook his head. "Northhampton will take it straight back to White. If Ruiz does too, if they think somebody suspects, they'll get rid of me and replace me with somebody else who takes orders better." A bitter smile twisted across his lips. "White doesn't like me to begin with."

"What are you going to do?"

"I'm going to look for proof. I'm going to stay over this evening after they've all gone to quarters, and I'm going to get into their files and find out what this stuff is, what reports they've filed, and what they plan to use it for. I'm going to find out what we're being exposed to. And I want you to cover me."

"Okay," Rick said instantly.

Gil smiled again, less bitter this time. "Maybe there's nothing. Maybe I'm just going crazy. But there's too much going on here."

"You heard about the Hendersons, didn't you? How their kids' swing set disappeared? You think that has anything to do with it?"

"No. Let's not get crazy with this. The Hendersons' back yard was just built over a tunnel, that's all, and it collapsed. They're lucky their kids weren't out there at the time."

"You think so?"

"Let's say I'm reasonably sure." Gil shook his head. "Damn, I don't like this. I don't want to do this . . ."

Rick kept silent, unable to help the other man.

Gil sighed. "We'll wait until they go back to the living quarters. It'll be just you and me—I don't want to get anybody else involved. There may be nothing there, after all."

"But you think there is."

"I think there is. And I think it's bad for all of us."

# 2

The portraits on the other walls brooded at Harry Kostner as he worked behind the big desk, glaring like hawks mewed up in frames by mistake. Looking up sometimes to follow a stray thought he found himself looking into the painted eyes, at the symbol over the model, and he smiled grimly.

The phone at his elbow rang twice, demandingly. He picked it up without moving his gaze from the portraits. "Yeah?"

During the rumble of speech from the other end of the connection, he allowed his gaze to drift down lightly, casually, to the model itself.

"*What?*" Rage blazed in the single word, and he caught himself with an effort. "You tried the new stuff yet?" A short pause. "You're waiting for EPA clearance. I see." His voice dropped, became honeyed.

"I can see how disappointed you must be. Takes a long time for the EPA to approve things. Years, sometimes."

His fingers, gripping the receiver, were red and white with pressure. "Yes, of course. Of course. Now, I'm just a layman, Doctor, but I guess I don't understand how you can hurt dirt. That's all we're dealing with here. Dirt."

The voice on the other end started to jabber, and he cut it off without raising his voice. "Well, I can certainly appreciate your position on this, Doctor. It's quite a disappointment to me, of course. I can't really afford to wait such a long time, and we both know that they're going to okay it eventually, aren't they? This is the stuff that really works. *Isn't it?*"

A short, weak answer.

"You know, I really wish you'd reconsider. It would look pretty strange, wouldn't it, to file this late in the process? And I know it would be a hassle for you to go find funding somewhere else. If you really *did* go to the government you'd have to file, of course. Full disclosure, and you'd lose all the patent rights.—*All* the rights. I'm disappointed, yeah. *I'd* hate to lose what I've put into it this far. I've been keeping up with your reports. They all look current to me. I'm going to quote from them day after tomorrow.

"It looks good, White. And if you think this is really the breakthrough—"

An excited babble.

"Well, maybe you need another test. Or two. You know, before you go through all that hassle. They're going to want to look at your data, right? Makes sense to get as much as possible . . . You'd look a lot better when you come in."

A pause. Thoughtful answer. The pressure on the receiver eased somewhat.

"That's right. What's the point to filing all that stuff when you aren't sure? Hey, listen, you want to run a couple more holes, I understand that . . . It does what? Okay, yeah, a few more tests. But if it *works*—hey, maybe we could find a way to do a large-scale test. I mean, *really* big. Impress the hell out of the bureaucrats—"

Another babble. Kostner's lips writhed back in a savage grin, but his voice sounded carefully uncertain.

"Hey, now—hey, man, that's a ballbreaker. Shit, that's big, all right. The whole damn mine? Can you make enough of the stuff? How much more? Shit, man, that's fucking unbelievable. You've got vision, man, that's all I can say. Yeah, it would sure cost less than reinforcing the whole mine . . . How soon?"

The answer jolted him. Now his enthusiasm was genuine.

"That soon? Really? Fan-fucking-tastic. That's great. That's really great. Yeah, I think we could do that. Sure. Sure. Listen, let's set something up tomorrow, okay, I'll come out there. I want to see this for myself. Yeah, sure. Fine. 'Bye."

He replaced the receiver in its cradle with an inaudible click and got to his feet, circling the desk and moving in on the model, touching the rooftops with a fingertip, moving a toy car a few inches down the dusty street, nudging the little figures on their way. He was absorbed in placing someone in the doorway of the ore mill when a tapping at the office door disturbed his concentration.

"Harry?"

"What?" He didn't turn around.

"I was just talking to Bobbi Jo. Down at the café?"

Kostner grinned a private, reminiscent grin that didn't appear on his lips when he answered his wife. "So?"

"Did you tell that Esher he could talk to Wanda?"

"To *Wanda*?" Harry swiveled his head to look over his shoulder at her, brows beetling. "What the fuck does he want to talk to Wanda for?"

"Don't know, Harry." She leaned hipshot against the door, showing off a length of tanned leg, and crossed her arms under her breasts, bringing them up, full. "What the hell would anybody want with Wanda?"

Harry grinned. "Damned if I know, sweetcheeks. Hey, you busy?"

She grinned knowingly. "What you think?"

"Be with you in a second."

She turned and swayed away. Harry straightened to follow her, gave one more look to the portraits over the model, one more glance to the model itself. He snorted, reached out, and flicked a finger against one of the tiny figures, a woman in a loud polka-dot dress. The figure went flying against one of the model houses and sprawled, broken. "Yeah, fuck you, Wanda," he muttered, and followed the woman out of the room.

# 3

Deep in the Earth, Spirit gathered, listened. Up above, someone was calling. The voice, the need, came down the chutes and winzes, drifted along the walls like fog, deep, deep, seeking. Through darkness—need needs no light—and the heat of the bowels of the Earth. Seeking.

And finding what it sought.

Deep in the Earth, the air took a shape.

Awakened, Spirit began a seeking of its own.

# Four

## 1

Esher switched on the tape recorder as he walked in the front door of the county jail, trusting that it would pick up from his jeans pocket as well as it did from his shirt front. A balding, young deputy with sergeant's stripes swung his boots down from the desk as he came in.

"Kin I he'p you?" he said, punctuating the courtesy with a stream of tobacco juice aimed at a receptacle hidden behind the furniture.

"Sheriff Bailey in?"

"Well, not 'zactly," the sergeant drawled insolently.

Esher studied him. The young man seemed to be laughing at him, as if the accent and the chaw and the weatherbeaten boots were all some kind of masquerade, and the young man wasn't really a typical local yokel at all. On the other hand, given how few natives there were in Nintucca, there probably wasn't any such thing as a 'typical' local yokel.

"Where is she?"

"Wellll, I suppose she's out." Another noxious stream.

"And when will she be back in?"

"Kind of hard to say. Sheriffs don't keep regular hours." Certainly not office hours convenient to the mere public, he might as well have added.

"Is she investigating the Evans death?"

The amusement, and with it the persona, vanished abruptly. "Listen, you're that Esher dude. I know you. You're supposed to be writing about the mines opening up again. You're not a crime reporter. So how about you buzz on out of here and leave this alone? It's none of your business."

"Well, that's kind of up to me to decide, isn't it?" Esher said deliberately.

Red-faced, the deputy got to his feet. "Get the fuck out of here."

"Let me get this straight. Local law authorities are refusing to investigate an unexplained death? Why is that, Sergeant—" Esher leaned forward to read the name tag—"O'Malley?"

"Nobody's refusing to investigate anything," said a new, feminine voice. "Luke, get rid of that damned cud. I told you I didn't want you chewing in the office."

Both men swung around as Laura Bailey entered. She was pale, with dark circles under her eyes, and her voice crackled.

"You were supposed to be making up another search roster," she continued, ignoring Esher for the time being. "Where is it?"

"Uh, right here, ma'am . . ." O'Malley stuttered, scrambling a clipboard up and thrusting it toward her.

"And have you got in touch with any of these people?"

"Uh, not yet, ma'am."

"Well, why the hell don't you go ahead and do that? Esher, in my office. Now."

She reminded Esher of a Marine sergeant he'd once interviewed. Somehow he didn't expect to be any more successful with her than he'd been then.

"How's Jessie?" she said, swinging into the chair behind the desk. "You and Rick took him to the doctor?"

He was surprised that she asked. At the riot, she'd shown no interest at all in the old man's injuries. "He's okay. I don't think he'll be pressing charges," he added nastily.

Bailey stared at him coolly. "No, I don't expect he will. What can I do for you, Esher?"

"I'd like to know what the hell was going on out there at the mine. What it was all about. For instance, how did Evans die? Can I get a look at an autopsy report? Was he inside the mine? If so, what was in that mine? Is there really something to be afraid of down there?" He listed his questions one after another, watching the expression, or lack of it, on her face. The woman was under incredible tension. He'd be lucky not to get thrown out, he decided.

"You running a tape?" she said at last.

"Yes," he admitted. As she continued to stare, he pulled the small recorder out of his pocket.

"Shut it off."

He did so, showing her the microcassette reels coming to a stop. Then he slid it back into his pocket, thumbing it back on as he did so.

"This is off the record, Esher. And straight. I just came back from the hospital. They took care of the autopsy right away—it's not like we have a lot of people die in this town. They said Evans died of cardiac arrest. His heart stopped beating."

That does happen when people die, Esher thought. "Bullshit."

"Exactly. Bullshit. I think, and the doc thinks, that the man was scared to death."

"Sudden attack of claustrophobia?" he hazarded.

"More bullshit. The man was a miner. He'd spent years under the ground. No, there was something else. There's something in that mine, about that mine, that literally scared him to death. He ran himself to death trying to get away. And no, I don't know what it is, and no, Kostner isn't going to listen."

"Did you go in and look?"

Bailey shrugged. "Yeah, as much as we could. But there's miles of tunnels down there. We found—didn't find anything."

Esher knew she was lying. There was something. But he also knew he wasn't going to pry it out of her, at least not right now. He decided to change the subject. "Could it be the same thing that got the kid?"

"Tessy Marie?" She flinched and stared at him hard. "We don't know what happened to Tessy. She's just gone. We're still looking, but I don't think we're going to find her." She drummed lightly polished fingernails on the desk, stopped. "And that's definitely off the record, understand?"

Esher nodded. Interesting reaction, he thought. She hadn't expected him to bring up the missing child, and she didn't like it. Maybe whatever she found had nothing to do with Evans, but instead was related to Tessy? If so, why keep silent? Unless

Kostner didn't want any association made between a missing child and the mine.

Later, he cautioned himself. Take it up again later. The sheriff looked like she would explode like old dynamite any minute. "Yeah, I understand. But this mine business—what's this 'beast' Gallita talks about? You said yourself you couldn't search the whole place. Could there be some animal down there?"

"Now that *is* superstition, Esher." She rubbed her eyes, blurring makeup along her cheekbone. "I want to deal with something we can put in jail, okay? Something we can fry, for preference. This stage of the game, I'm a great believer in the death penalty."

Esher nodded again. "But not in assault and battery charges." Not against Harry Kostner.

She took a deep breath. "Not in this case, no. Not unless Jessie presses charges."

"Kind of hard to guard justice in Nintucca, isn't it, Sheriff?" He couldn't resist the tone of mock sympathy.

"You think you'd do a better job?" she flared. "Now, you got anything more to say? Because I don't. I want to go home and fix dinner and talk to my daughter about something besides people dying, like I used to be able to do before all this trouble started. That okay with you, Esher?"

He nodded reluctantly and left.

# 2

"Mrs. Kostner?"

The woman in the booth looked up from her dinner, still chewing a too-large mouthful of steak. Her head bobbed in an upward nod of recognition, and she waved him into the seat across the table from him. By the time he slid in she'd swallowed.

"Mr. Esher! They said you were looking for me. Come to get that interview, huh?" Setting the fork down, she reached for the salt shaker and poured a small hill onto the corner of her plate. "Well, you came to the right place. Anything you want to know about Harry, I can sure tell you." Picking up one of the home fries, she dabbed it into the salt, creating a small volcanic depression. "You eaten yet? Steak's good tonight. Steak's good every night, but then, what can you do to steak, right? Though I used to fry it too much. I guess you can ruin a steak if you overcook it. I never was much for Home Ec, never did like it. My mama did all the cooking and made me do all the dishes, so I'm a whiz at doing the dishes. Or they've got a pretty good chef's salad. Lots of good stuff in it. I eat out here almost every night."

Popping the fry in to her mouth, she paused to watch the effect of her torrent of words, much as she had done earlier. Esher grinned.

"I guess I'll have the steak, then. And some potato salad. As long as it doesn't have lettuce," he added. "Yeah, I wanted to interview you."

Wanda nodded vigorously and waved her hand in the air; a teenage waitress appeared as if by magic. "Mr. Esher wants the steak, Vonne. And potato salad, not the regular dinner salad." She swiveled toward Esher. "You want dressing with that? No, I guess not, not if you don't want lettuce. But the Thousand Island is good. Course, it comes from the bottle, how can you go wrong with that, right? Vonne's mother makes the Italian herself. I always thought it tasted a little funny myself—"

"That's fine," he broke in. Vonne rolled her eyes and wrote his order down. Wanda kept right on going.

"And you could order beer to drink, or wine. But that's right, you don't drink, do you? Lees, the bar waitress, told me," she explained, and then redirected her remarks to Vonne. "He drinks ginger ale."

Suppressing a surge of anger—obviously the whole town knew, and hadn't he said it himself, publicly? What did he have to be angry at?—he shook his head. "Coffee, black."

Vonne nodded. Unabashed, Wanda rolled on.

"And he'll probably want some dessert. That's a big steak, but it's only a steak, after all. This is a big guy. Make sure you put extra ham in his potato salad and lots of that white cheese stuff. Last time one of the guys ordered the salad it had hardly any ham at all, just those eggs and lots of potatoes. I was just telling him how good that salad is, so you better not make a liar out of me."

She switched off again. Vonne raised one eyebrow at Esher.

Esher nodded. Vonne wrote. She raised an eyebrow one more time, and he shook his head. She left.

Esher turned back to Wanda just in time to catch the faintest smile hovering on her lips.

"I think I'll like the potato salad," he offered.

"Yeah, but don't blame me if you hate it. What do you want to know?" She picked up her knife and fork and began cutting up the rest of her steak.

"Well, how about Harry? When did you meet him? How long were you married to him?"

She snorted in an unladylike fashion. "I grew up with the son of a bitch. I was born here in Nintucca, went to school with him. Elementary, high school. College." The steak was being carved into progressively smaller pieces. "Yes, sir, Mr. Journalist, I went to college. In California. I majored two years in education. Then my mama got sick and I came back home. And Harry and I got married."

"When your mother died?"

"Oh, no, she didn't die for years. I stayed with her when Harry went back to school. She left me her house, y'know. Free and clear. Made me promise I'd never let anybody else have it, and boy was that a smart promise."

"Harry went away to school and left you here?"

The knife clattered down and the fork stabbed into a tiny square of meat. "He did. Finished up his degree and got his master's in mining technology, and he came back home again. He wanted to open up the mine again clear back then, but his mama wouldn't hear of it. She'd have screaming fits when he even talked about it. One time, he almost had some people interested, but he needed some more money. Tried to get me to sell my house and give him the money—this was after my mama died. I wouldn't do it, and he divorced me. His mama found out about his syndicate, had herself a heart attack, and he had to quit again. Then *she* died, and I guess he started investing and stuff." The piece of meat went into her mouth and she chewed it four times and swallowed.

"What was he investing in?"

"Kostner stuff. Land, cattle. Banks mostly. Harry was real good at foreclosing." A home fry missiled into the salt volcano and shattered it. "I really thought he'd forgot about the mine. Then that government stuff started going on outside of town—

you know, the site, out where Rick and those guys work?—and a few more people came in and all of a sudden he really started talking up the mine again. Brought geologists and everything. The more people the site hired, the more he talked about the mine. Well, look at you. He brought you in."

"I came on an assignment from *Town Life*. I don't work for Harry Kostner," he objected mildly.

The fry screwed down into the remains of the salt pile. "*Sure* you don't," she said.

"Well, if I'm supposed to be working for Harry, how come I'm talking to you?"

The potato salad arrived, a yellow-white mound dotted with pimentos and pieces of pink ham and smelling of vinegar, and was set in the middle of the table while Vonne set out a paper place mat, utensils, a full glass of water, and coffee. Wanda resumed work on her steak and watched.

"I don't know," she said at last, after Vonne left. "But I know *Town Life* wouldn't have sent you if Harry didn't think he could handle you."

"Well, maybe Harry was wrong."

Wanda clearly doubted it, but her raised eyebrows made it obvious that she was far too polite to say so.

"So Harry started talking about the mine again when this site started up? Any connection?" He poked in the salad for the ham. There was lots of ham. Lots of the white cheese stuff too.

For the first time, the woman seemed uncertain—not about what to say, but whether to say it. "Well, you know how it is in a little town like this one. Everybody talks. Everybody guesses. Everybody thinks that White's really working for Harry. But it isn't like anybody *knows*."

Studying her, Esher was certain that she did know. And she wanted to tell what she knew, preferably to the whole world. And what she told would not be complimentary to Harry Kostner.

"It would be awful hard to prove, that the two things were connected. And even if they were, what's the crime?"

"How about misappropriation of government funds?" Wanda's voice was almost a whisper. "How about fraudulent environmental impact statements? People go to jail for that these days."

"Still, awful hard to prove." Vonne came by with his steak,

and Wanda made herself busy eating until the waitress was gone. All the conspiratorial instincts of a school kid, Esher thought. But he liked her all the same.

As he had hoped, she responded to the probe. "Yeah, but if you had stuff in writing, you could, couldn't you?"

"Depends on what it is." He took a large, casual bite of potatoes and mayonnaise and pretended not to watch her.

"Well, I know Harry left some notes at a board meeting at the bank one time, and they were written on site stationery. So he must have been out there sometime. It would be just like him to rip them off for some paper. Harry's a cheap bastard."

"Is that all?" He let disappointment show in his voice.

She shrugged, her sable hair falling across her shoulder. "Maybe. Prob'ly."

There was more. He could taste it as surely as he used to taste whiskey, there was more; but if he pushed now, she'd go skittering away and never produce. "Well, okay. Listen, let's talk about some other things, okay? Why don't you tell me about Nintucca. What was it like growing up here?"

With that she became animated again, and kept talking until his pocket recorder had reversed itself and run all the way through, and he begged off from any more anecdotes and pleaded exhaustion.

"Are you going home now?" he asked at last.

Wanda looked at him as if he'd lost his mind. "Of course not. It's only ten-thirty, and I haven't played anything yet." She cocked her head, considering. "Tell you what. You meet me here tomorrow around lunchtime and maybe I can tell you some more stuff about Harry, okay?"

Bingo, he thought. "Okay—"

# 3

The only way to call out of the Rowdytown Hotel was through the switchboard operator at the front desk. And the switchboard operator, Harry Kostner's daughter, wasn't interested in placing any calls back East for the journalist guest. Esher tried five times before giving up in disgust.

He bent over the keyboard of the laptop, typing furiously,

swearing as his fingers, used to reaching for keys more widely spaced, stumbled and tripped. There was too much he wanted to say. He wanted to write about Jessie Gallita, beaten to the ground and struggling up again. About the network of gossip in Nintucca that webbed up a stranger. About the hopes for jobs. About hitching a horse to the porch of the casino. About mysterious testing going on out in the desert, about which everyone seemed to know and nobody wanted to talk about. About the desert itself, white and yellow and sere. About what a man looked like when his heart had burst with terror.

About the single-minded drive to re-open a mine, re-create a town.

A fief.

Where something terrible—something unnamed—was going on.

He wrote with a passion, nearly screaming with frustration when the characters on the backlit screen turned out jumbled and senseless and had to be done over. It was a wonderful feeling, one he had thought long dead, and Harry Kostner wasn't going to like it one bit.

The phone rang. His left hand kept moving over the keys and he reached for the receiver with his right, not really concentrating. "Yeah?"

"Hey, it's Rick. I was talking to Gil a little bit ago, and there's something—" the deep voice paused, and he could hear Rick swallowing, as if his throat had constricted on the word— "he says that there's something out there you might like to see. A little . . . strange."

It took a moment or two to grab his attention. "Out at the site?"

A wary pause. "Yes and no. They're not actively working at this particular place right now. Anyway, I thought we could go out there tomorrow afternoon and I could show you this thing."

"What kind of 'thing' are we talking about here?"

"Dead horse." Clipped, abrupt answer that made Esher even more confused.

"You want to show me a *dead horse*?"

"Yeah. I think you'll be interested."

Esher stared at the last paragraph on the laptop screen and wondered why he should be interested in a dead horse.

"Okay," he said at last. "I'll bite. Why am I going to be interested in a dead horse?"

"I'll show you, and you can tell me."

"Shit . . . Okay. I've got some more stuff to look at in the library in the morning. I'll meet you, okay?"

"Fine."

Connection broken, mood broken. The white fury of putting words on paper was gone. Only the questions were left.

# Five

## 1

Night was comfortable. It floated with the drifts of air, twisting in alleys between houses, rising and sinking without aim. A cat, sensing it, yowled with fear and fled, but it could not go far enough and the thing tasted of its fear. It followed a couple walking home, touched lightly the hairs on their necks, and faded back again. Searching. Angry. Hungry.

It was fully awake now, for the first time in a long time, and for a long time it had not been fully fed.

It followed a small blond boy who bicycled aimlessly along an abandoned road, watched him as he looked behind him and to either side, searching for someone who was not there. It reached out to the boy and then stopped. It did not understand why, but part of itself rejected its own hunger, here at least. For now.

Angrier now, it returned to the town, to the artificial constructs made of its own blood and bone, hunting.

It was almost strong enough now to take what it needed, to silence the voices demanding obedience, pulling it in opposite ways. Almost strong enough to be free to do what it would. Almost.

It found a house, found traces of ancient ties. It took a shape, settled on the porch.

One more feasting.

# 2

The single-wide trailer sat on blocks in the middle of dirt unrelieved by plants, trees, even rocks. It was as if the whole area had been scoured clean of any life; even the bluetails avoided this yard, as if they knew that there was no shelter here from marauding hawks, cats, children, all the creatures that would make a lizard's life miserable. An owl drifted overhead, the white tufts of its ears gleaming in the moonlight, and cried mournfully.

The casual observer would see that the beige paint showed signs of recent touching up, probably due to a sandstorm gritting down to the base metal. A bay window thrust itself importantly out beside the front door. There was supposed to be a porch, with an overhang to provide shelter; instead a set of wooden steps, surprisingly solid, led up to the door. Everything about it said that it was a temporary home, a home for a person who didn't plan to stay long and wasn't too particular about his choice of quarters for the time being.

But the message would be misleading. Inside, it was cool and dark and inviting, furnished with deep-cushioned rugs and heavy, dark furniture, well worn but solid, comfortable. Two large-leaved rhododendrons on tall stands occupied corners. Bookcases lined the wall opposite the bay window, filled to overflowing with volumes that had been read more than once and carefully double-stacked away. Over the entrance to the kitchen area hung a landscape, New England hills in autumn with trees afire with changing colors and a gentle fog swathing them against the rays of a rising sun. A glass trophy cabinet half hidden behind the leather couch held plaques and statues of men holding guns. The bay window, and all other windows in the trailer, were shut tight and shuttered by venetian blinds and curtains, not letting a trace of Nevada moonlight in.

Gil Santillanes unbuckled the gun belt, let it slide to the couch, and stretched, rotating his shoulders. There was something to be said for an office job, he thought, picking the belt up again and hanging it on a hook beside the door. Sitting in a truck with iffy air-conditioning all day in the desert heat, watching other men do hard physical labor—he shook his head and wondered why in the hell he had ever envied them.

He had spent his fair share of time in an office, though. Then he had chosen hard physical labor, in an effort to work things like the murders of children out of his system. And finally he was brought to sitting in a truck, watching other men sweating in the sun.

Turning on the air conditioner and all the lights in the trailer, he moved through living room and hallway and back to the bedroom. One wall of the bedroom too was lined with books; another supported rack after rack of houseplants under a lighting arrangement. The other two were crowded with paintings, sketches, all of other places where the land was green and water stood in lakes without evaporating.

Stuffing the khaki uniform into a hamper, he stepped into the locker-sized bathroom to turn on the shower and soap away another day's dirt and sweat. Emerging into the bedroom, he pulled a clean set of clothes out of a bureau and stretched, noting with amusement that he didn't even have to towel himself dry—most of the water was gone already.

The trailer's kitchen was barely the size of a shoe box. He opened the cupboard and scanned the shelves, was interrupted by an indignant yowl at his feet.

A small brown cat looked up at him accusingly.

"If you didn't flop over at my feet, I wouldn't step on you," he informed the cat without sympathy. "Turkey bits tonight. That's for you. Omelet for me."

The cat found this acceptable. Gil scraped and mixed. Eventually, both fed, plates clean, the cat leaped into the man's lap and balanced, standing on his legs and staring into his face.

Gil looked into the golden eyes and made no attempt to touch the animal. "You're welcome."

The cat meowed once and leaped down again, crossed to the couch, and curled up, content.

Smiling to himself, Gil cleared everything else off the kitchen table, pulled out a bottle of dark beer, and spread an old, much-washed dish towel out. From a cabinet over the sink he pulled two flat metal cans with thin plastic-capped spouts and set them on the table. Beside them went bronze-colored wire brushes, a twelve-inch plastic rod, a small piece of plastic looking like an ankh without the crosspiece, a small box. He set everything out as carefully as an altar boy might have arranged candles and cruets.

Reaching into the catch tray for a plant on the windowsill, he pulled out a small key and started to unlock a second glass-fronted cabinet. The cat yowled.

Nodding agreement, he went over to the stereo and paged through a stack of CDs. Making a couple of selections, he put it on and went back to the cabinet, withdrawing three handguns and setting them on the table. As the opening notes of Fresh Aire IV echoed, he began to break the guns down, humming along with the music.

The single-shot was the easiest; his target gun, the one he used when he wanted precision, instead of brute force. In many ways it was his favorite. The frame still held the .22 barrel he used the last time he went out target shooting; he'd cleaned it after that session too, but nonetheless went through the motions, because the motions were the important thing tonight.

"Remember always," his *abuela*, his grandmother, had told him when he was six. She had punctuated her words with a long bony brown finger jabbing into his chest. "Remember always, you must be prepared to fight evil. There is much evil in this world, evil that there are no laws against. You must be prepared to fight it. But if you are pure, God and all his Holy Saints will be with you, and you will triumph."

He didn't know how pure he'd stayed, but he was good at being prepared.

The gun broke open like a shotgun, and he levered the barrel up, peering through it at the kitchen light. Opening up the box, he took a circular piece of white flannel and threaded it into the loop of the ankh piece. Setting it aside, he attached one of the brushes to the rod, running it up the barrel for form's sake. He never allowed his guns to get *that* dirty, but things must be done in the proper order. He replaced the brush with the plastic piece, dampening it with solvent, interrupting his contented humming with a wrinkle of the nose for the stink of the solvent.

Brush again. A new swab, scrubbing the remains of the solvent away. Still another swab. Scrubbing the receiver face. Finally, a light coating of gun oil from the second can for both face and interior. Weapon clean, he set it carefully aside and picked up the revolver.

The .38 had seen more use; the grips were worn and

yellowed, the hammer nicked by some forgotten accident. Flipping open the cylinder, he inspected it automatically. His hands moved over the gun with a life of their own, his eyes half closed, his torso swaying an inch or two to the music. Brush and swab the barrel and forcing cone, unscrew the barrel for good measure and check the threading, scrub away imaginary dirt under the plates, and end with the thinnest coat of gun oil.

It was mindless work, work that he had done a thousand times and probably didn't need to be doing now, but he didn't want to read, didn't want to go out drinking. He wanted to occupy his hands and empty his mind.

He had no particular opinions one way or another about White, or about the testing out at the site, or even about Kostner's reopening the mine, as long as it didn't threaten himself or the men he was responsible for. But coming home tonight he had found himself looking into the rearview more often than usual, watching for something. Listening for something. Knowing there *was* something.

He remembered coming back home to show off, standing at attention in his shiny neat Military Police uniform in front of the little, dried-up woman brown as a fallen leaf and about as substantial; but her bony finger still hurt when she poked him in the chest, peering up at him, up at him because now he was tall and she was so small. "You know how to use that gun, child?"

And he had somehow kept from smiling as he answered, "Yes, *abuela*."

"Good," she had said. "You keep it ready. There are evil things, child, evil things there are no laws against. You be ready for them."

"Yes, *abuela*," he had said.

He'd found evil from time to time, but he hadn't had to use the guns. Evil in the face of a child killer, evil in a dark place under the ground. He was pretty sure he had found evil here, too. Perhaps not. But it never hurt to be ready.

He'd almost hit a calf scampering across the road to get back to its mama tonight; the jolt of adrenalin that had given him had wound him up too much to want to be around people. And the documents. They hadn't been reporting, but Paul Northhampton was enough of a scientist to keep careful records of the effect of the green liquid—dead antelope, poisoned trees, seepage in places far from the drill sites where the stuff had been injected. It was time to turn a spotlight on his employers, even if doing so tore his loyalties in half. No, he didn't want to be around people tonight.

Only Rick, who'd been with him as he read the papers, would understand, and Rick would be wrapped up in his Marianne if he had a God's lick of sense. Which the kid did, after all. It had been his idea to show the reporter.

Wiping his hands on the cloth, Gil took a deep drag of his beer.

There had been a lot of animal activity out at the site today; he'd seen five or six coyotes running scared, some rabbits, even a big ugly wolverine clawing at the earth. Maybe looking for one of those rabbit families.

Maybe trying to find a safe den.

Not in this earth, buddy, he said silently to the memory. There's no safe place in this earth. Not when skeletons get up and walk.

Finally, the complicated one, the automatic. This was a newer gun that had seen more recent use. Pieces of metal were scattered across the towel; the stack of used swabs grew ever larger. Breech, slide, bushing, barrel—he caught the spring as it leaped out from the frame. Brushing. Swabbing. Each piece treated separately, carefully, and set aside. He cleaned out the underside of the slide with an old toothbrush grey from much use, and inspected all of the pieces. Almost done.

He could do the long guns next, he thought. Or find something else to do. Go by Sexy Sadie's and get laid—not a bad idea either, he thought, and smiled. He wondered if Rick had taken that dude Esher by Sadie's yet. Maybe not—Marianne would kill him—but he'd probably told him about it. He couldn't imagine the Easterner not being curious, not wanting to check out a genuine Nevada brothel. He remembered what it was like the first time he'd ventured past the pastel-green door, and smiled again. Yeah. Maybe Tillie'd be free. Finish this up, get the crap off his hands—

The music came to an end, and he wiped his hands on a towel and got up to replace it with something from Mahler. The Seventh, with the tragic minor ending suitable for mourning Evans or someone else he didn't know well. As he turned back to the table, he saw the brown cat sniffing at the gun barrel.

"Hey, get out of there!"

The cat ignored him, touched the metal with one velvet paw, nudged it a few millimeters along the dish towel.

"I said cut it out! Off the table!" Pulling another towel off the oven door handle, he snapped it in the air.

The cat glanced up, slit-eyed, and snarled at him. The towel sagged in his hand as he stared. He and the cat had an agreement: he fed it, forebore to touch it, and it deigned to live with him. But it had never acted this way before. "Cat?"

The cat bunched itself together, the fur along its spine standing straight up, its tail puffing to five times its normal size, and yowled again, a low war cry rising to a chilling scream. Light gleamed from the ivory fangs, the tiny hooks covering the bright pink tongue. He thought about rabies. But its actions were too deliberate . . .

"Cat?" He stifled the urge to step back, away from the furious animal.

Snarling again, the cat deliberately batted the recoil spring off the table, sending it spinning across the carpet and under the couch.

"Damn you—"

As the cat began to shove the gun frame off the table, he stepped forward. The animal spun and snarled and he stopped again, watching as one by one every piece of the gun hit the floor, followed by cleaning rods, brushes, swabs, and cans of solvent and gun oil, the cat spinning and snapping and striking at the metal as if it were alive and an enemy and had to be destroyed.

The liquids spread and stank, the odors fusing and spreading like a noxious mist over the table as the cat methodically shredded the dish towel to the music to Mahler and he stood there watching, paralyzed.

And then, when there was nothing left on the table but damp scraps of cloth, the cat stepped delicately away, shaking drops of clear liquid off one hind leg and turning its head to groom down the middle of its back.

"Cat?" he whispered, finding his voice at last.

The golden eyes regarded him peacefully, and the cat sprang down and butted its head against his ankle before leaping back up to its accustomed place on the couch to return to its interrupted sleep.

# 3

Coin, coin, coin, coin, coin. On the screen, cards *thwipped* into place: two threes, a king, a queen, a jack. Followed by "Sorry, you lost! Try again?" in large clownish red letters.

Wanda Mirielle paid no attention. Already she was feeding more coins into the video speaker, the dollars sliding down the metal throat one after another with a soul-satisfying series of *clunks*. Even as the next series of cards flipped over, her polished nails were scrabbling at the bottom of the cardboard bucket for the next five coins.

And five more. And five more. And—no more. Her nails, long and carefully manicured and painted Adobe Rose, scrabbled in vain. Next to her, someone hit for four of a kind, the jackpot laughing into the stainless-steel bowl as an announcement that someone else was winning. Someone else, not her. Exasperated, she shoved the cardboard bucket in with the discarded coin wrappers and used ashtrays and empty complimentary drink glasses between the two machines and reached for her purse, poking around in the depths, looking for another dollar.

Nothing. She closed her eyes in momentary defeat, opening them again as the winner next to her slid out of his seat. But he hadn't overlooked anything in the bowl—no stray dollars looking for a home—and her shoulders slumped as she levered herself off the stool and started for the door. It was only eleven o'clock and she was wiped out already. Not fair, dammit. The guy had been sitting at her machine. It should have been her jackpot, not his. Even if it was only a lousy four of a kind.

"Wanda? Wanda, honey, you goin' home already?" The speaker was a neat brunette wearing the apron of a casino change girl. "Now, Wanda, don't you go looking so sad. Your luck's gonna change." She pulled Wanda over into a reasonably quiet corner by the change counter and patted her on the arm.

Wanda straightened up automatically and brushed a wisp of hair out of her face. "Oh, it's just one night, Linda. I was down to Vegas last week and I hit a royal and two straights. Came home with four thousand dollars! I really needed it too. I had to get the car fixed and—you know."

Linda nodded sympathetically. "You go down there with that Perry from the site? Did y'all have fun?" Her hands were thrust deep into the pockets of the apron, juggling the rolls of coins out of Wanda's sight but not her hearing. Her eyes canned the crowd as she talked, looking for a gambler running short of change, somebody who might hit it big and be good for a tip.

"Oh, Perry's no fun. He wanted to go to some lecture or something, and I wanted to go dancing and gamble. And after the lecture he wanted to go bowling at the Showboat. Hey, if I want to go bowling I can do it right up here. We've got our own bowling alley. We don't need to go to Vegas.

"Did you see that new guy? That Esher? He's writing about the mine for Harry. I might ask him out. He's cute. And I could tell him lots of things."

This got Linda's full attention. The rattling coins stilled. "Wanda, you wouldn't. You couldn't ask a man out, that's—that's low class. Besides, Harry would have a fit. The guy works for him."

"No, he doesn't, I'll bet." Wanda hitched her massive purse, a square collection of multicolored leather patches, higher on her shoulder. "I like him. I bet he doesn't work for Harry, even if Harry thinks so. And what's wrong with asking a guy out if you think he's cute? I swear, Linda, you're living in the Fifties."

"Wanda, you're a libber." But the insult was soft, between friends. "Trust me, you don't want to go out with this guy. He's a drunk."

"He *is*?" As fascinated as if she'd never heard the rumor before, Wanda pulled her into the doorway of the change booth, ignoring the glare from the change boss. One of the delights of Wanda's life was hearing rumors—particularly her own—from a fresh source. The fact that this one wasn't one of her own lessened her pleasure only a little. "What did you hear?"

"Lees, over in the bar. She says the night he came in, he had a drink with Mikey and Gil and Rick and Marianne, but all he had was ginger ale. He even came right out and said he wouldn't have a beer 'cause he couldn't handle it. And you know what *that* means."

Wanda nodded. "Boy, do I. Harry used to—" Belatedly, she stopped herself, reconsidered. "But if he's not drinking, he's all right. Drunks only get bad when they drink. They can be real nice other times."

Linda sighed and went back to rattling her pockets. "Wanda, honey, don't do it. Okay?" Then, making an effort to change the subject, she said, "Did my order come in yet? I wanted to have those earrings for the party tomorrow."

"I don't know, I haven't been home yet." Brought back to the mundane, Wanda hitched her purse up again. "I'll check. I'll bring them by tomorrow. Yours too, Etta," she called to the fuming change boss. "You had that new lipstick and blusher, right? It should have come in yesterday, so I'm sure it all got in today. If you really like it you can order the nail polish that goes with it. It comes in a set. You can save five bucks if you do the whole thing."

Etta grunted, and Linda whispered, "I gotta get out there. Talk to you tomorrow, Wand'." She slid out of the doorway, leaving Wanda standing alone, staring at the rows of machines and listening to everyone else's jackpots clattering cheerfully into the bowls.

Someday Nintucca would have streetlights, she thought a few minutes later as she left the casino. Not that she needed them; she'd walked this way almost every night for more than twenty years, ever since she turned twenty-one and could go gamble legally. She didn't even have to think about that pothole coming up on the right, or stepping around the coil of rusty barbed wire the Stephensons left beside their driveway. It was as if her high heels had eyes of their own and could see all the obstructions on the familiar path.

But someday, Nintucca would have lighted streets, just like Reno and Vegas. If the mine opened up again, Harry'd have to pay more taxes, and wouldn't *that* burn his shriveled little soul—but he'd do it, because people would be coming to his town and he'd want to keep up appearances. Appearances were real important to pricks like Harry.

And if it *didn't* open up, that would hurt even worse. Humming to herself, she wondered what new mischief she could set up for Helen and Jerry. She supposed she ought to feel ashamed of herself for manipulating those poor misguided idealists, but shame was not an emotion Wanda Mirielle was acquainted with.

She unfastened the gate to her front yard and swung it shut behind her, still thinking about Harry. Thinking about the time he'd tried to tell her she'd have to sell this house, her own mama's house—to him—to pay her gambling debts. That son of a bitch.

The screen door sagged open, held ajar by a large box. Swinging her purse over one hip to balance, she picked up the package and shoved the door open. One of the nice things about Nintucca, she thought. No streetlights, maybe, but you didn't have to lock your door. A riffle of mail had spread out underneath the mail slot; she scooped it up in passing.

It was the shipment from the company. Setting box, mail, and purse on the kitchen table beside the stack of catalogs, she went to the back door and called out. There was no immediate answer. Calling again, she left the door open and went back to the table.

Bills. A second notice on the mortgage—well, she had some money left from the Vegas trip, she could catch up on that. Maybe taking out that equity loan hadn't been such a good idea, but she'd been sure she'd be winning big again in just a little while that it didn't seem like much of a risk at the time. Gas card bill—now, there was one for you. Gas down in Vegas was fifteen, twenty cents a gallon cheaper. Old man Hawkeins could whine all he wanted about the cost to truck the stuff up here but that didn't make it right. It wasn't right.

Credit card. She barely glanced at the balance and stuffed the bill back into its envelope, and used bill and envelope and all for a bookmark in the Old Pueblo Traders wish book sitting open on the kitchen table. Water bill. Electricity. Why did they all come at once? The bills went flying just as the back door edged open.

"Paco? Oh, Paco, there you are. Did you miss Mommy? Sure you did, my baby did. Oh, you're all dirty. Here, let me brush—"

The poodle twisted out of her arms and scratched energetically at one ear.

"Is Mommy's baby hungry?"

The poodle, a nondescript, unclipped dusty brown animated mop, yelped agreement.

"Okay for a Mommy's baby. There's some nice doggie food here. Do you want to finish the Liver Chops?"

Paco yapped assent.

Wanda got the can out of the refrigerator, scraped the contents into a ceramic bowl and put it in the microwave to take the chill off. Paco yipped and jumped up on a chair, sniffing at the contents of the table.

The microwave pinged. Wanda removed the bowl and mixed the part of the dog food that had been successfully heated with the part that was still ice cold, and put it back in. "Almost ready, baby. Is Paco hungry?"

Paco, sniffing at the box, snarled.

"What?" Surprised, Wanda swung around to stare at the dog. "What was that for?"

The dirty brown muzzle edged nearer the package. The dog's entire body was tense, the brown wool on his withers bristling.

"Paco? What did they do, send some of those perfume samples you don't like? Well, that's naughty of them. I told them not to do that, I told them you didn't like them. But they never wrote back. I'll bet they've got a new person in shipping, Paco, that's what it is, and they put some more of those nasty perfume samples in my shipment. Come on, baby—" As she reached to remove the dog from the chair, Paco snarled again and dodged out from under her arms and out the door again. The microwave pinged again.

"Paco, your dinner's ready!"

There was no response. Brows knit, Wanda took the dish out of the microwave, mixed it again, and set it outside the back door. Paco would come and eat when he was hungry, no doubt. But he was acting awfully strange. Maybe when the vet came back to town next Wednesday she'd have her look at him.

Meanwhile she needed to get something to eat herself. Picking up the scattered bills, she stacked them neatly on the corner of the table, next to the catalogs. No new catalogs in the mail today, she thought sadly as she fixed a sandwich. Yesterday there'd been one from The Diamond House. That was still in the bedroom, though. She'd fallen asleep right in the middle of the section on furs. There was a beautiful Russian Sable jacket . . .

She munched reflectively at her sandwich, staring at but not seeing the box. Now, that jacket, it was only twelve thousand dollars. If she could go back to Vegas, maybe hit the big one at the Flamingo, she could afford that. Pay off the mortgage too. Take that trip to the Caribbean. Maybe that Esher would take her down there when he finished up his stories. Not to the Caribbean, of course, she wouldn't want to go to the Caribbean with a drunk, but he could take her down to Vegas. He'd have to go there anyway to go home. Unless he was leaving out of Reno. But she could play the pokers at Harrah's, even though they weren't as lucky for her. She couldn't pick out the right machine at Harrah's for some reason.

Sandwich finished, she cleared away the mess and started on the box. Slitting the opening, she removed the packing slip and the bubble wrap and began setting out the contents, one at a time. Lipsticks. Perfume bottles. Jewelry. Pretty soaps. A whole new sample case of makeup.

Wanda conscientiously checked everything against the packing slip and started sorting through her order forms, checking to make sure it was all there, checking the inventory. The shipment came with a supply of little bags to sort the orders, and she checked them all off and began bagging, an item or two here, three there. If she could only talk Bobbi Jo into increasing her order—the woman was as homely as a grandmother hog, but she kept thinking all she needed was a little lipstick and the men would fall all over her. Well, they wouldn't, that was all there was to it. Now Etta, Etta knew how to order. Twenty dollars at a crack, at least.

Maybe when they opened up that new hotel, the fancy one in the plans, she could tell Bobbi Jo she needed some nice earrings to get that desk job. It would pay better than waitressing. Maybe with a necklace she could even be assistant manager or something. Unless Harry's brat Sherry was going to get the job. If she could talk Bobbi Jo into a really big order, maybe she could take off a couple days and pay her own gas down to Vegas.

Orders bagged, she turned to the new sample case. This was the most fun part of the job. She took it into the bathroom with her and set it on the tank cover while she splashed water and soap on her face, removing the layers of makeup, blusher, foundation, wiping at her eyes with the eye-makeup remover, until the naked face of Wanda Mirielle Kostner stared back at her out of the mirror. The face nobody ever saw but her. Not even Harry, not even when they were married. This was not the face—with thin scraggly brows, invisible lashes, red blotches that wouldn't go away, circles under her eyes—not the face that Wanda Mirielle Kostner wanted to be known for. Not at all. Beauty was only skin-deep, maybe, but confidence was a new eye shadow. And with the sample case all things were possible.

Besides, she could make honest recommendations to her customers if she tried things herself. And above all things Wanda prided herself on being absolutely honest.

It was wonderful. There were new shades of foundation and makeup, shadow, blush, mascara, eyeliner pencils with gleaming blue-and-silver-striped caps. Even a little pencil sharpener to go with them. And lipsticks, thirty or forty little sampler lipsticks, five in each shade so she could try them and then have an absolutely fresh one to show her customers. She twisted one open and looked.

Dark red. Almost black. What an ugly color, she thought. Still, sometimes they looked one color in the tube and different on your face—She daubed it on.

It really *was* dark. Too dark for her fair complexion. A little runny too, and it tasted—was this one of the flavored line? She examined the tube and couldn't tell. Well, if it was supposed to be flavored, it had gone bad. Tasted metallic. She couldn't recommend it. Not at all, not even to that hussy Harry was living with. Taking a tissue, she wiped it away and explored further.

Some stuff to take away the circles under the eyes. She applied it, examined the results with a critical eye. Seemed to work okay. Then foundation—boy, that was really pale. She left the box open as she went on to the powder. Once again, too pale. It made it look as if she hadn't got all the lipstick off. She gave another halfhearted scrub to her lips and tried the mascara. Now, *that* was dark!

There were bubbles on the top of the foundation. Funny.

Eyebrow pencil: steel-blue. Hmmmm. Sharp point, have to be careful with that. Pulling her eyelid taut, she applied the edge of the pencil just above her mascaraed lashes.

For a moment it didn't even hurt. Even when she looked at it and saw, not a gunmetal-gray line but a line of welling blood, she couldn't take in what happened. Then it began to bleed, dripping down her face onto the pale, pale foundation, the dark, dark red lips. The makeup on her face began to bubble in a weird cadence with the makeup still in the box.

She screamed, knocked over the box of face powder, screamed again as the spray of white on the bathroom rug began to transform, turn dark, turn into little hungry squirming red things working their way through the fiber. But it was hard to pay attention to them, because the makeup on her face had changed too, as the sliced-off edge of her eyelid dripped lashes across her face and the powder changed, the foundation began to eat away at her, all the way through beauty and down to the grinning bone.

# 4

In an old house in another part of Nintucca, an old man knelt before an altar in the back room of his house and wept. And before him, the air shimmered, and thickened, and changed; shadows of shapes, vast images of mountain and eagle and waterfall and badger and even a small blonde girl twisted and changed. The old man pleaded and cursed. And the Spirit tore loose, and laughed.

# THURSDAY

# One

## 1

The sky was gray and lowering, with an unlikely chill in the air, as Esher climbed into the pickup beside Zimmermann. Rick was wearing a sheepskin and denim vest and a gray felt cowboy hat against the cold.

"What's with this weather? I thought this was supposed to be desert. It hit a hundred yesterday and it can't be more than forty-five out here now."

"Storm coming in from the White Mountains," Rick said, but he sounded uncertain. "Never seen it drop like this, though. This is more like the weather we get in the late fall or winter."

"Goes with the mood of the whole damn town." Esher had got up early to eat breakfast in the hotel restaurant, and every person he'd seen looked as if they'd lost their best friend. People spoke to each other in low voices, glancing often over their shoulders. The spiritual gloom was as palpable as the physical.

Esher started to ask his companion what it was all about, what was so important to see out at the site Rick had until yesterday been trying so hard to keep him away from, but the younger man's lips were pressed tight together, his face lined with anger. Esher decided to leave him alone. He would find out eventually.

189

A gust of wind and sand slapped the side of the truck, pushing it halfway across the road. Rick fought it back under control. They headed out of town, past the bowling alley and the brothel, and out onto the empty road.

They saw four or five cattle bunched together, heads lowered against the wind. Nearby a calf lay flat, a buzzard perched on its withers raising its head to stare after them. Esher was almost sure he could see something long and wet hanging from the bird's beak. He grimaced. A band of scruffy-looking horses, one still wearing the remains of a bridle, spooked and raced them along the road for a quarter of a mile and then veered off. Rick cursed under his breath and slowed in case the animals decided to cross in front of him; when they went the opposite way he sped up again and didn't give them a second look.

It was a long ride, and as they drove Esher realized he was sick of Nevada—sick of the endless stretches of yellow and white and dull greenish gray, the mountains that were always a promise off in the distance but never seemed to get any closer, the tired people and the tired buildings and tired animals. He wanted rain, and green things. He wanted to look at giant shovels tearing strips off of hills in search of coal. He wanted tall buildings all around him to keep him safe from the horizon. Nevada was too much for him. Nevada was too big, too empty, too dry, too different.

Too alien.

They came to the turning place marked by the aluminum drill rig, where a faint dirt road split off the highway. A kit fox sat under a Joshua tree and watched them, huge bat ears alert, a wise expression in the tiny black eyes as if it knew something they didn't, something terribly sad. Esher looked out the back window as the fox receded. Its expression never changed.

The truck began jolting and jerking from one shoulder of the road to the other. Esher clutched for a handhold.

They came around the hump of a small hill—a pile of tailings, Esher recognized, and felt obscurely proud of himself for doing so—and pulled up beside a clear, flat, shallow depression in the earth. A days-dead foal lay near the center of the depression, its legs sticking straight out and its belly bloated from decomposition. A flock of ravens stared at them; as they got out of the truck the birds hopped away a few feet and then, as they came closer, grudgingly flapped about fifteen feet away, cawing insults.

The stench sent both men gagging. Esher held both hands over his mouth and nose in a futile effort to keep it out.

"So what the hell do you want me to see?" he said, voice muffled. Glancing up at the sky, away from the pathetic body, he noticed that it was getting darker. In the distance he could hear rumbling. Thunder, he thought. That's all we need—a desert storm.

Rick pointed at the rusty circles of chemical drums, the marks of the metal shed's foundation, and then trotted some twenty feet away to pick up a dried cholla branch, bone-white and riddled with holes like Swiss cheese. He paused, filling his lungs with relatively clean air, then came back holding his breath. Before touching the remains, he jabbed at the ground beside it, then scraped at it hard, using the stick, his boot heel, finally a Swiss Army knife blade. Nothing marred the white sand. Frustrated, he jabbed hard, straight down.

There was a sound, almost like a moan.

Then green stuff began bubbling from the hole, a trickle at first like pus from an infected scab, then more and more. Rick jerked back as the hole he had made widened, the hard shell of desert crust breaking open to release more and more thick, stinking green ooze, hissing as it erupted from the earth.

"Don't touch it!" Rick warned, when David would have prodded the stuff with the toe of his shoe.

"Why? What the hell is it?"

Rick didn't answer in words. Using the stick, he flipped the foal completely over, revealing the skeletonized side, with the ribs melted over the body cavity like old wax. Making sure David got a good look, he waved him back to the truck, where they could breathe more easily. The suppuration was slowing as they left.

"*Je*-zus. What the hell is it?" Esher couldn't take his eyes off the foal's body, now sinking into—dissolving into?—the green pool. Once the men were back in the truck the ravens returned, but they didn't settle on the bones, he noticed. They pecked at the earth well outside the depression, images of frustrated fury, and finally flew off in a tremendous clatter of wings.

"Gil and I think White had a chemical leak here," Rick said. "The foal wandered into it. We think he breathed the stuff, and he just toppled over and it ate him." The young man's voice was shaking just a little, whether from fear or outrage or plain anger was impossible to tell. "We—Gil and I—looked at some records last night in White's office. It's not just the places where they pump it into the holes. It's all over. Everywhere there's a new break in the surface, things are dying."

"White would have to report a contamination like that," Esher said, feeling foolish as he did so. Rick gave him a look of scorn. "These are the stabilizing chemicals he's been testing?"

The other man nodded. "It's what he's using to keep the tunnel walls from giving way. And Gil heard him talking to Kostner. White and Kostner are planning to test this stuff on the walls of the Heartbreak."

That was what Wanda was hinting about, Esher realized. Not just illicit exchange of information. Conspiracy.

Esher thought of the illegal chemical dumps he'd seen back in Pennsylvania, New Jersey, New York. Why had he thought Nevada would be any different? Because the West was clean and young and the East was old and corrupt? That was the image, not the reality. The West struggled with its own questions of radioactive waste and forest fires and chemical spills. But this—this was worse than anything he'd ever seen. He pointed to the puddled bones. "Christ, if that's any evidence, it'll kill everything it touches. Look. There aren't even any plants in that circle. The ravens won't even touch it."

"The guys who use it dress up like spacemen."

"The miners won't, though—And the first time they stick a pick into the wall—"

"Yeah." Rick's tone was bleak.

"Does White know about this? Does Kostner?"

Rick nodded. A whisper, a vibration of sound from the green pool caught their attention. It was sinking back into the ground, leaving only a wad of warped bones for witness.

"I know you don't want me out at the site, Rick, but I think I'd better go talk to Dr. White and find out what's going on. You can take me back to town and I can get my own car—"

"No, I'll take you." Rick sounded as if he'd come to a decision and was at peace with himself. He yanked the truck into gear and pulled it far around the small body and back onto the dirt track.

# 2

". . . twenty or thirty people . . ."

". . . they live out there . . ."

Remembering bits and pieces of the conversation from his first night in Nintucca, Esher was surprised at first by the extent of the building at the site. It must have employed quite a few people to put the buildings up, at least for a week or two; he counted nine identical beige temporary buildings arranged in a circle around a water tank on stilts, and clustered around which were two dozen pickup trucks and vans like chicks around their mother hens. The compound was surrounded by a fence with a barbed-wire crown. Someone left one building, entered another; otherwise there was no sign of life.

A man wearing a khaki uniform and mirror sunglasses—hardly necessary in the dusky light—and carrying a rifle stepped out of a guard shack at the gate to the compound. Rick pulled up. "Hey, Ernie. The Man in?"

Ernie shook his head. "Out for a test."

Rick arched an eyebrow. "You're kidding me. He's actually watching a test? What site?" Esher was amazed at the apparent casualness of the question.

"Who's he?" The barrel of the gun did not quite point at Esher.

"Man who needs to know."

Ernie thought about it, working his jaws around a wad of either gum or tobacco.

"Come on, Ernie. If the Man's not here, we're not going inside the fence. What site are they working?"

Ernie shrugged. "Little Sheba. But you didn't hear it from me."

"Not a thing." He reversed and pulled away.

"What's Little Sheba?" Esher said as they navigated a fairly good road.

"It's an old mine." Rick yanked the gearshift.

*Rumble.*

# 3

Aged fingers stroked the yellow and white fur. The quavering, singsong voice was pleading, with the hopeless sound of one who knew that it was too late. "Spirit of Earth, Badger, Bear, Spirit of all things of the Earth . . ."

The clay cup rattled on the wooden table. Jessie Gallita touched the long black claws still attached to the foot ends of the pelt. There was a sound that might have been laughter, as if an earthquake had laughed. The old man's voice grew more desperate.

"Spirit of Earth, be healed, be not infected with the madness . . . Spirit—"

Before him, the air began to tremble and thicken.

# 4

Little Sheba had been worked in the late twenties by two middle-aged Chinese and one starry-eyed youth from New York State. The New Yorker had quit early and gone back home "before the skin dries off my bones"; the Chinese had continued working, chasing a thin, elusive vein down sixty feet, until one man was bitten by a mine rattler and the other decided the metal in the Little Sheba never was going to come back. It had lain abandoned ever since, so unproductive not even the Kostner family wanted it. The outside was a partially caved-in hole in the hill resembling the first mine Esher had investigated.

The Generous Lady hadn't been quite so popular, though. Far from being deserted, the Little Sheba was surrounded by vehicles and small tanker trucks and clusters of men waiting around, keeping an eye on a smaller, central cluster focused on a man in a lab coat who was consulting pages of computer printout and ignoring the man at his elbow jabbering into his ear. Behind the trucks a drill rig had frozen in the act of its downward plunge; behind the drill rig stretched miles of high desert, dappled by patches of dry white sand that might have been a lake bed or a swamp several million years ago.

Esher reached into his pocket and switched the tape recorder on. There was something funny about the air; he pulled in a deep breath, trying to figure out what, and remembering the foal, blew it out again like a snorting horse.

No one seemed surprised at the arrival of one more vehicle; some of the bystanders noticed Esher, nudged their less alert fellows. The awareness flowed in a silence-making ripple right up to the ankles of the man in the lab coat and stopped.

The man beside the scientist's elbow tugged at his sleeve. He made an irritable answer and then looked up to see Esher and Rick coming up to him.

"What the hell is this? Who are you?" He thrust the printout into his companion's hands and stalked over to them. "Where the hell is Security?"

"My name's David Esher. I take it you're Dr. White?"

White looked around. "Security!"

"Oh, I'm here," Rick said. White looked at him, then recognized him.

"What the hell do you think you're doing, bringing unauthorized people out here? Are you crazy? You're fired!"

"I kind of figured that." Rick kept his voice low and even. Esher was suddenly glad that the guns were back in the truck. Rick sounded too calm.

"Dr. White, I'm a journalist. I'd like to ask you some questions about the chemicals you're using. Are you aware of possible harmful effects—"

White's eyes bulged and his face went crimson. "A journalist! Journalist! You're that writer Kostner hired—he promised you'd stay away from here! Ruiz! North ampton! Get this man out of here!"

Esher stood his ground. "It's public land, Dr. White."

The ground rolled under their feet. Esher heard someone murmur, "Test Site. Must be unscheduled—"

Wind shuddered along the ground and died.

"The stuff is mixed," announced a latecomer, coming up to them. "Let's get going—hey, what's going on?"

"This man is a *journalist*," White said between clenched teeth. "He wants to write an *article*. The process is not ready for public review, Mr.—"

"Esher." Esher looked around at the other men. Their attention had been distracted from the confrontation, but he couldn't tell by what. Beside him he could hear Rick breathing, slow and controlled, like a man clamping down on righteous anger.

"Well, we'd better get our asses in gear anyway, journalist or no journalist," the latecomer said. "We can't keep this in the tank very long."

"And you are?"

"Perry Ruiz," Rick said in an undertone.

The latecomer gave Esher a measuring look, Rick the slightest nod of acknowledgment. "I'm just a joe trying to do a job, and if you'll pardon us, mister, you're in the way. Now come on, boys, suit up and let's get those sprayers loaded."

White ground his teeth in frustration, and Esher and Rick were elbowed back out of the way by the movement of the men around them. White shot them a glare and then was swept up in the movement himself.

"Men dressing in shiny, white suiting, with hoods and glass masks," Esher dictated into the recorder. Rick gave him a startled glance but kept quiet. "Clustering around a tanker parked next to a drill rig. It's very dark out here today, can't even see the edges of the clouds; if we were back East I'd expect thunder and lightning, but there's nothing, only the occasional faraway rumbling and the movement of the earth beneath us, which one of the men here attributed to testing at the Nevada Test Site. The Nevada Test Site is where underground nuclear testing takes place.

"They're loading hand sprayers now, they look like five-gallon tanks. Look heavy, too. One man dropped—no, he's got it. You can smell the stink of the chemical, very bitter, almost like tear gas." He worked his tongue, trying to bring up some saliva. The chemical was worse than tear gas. It left the taste of rotten meat in his mouth. He paused, watching the activity, trying to make sense out of it. "Dr. White is unwilling to talk to me about this test.

"The air is funny. I can't figure out what—"

"Too dry," Rick interrupted. Esher held the microphone toward him. "It's too dry. Before a storm like this you'd expect the air to be damp. There's no humidity."

"That's Rick Zimmermann, who's been helping me research

these articles. —Now they're bringing up a smaller tank mounted in a cart. Having some trouble with the connections, it looks like. They're wearing heavy gloves, trying to manipulate a long green hose with red markings, about four inches in diameter, from the big tanker to the cart. It appears to be under high pressure. It's giving them some trouble."

*Rumble*.

The ground shuddered again, and Esher steadied himself on the fender of the truck. Rick shook his head. "That's no nuclear test—"

The earth rocked, swayed. The men around the cart staggered. The hose tore loose, whipping through the air like a snake, spraying a viscous green liquid through the air, across the men gathered around, across the earth.

The earth snarled.

One man screamed as the liquid soaked through his protective suiting, and began to claw off his hood. Two others tried to restrain him, while the rest tried to get the pressure-driven hose under control. It whipped across the drill rig, and green liquid began to run hissing down the metal struts.

The earth heaved and shuddered. The foundation around the drill rig began to crumble, and the rig began to sag sideways. The man who had removed his hood was caught by another lash of spray and collapsed, half his skull exposed and gleaming white as if it had been polished in an acid bath. The rest abandoned him and ran.

The air thickened behind them. The ground rose up fifty feet in front of them and curled back down to where Something was growing out of the dark air, taking a form that was no form, with eyes that gleamed as hot as stars and claws of wind that shoveled the fleeing men toward it, toward the deeper darkness out of which it was made.

Esher shrank back against the side panel, recorder forgotten, his lips moving in what might have been prayers or curses or pleas for his mother. Beside him, Rick trembled and cursed.

The ground belched and swallowed, and the drill rig slid out of sight, dragging White and four other men clinging to its struts with it. A bubble of green formed around them, and Esher could see the viscous stuff coating them, bubbling where it hit buttons, zippers, pocket protectors, soaking in where the only resistance was skin, eating them away even as they screamed and melting their bones like wax.

The remaining men scrambled at the upcurling ledges of sand and stone that steadily pushed them back and down. One of them called out to them, and Rick yelled wordlessly and ran up the crest of the wave to sprawl out, reaching for the last man's hand as he slid back and down and under the ground as if swallowed by quicksand. The rumbling that was not thunder continued, rose to a shriek. Rick struggled, swaying, to his feet and looked back at Esher, without panic, as if wondering abstractedly if he was going to come and help.

The ground buckled beneath him and threw Rick forward and down, rocked Esher to his knees.

By the time he regained his feet, the ground was silent and still and quite, quite empty.

# TWO

## 1

The darkness followed David Esher up the road, and there was no bottle under the seat to pull out and drink and make things clear. Or to make them blurred. He wanted them blurred. He wanted to not see Rick Zimmermann, looking at him with that strange calm and the question in his eyes. The face would not go away. It would not.

And the road before him remained unblurred and the darkness behind him howled and pursued, and the accelerator pushed back against the sole of his right foot. His fingers bit white into the steering wheel and he hunched over and moaned and flinched away from the form behind him.

It fell behind as he reached the paved road, and the truck lunged forward, tires finding smooth pavement and gripping instead of jouncing from one rock to another. He licked his lips and risked a look in the rearview mirror.

It seemed to be fading. Fading . . . He almost expected a shadowy fist shaken against the sky, but he couldn't have seen the black against blackness anyway. He was outrunning it. He was heading for town, where people were.

There was ice in his belly.

He tried to swallow.

He could still see Rick's face.

And he would have to tell—

199

He could not tell Marianne—

He needed to hide. He needed oblivion, with an urgent craving that would not be overcome, would not go away.

He needed a drink, and this time there was no reason any more not to have one.

The road rose with the hill and curved, and a pink building came up on his left—a building with lights and people—and he cursed and swerved, skidding into the parking lot of Sexy Sadie's Rooster Tail Bar.

# 2

He slumped into the second booth and rolled his head against the leather back, staring into the chandelier, trying to burn the face out of his vision. It wasn't working. He looked around and shivered. The bouncer, who wore a green apron over his jeans and a T-shirt several sizes too small to show off his muscles, swept out a corner of the lounge area with a worn yellow broom. Esher and the bouncer were the only men in the place.

Looking back at the chandelier, he blinked and stared harder. He almost had it—almost obliterated the memory— when his vision was blocked by a shelf of breasts leaning into his face.

"Why, if it isn't Mr. David Esher, come to visit us! Mr. Esher, would you like your regular drink? And is there a particular waitress you'd like to have serve you?" The voice was raddled by years of cigarette smoke.

"Regular?" he asked, shaking his head and pulling back. Sadie was on the bar herself tonight, dressed in a flimsy black teddy that supported but did nothing to conceal her breasts. Her nipples were rouged. Esher found himself staring at them, wondering if she had a special rouge or just expanded the possibilities of face makeup. Sadie smiled and jiggled gently. She smelled of light sweat and baby powder.

"Your ginger ale, rocks. Or would you prefer something different tonight?"

He pulled in a long shuddering breath, the images of darkness and screaming men coming back again, too close to deal with: "No. Not ginger ale. Bourbon, straight up. Double. Until I tell you to stop."

Sadie looked uncertain. "Bourbon? Well. Sure. And your waitress?" She stepped aside and back, giving him a view of the lace-clad women standing lined up against the wall.

Jody, Missy, Kitten, Sweet. As he watched, Sable came out of the door behind the bar and joined them. Rick had named and described the girls well enough to recognize, laughing and turning red when he'd asked if the young man had sampled them all.

Rick, looking at him so calmly—

They shot him glances from under heavily mascaraed lashes, posing provocatively, breasts or hips outthrust, smiling just enough to let him know they knew he was watching and didn't find it unpleasant. They were dressed in short silk jackets, each in a different color, loosely tied at the waist and gaping open, revealing and not revealing everything underneath. They wore silk stockings and stood hipshot on three-inch heels, pivoting and posing for him.

The bourbon arrived and he picked up the glass and swallowed half of it in one gulp. The girls oohed and giggled, impressed. The liquor burned his throat and he choked a little on it, but he knew how to get over that, and he swallowed again, a little less this time, and it hit his stomach and glowed, beginning to melt the ice. God it was sweet—

He could still see Rick. White. Ruiz. The drill rig, slipping silent into the sand.

"Hey, Sweet." His voice sounded unnaturally loud. The smile on the blonde at the end of the line widened, and she tossed her hair and stalked over to slide into the booth, taking his hand. Her toes walked up his shin. He thought she must have got rid of her high heels somehow.

"Hey, you're that writer, aren't you?" she said. Her voice was naturally higher-pitched than the tone she was using now. The other girls along the bar shrugged and began to talk to one another, paying no further attention to him. "Want to buy a girl a drink?" She licked her red lips. "Maybe take a look at the menu?"

He finished the first drink, beginning to feel light-headed. "Menu."

"Umm-hmmm. It tells you all the things you can . . .

order." Her toes began to rub the inside of his thigh. His fingers clutched at the second glass.

Sweet began to look worried. "Now, you don't want to do all your partying out here, do you? I didn't know you even drank that stuff. I thought you drank ginger ale."

"I hate ginger ale," he admitted, and raised the glass to his lips. He swallowed again, and again, the liquor warm all the way through him, down each vein to the fingers and toes and up to the brain. The golden crystals of the chandelier blurred. So did the memory of Rick's face. He finished the drink, slapped the table for another.

Sweet pouted. "Do you hate me too? C'mon, honey, let's go in back and have ourselves a little private party." Over at the bar, Sadie was glancing at her watch.

"I don't want a party. People died today. How can you have a party?"

Sweet frowned, threw Sadie a worried glance. By the time she turned back to Esher, the practiced smile was back in place. "Okay, honey. We won't have a party. Why don't you come with me and tell me all about it?"

Reaching out with one unsteady hand, Esher grabbed the woman by a spaghetti strap. She jerked back and it broke, leaving him blinking at the strand of black in his hand and Sweet's exposed breast. He was drunk, he realized. It wasn't fair. He didn't used to get drunk so fast. On one drink. No, two drinks. Still.

Before Sweet could do more than yip in surprise, a figure loomed over them both.

"Excuse me, sir," he said, his voice surprisingly light. "That's not gentlemanly behavior. We're going to have to ask you to leave."

Sweet looked up at the bouncer and over to Esher and licked her lips, leaning back in the booth to watch. The bouncer placed his hand on Esher's shoulder.

"They all died," Esher said, owl-eyed. "It was—"

"Come with me, please, sir. We'll go outside now."

"*No!*" Esher lunged up, past the bouncer. "Not outside! I'm not going to go outside!"

"Come along, sir." This time the bouncer tried to grasp his arm.

Esher yanked away, staggered to the bar, and looked around

wildly. The other girls scattered. The bouncer paced after him, a massive bulk casting a shadow before him. The shadow touched Esher and he screamed, remembering another shadow, and reached for a Seagram's bottle, smashing it against the polished wood of the bar in a rotating blow that left a ring of ragged, gleaming edges and a shower of whiskey across the length of the bar. The smell rose like a cloud around him.

"I'm not going outside! That thing's out there! I'm not going out!"

The bouncer stopped. Behind him, Sadie reached for a phone. The girls muttered. From the booth, Sweet said loudly, "He sounds just like that nut Gallita."

"Now, sir, why don't you just put that down before somebody gets hurt. We don't want anybody getting hurt, now, do we? Come on, sir . . ." The bottle wavered, dropped a fraction of an inch, and the bouncer stepped inside it and swung.

Ducking away, Esher swung back with the hand holding the bottle. The edges glowed red, and the bouncer shrugged one shoulder and moved in again.

"Stop it!" It was Sadie, reaching for her bouncer's bloody arm. "Stop it, O'Malley's on his way."

"I think I can take him, ma'am." His voice never rose above a conversational level, expressed no pain, no anger, merely an opinion.

"I'm *telling* you, stop it!"

"Yes, ma'am." He stepped away.

Esher sagged and tightened up again. "I won't go outside. It's dark outside."

"Nobody says you have to go outside," Sadie crooned. "Nobody says you have to go in the nasty old dark."

Esher watched her with wide, frightened eyes. The old lady moved in on him, still crooning, and reached out for the broken bottle. He flinched and she waited, patient, and when he was calm she moved in again, until her hand was on his and on the neck of the weapon and his fingers fell away.

"You want another drink, Mr. Esher?" she crooned, moving still closer until he was trapped between her billowing flesh and the bar, her face inches from his. "A nice drink?"

"Yes," he whispered.

Sadie snapped her fingers and a glass appeared in her hand,

and she held it to his lips and pressed until his head tilted back and he drank.

Or started to drink. As he opened his mouth the door of the brothel opened, admitting Deputy Sergeant O'Malley, and Esher shoved the woman away. She went sprawling against the booths. O'Malley and the bouncer moved in.

# FRIDAY

# One

## 1

He woke up in the drunk tank. A drunk tank in Nevada smelled just like one in Pennsylvania or Ohio, stinking of urine and vomit and sweat. A large puddle over in the corner was probably the source of most of the smell. A huddle of rags next to it represented its origin. Esher had been in a number of tanks from time to time in Ohio and points East; the bum on the floor would have looked at home in any of them. And might have been "at home," for all he knew.

Esher rolled to a sitting position, gagging, trying to hold his head together. He couldn't remember exactly what had happened at the brothel. He remembered all too well what happened before he got there.

Was it hours ago? Days? He couldn't tell. Hours, probably, judging by his hangover. It must be Friday, then. Friday morning. The day Kostner was going to meet with his investors.

It looked just like an Eastern drunk tank, too. Same institutional gray-green, chipped paint. Obscenities scratched into the walls by someone's fingernails; they didn't leave you a pencil to make your feelings known, not even shoelaces to use the aglets. Somebody must have been really angry to scratch such a long comment in the wall; in places it was stained black with dried blood where the writer's instrument

had worn out. His wallet was gone. His shoes were gone.
Everything was gone except his memory, his headache, and a
raging thirst.

The huddle in the corner didn't move. Esher pulled himself
to his feet and moved over to the single bunk. It wasn't much
better than the floor—springs jabbed out of it at surprising
angles—but at least it wasn't wet. Sitting down sent a jolt of
pain up his spine and into the base of his skull and he
whimpered, leaning very carefully against the cinderblock
wall, eyes closed, trying not to jar himself any more.

*"He sounds like that nut Gallita."*

The sentence came out of nowhere. Somebody had said that
about him last night. He'd been trying to tell them, and they
said he sounded like Gallita.

He supposed he did. Now he knew what Gallita was talking
about. He had seen the Beast with his own eyes. If the old man
was crazy, then so was he; it had been no natural thing that
dragged those men to their deaths. It was not just the
chemicals; it was what the chemicals woke.

An idea came to him through the pain: Find Gallita.

He opened one eye and saw that the bars were still there,
shut it again.

The cell remained closed, the corridor outside it empty, for
several more hours, during which the huddle on the floor
grunted once and rolled over, and the puddle on the floor with
its accompanying odor increased perceptibly. Esher was beginning to draw unfavorable comparisons between Nevada and
Ohio official hospitality when the steel door at the end of the
corridor opened.

It was Marianne. Beside her, a grim shadow, was Gil.
Squeezing his eyes shut didn't get rid of them.

Next to them O'Malley stood, jiggling the keys. "Come on,
man. You planning on spending all day in there too?"

Muscles stiff and protesting, Esher dragged himself off the
bunk. O'Malley escorted them out to the desk, where he got
back his shoelaces, wallet, keys. The wallet still had his cash.
Esher still had his headache, his thirst, and his memory.

Shoes laced, he followed Marianne and Gil outside. He
couldn't focus on the almost-empty streets. The passersby
walked around the three of them, ignoring them, all but one

small blond boy on a bicycle waiting patiently for them to get out of his way. "Uh, thank you—" he began.

Gil made an abrupt move, silencing him.

"David, where's Rick? You went out with him yesterday and I haven't seen him since." The young woman's face was tight and anxious, pale with worry.

He swallowed a dry lump. "I don't know how to tell you."

Gil's voice was low and rough, his anger more apparent than Rick's had been. "White's gone too, and a bunch of men from the site. The Sheriff doesn't know it yet—she's been working on some other problems. But my man at the compound told me he sent the two of you out to the Little Sheba, and there's nothing out there. Any more."

Marianne, listening, was shaking. "Gil said there was a rig out there, a tanker. But there's nothing there."

Esher tasted dust on his lips. "I—I don't know how—let me get a drink. I can tell you if I have a drink." He heard himself, hated himself, didn't care. He couldn't say those words without liquor.

"No, God damn you." Her voice rose to a shriek. "I heard about you at Sadie's last night. You came up there driving Rick's truck and got drunk. Where's Rick?"

He shook his head. "I can't tell you. You won't believe me."

She slapped him so hard he rocked backward two steps. It cleared him enough so he could see her standing, arms akimbo, staring up at him furiously, eyes glittering. "Where is he?"

"He's gone," he said, holding his jaw. "The Beast got him."

To his surprise she believed him. She exchanged a glance with Gil, who said, "Jessie's Beast?"

Jessie's Beast. The Beast the old man was always talking about . . . It was real. It was *real*.

He nodded, straightening. The words said, the thirst was receding, by inches.

"Can we get him back?" She didn't believe that, he saw, but she had to ask anyway.

"No." Rick had known, he realized. Rick had known when he tried to rescue his friend that there was no hope and that he himself was doomed. But he had looked back, curious, to see what choice David Esher would take. What choice the drunk would take, he thought bitterly. All his dreams of his life finally turning around were dead, as dead as the men at the site, as dead as Rick Zimmermann.

Marianne made a noise that might have been a sob, might have been a gasp, and bit at her hand. Gil, standing by, made no attempt to comfort her, simply standing by like something solid, dependable and immutable, if there was anything immutable left.

After perhaps ten seconds she lifted her head again. "I'm going to talk to Jessie."

He nodded again. "I want to talk to him too."

"It's none of your business!" she snapped, tears rolling down her cheeks. She dashed at them angrily and then ignored them, letting them flow.

"I was *there*, dammit. Whose else business is it? He wouldn't have been there if it weren't for me." He looked defiantly at them both. There was something wrong with his logic, but Marianne, at least, accepted it. "What about you?" he challenged Gil.

"I'm going to find Harry Kostner." The flat, empty brown eyes held him for a moment longer, and then Gil turned away. Gil wasn't in his site guard uniform, David noticed through the pounding behind his eyes. But the dark man was still wearing a gun.

# 2

No one responded when they pounded at the door of the Gallita house. The front door was locked. Marianne led Esher around the side and tried the back. It opened without resistance.

The door led into the kitchen, a small, spotless room filled with the good odors of past, spicy meals, garlic and onions hanging in baskets from the ceiling, soap and clean water. Marianne barely gave it a glance before going into the living room, seeing that it was empty, and moving down the hall toward the bedrooms. Esher followed more slowly, feeling uneasy about intruding. Besides, the house felt—strange.

"Jessie!" It was Marianne's voice, sharp, calling. She opened doors, looked, closed them again and went on to the next. "Jessie?"

If the old man was home, why didn't he answer? Esher wondered. Was he sick? Why didn't he come out to find out who had invaded his home?

"Jess—Jessie!" Marianne had reached the end of the hall. "David! Come here, he's—I think he's hurt, or sick or something—"

He barely noticed the furnishings of the room as he helped the girl wrestle Jessie to his feet, out to the living room, and onto the couch. Part of his mind was thinking, you ought to call the hospital, you shouldn't move him; the rest was, Don't die yet, old man, you have to tell us what's going on here and how to stop it!

Marianne got a glass of water from the kitchen and came back with it, pushing it against the cracked lips until they opened, tilting it a very little until his throat moved, accepting; giving him more as he was ready to take it until finally his eyes opened and he looked at them, his once-vivid blue eyes dull. A gleam of what might have been recognition entered them.

"I saw the Beast, Jessie," Esher said. "I saw it kill."

The faded eyes closed again, and a sound that might have been a moan escaped from him.

Marianne's words sounded even and uninflected. Looking at her, Esher could see the similarities between her and her lover, the passionless passion that led to inevitability. "It killed Rick, Jessie. This Beast of yours killed my Rick. How do we kill it?"

The old man turned his head toward Marianne. "Can you kill greed, little one? Can you kill the Earth?"

Her hair whipped back and forth in denial. "Don't tell me that, Jessie! I want to know how to kill it."

Esher put a hand on her arm. "Jessie, we have to know if we can destroy this thing. We have to know what it *is*. Because it's not going to stop now, is it? It's going to come back."

The old man's head moved up and down. "Yes."

"Well, then?"

Jessie gestured for more water. Impatiently, Marianne gave it to him, the glass clicking against his teeth as she held it. Jessie looked at her reprovingly. David took the glass from her and set it down. "Now, Jessie?"

The Basque took a deep breath.

"Certain places in the Earth are strong places. They have power. All the ancient peoples, the peoples in touch with the

Earth, know this, the Indians here, the Druids, in the old country the Basques. You would call it magic. Foolishness." His gaze challenged them. They said nothing.

"Earth itself is a power, like air. Fire. Water. Once, Earth, like all these powers, had awareness and wisdom. It took the forms of strong animals to speak to the ancient peoples, because Earth was too great for a man to know. We saw the wolf, the bear, the badger, and we knew who they represented.

"Now it is mostly dead, killed by cities and fields, and we feed on it like vultures feed on a dead calf. But in some places, empty places, places that were always very strong, the spirit of Earth still lives. It has been sleeping, long, long. But we have wakened it again . . .

"Like any living thing it will protect itself. If it is tortured—by men digging out and melting down its bones, soaking it in poisons, ripping away its skin—it seeks revenge. Earth is no longer wise. It has gone mad, like the animal in a trap that maims itself in its pain, its need to be free." He glanced back at the room at the end of the hall. "It looks for the Beast in man to take into its madness and make it stronger."

Outside, a rumbling. Jessie laughed, a small laugh of one vindicated.

It could have been thunder, David thought, but he knew that it wasn't.

"We have to kill it before it gets any worse—" Marianne whispered.

Jessie laughed again. "How? When the government men pour sickness into the ground, and Kostner drills his new hole that will take him to the very den of the Spirit itself? There will be no sacrifices then that will calm it. The Spirit that is the Beast has Kostner. They are both mad and they feed upon each other. The Beast is in Kostner. And when Kostner enters the heart of the Beast, nothing will stop it. Nothing."

"Jessie, there *has* to be something." Marianne's voice was determined.

The old man licked his lips. "If you can find it, trap it. Lock it into the Earth. But first you must find it."

"*Find* it?" The scene at the Little Sheba flashed before his eyes—the blackness, the formless form sweeping little, insignificant men and machinery into itself. "Find that—thing?"

"Find the man it's taken," Marianne said. "That's it, isn't it,

Jessie? David, come on. We'll send a doctor to you, Jessie, when—we'll send a doctor."

Jessie smiled, the corners of his mouth twisting.

# 3

At the window, a towheaded boy listened, came to a terrible conclusion. And picked up his bicycle and rode.

# Two

## 1

"He's at the Heartbreak. He has to be. He was having his investors' meeting today." Wordlessly, Esher reversed the car and headed out to the mine. Marianne said nothing, holding on to the dashboard against the jouncing, her attention turned inward. He couldn't tell if the long ride took hours or only minutes. Time had lost its elasticity and was hanging over them in folds.

"Now what?" The words came out of his mouth against his will.

They saw the same scene that had surrounded the Heartbreak the last time David was there. A crowd of people milled about a ragged pair waving signs, a pair David belatedly recognized as Helen and Jerry from the Friends of Dirt, Grass and Trees. Miners and environmentalists were shouting at someone at the mouth of the mine. Pulling up to the assayer's office, on the other side of the crowd, was a dusty limousine.

"It's Helen and Jerry. They're picketing. And the construction men—they don't want to go in either. They must have heard about what happened to Wanda."

Esher, who hadn't heard what happened to Wanda, decided not to ask. The two stared despairing at the lines of shouting people waving signs and fists at the crushing mills and ore cars. The air around them seemed dull, weighty. Esher remembered the Little Sheba and swallowed a curse. "That limo—those must be Kostner's investors, coming in from Vegas or Reno."

Marianne jerked upright as if stung. "Wait. There's another way in. I remember R-Rick and Mikey showed me—"

She guided him away from the demonstrators, along a long-abandoned road, the small car rocking and jouncing. Esher ignored the possibility of a blowout and drove too fast, sweating.

# 2

"Look at those assholes," Kostner said, staring down at the line of posters and signs and fists from the threshold of the mainframe. "Slobs, every one of them. They'll work for somebody else every day of their lives and be grateful for it."

Laura Bailey glanced at him from behind mirrored sunglasses, rested one hand on her revolver in its holster, and said nothing.

"You hear something?" Kostner spun around and looked down the mine entrance. "I heard something . . ."

"Over all this?" Bailey shrugged. "I don't think they're gonna come any closer. They're spooked."

"There's somebody in there. Somebody's in—"

"Mr. Kostner—"

"—*my* mine—"

# 3

Behind him, Gil Santillanes moved from decaying wall to machine like a shadow among other shadows, closer and closer behind them. He saw Kostner look around suddenly to the mine as if something had called him, and he swallowed dryly and reached for his gun. But Kostner spun and dived inside.

Under the ground. *Things* lived under the ground. Here, as

in the tunnels of Vietnam. Gil had learned the hard way that his grandmother was right, that there was evil there were no laws against, and he had taken on the role of guardian with the oath of law enforcement.

He had tried to forget that, and his friend had died for it. And he could feel the jabbing of his grandmother's bony finger in his chest.

He didn't want to enter the headframe. He was afraid.

He knew it, accepted it, and followed Harry Kostner, slipping behind Bailey as she was distracted by the surging crowd and the neatly dressed handful of men in three-piece suits coming from the limousine.

# 4

"Here," Marianne said.

David skidded to a stop beside a now-familiar mine hole, the entrance to the Generous Lady.

"Wait a minute. I want to get something—"

He followed her into the shack to find her putting on a miner's helmet, slinging rope over her arm, a knapsack on her back, and struggling with a small, heavy box. "What are you doing?"

"Take a hard hat," she ordered. "If Kostner thinks he's going to drill that shaft, he's mistaken."

He wet his lips, realizing what she was carrying.

Dynamite.

"Do you really think—"

She stopped to stare at him, pushing a lock of blonde hair up into the helmet. "Yes. I do. Don't you?"

He followed.

It was dark inside the mine, darker than anything he had ever experienced. It took several minutes before he learned to let his eyes follow only the beam of light from the lamps. Marianne's whispered directions took him against one wall or another, grateful for their solidity, painfully aware that they weren't solid at all as little rushes of pebbles and dirt splattered down on his shoulders. Their words echoed back and forth, hard to understand even though they were within arm's reach of one another.

"How much farther?" he said at last. He had lost count of his steps long ago.

He was not comforted by her answer: "Long way yet. Haven't even gone down to the first—here. Here's the ladder."

All he could see was a hole. The lamp beam traced it, four feet square; he could put his hands on his hips, stick out his elbows, and bruise them both. Marianne set down her box and crouched by the shaft. "The guys, Mikey and Rick, put in a new rope. Listen, you put one hand on the rope and one hand on the ladder. That way if either of them gives, you won't fall so far."

David remembered Rick saying Marianne had gone with them into the mines. She sounded quiet and sure of herself. But he couldn't help asking, "How deep is it?"

"To the next level? 'Bout forty feet." Opening the box, she shrugged out of the knapsack and began transferring short, round cylinders from the former to the latter.

"Is that what I think it is?" Esher said, willing her to deny it.

Marianne's eyes gleamed. "How else you gonna blow a mine?"

"You better let me carry it, then." He couldn't believe the words came from his own mouth, but he couldn't stand the thought that this slip of a girl would carry dynamite on her back when all he could do was get drunk and thrown out of a bar—Something rustled in the dark behind them. Bats, he told himself, and refused to look back.

"Ever handled this stuff?" Marianne was saying.

"No."

"Then don't be stupid."

"Have *you*?"

A pause. "A few times. That's more than you. Besides, who's gonna handle Kostner when he shows up?"

"When," David noted. Not "if."

"Somehow," he said dryly, "I think Kostner's the least of our worries."

# 5

He could see Kostner at the cage, fighting the door latch, the man's own frenzy obstructing him. He had to yell to be heard over the sound of the generator. "Harry!"

Kostner looked up, saw the gun in his hand. "Who—Santillanes? What the fuck are you doing here?"

"I know what's down there, Harry. I know what you're doing." The lights were brighter than the gloom outside. Almost bright enough to fool himself into thinking he wasn't really standing in a cave. "You can't control that thing, Harry. It's killing—"

"Wanda, you mean?" The hawk-eyed man laughed. "I know what's down here better than you do! Better than Gallita! It's going to show me the silver! All the silver in the ground! I have deal with the Beast! I get the silver, and it—your friends are down there in my mine, Santillanes, and I'm going to feed them to the Beast!"

He hit a switch from inside the cage, and all the lights went out.

Gil jerked as the darkness closed in. He could see the red light at the top of the cage descending into the hole, the rattle of the winch as it was lowered into the shaft. And the laughing face of Harry Kostner as he dived into the earth.

Muttering a prayer in the half-forgotten New Mexican Spanish of his childhood, Gil reached for the rungs to follow him down.

# 6

Stuffing a handful of fuse into the sack, Marianne Bailey slung it onto her back and stepped onto the ladder. Esher watched her step down, down, until all he could see was the light originating from her metal headgear, and the reflection of his own light off it. It was a very narrow hole.

And he was very much alone at the top of it. He stepped onto the ladder and grabbed at the rope and started down after her, eyes stretched wide in an effort to see. After a dozen rungs he realized there was no point and squeezed his eyes shut instead. It was comforting, somehow. One step at a time, one foot probing for the next step, one hand clutching at the knots that studded the rope at regular intervals.

Before he knew it the rungs ran out, and he stumbled as his leading foot hit solid ground. He opened his eyes again and blinked at the sudden brightness of the carbide lamps.

"This way," Marianne said. He had to strain to hear her; she started off immediately down a side tunnel at a quick trot.

"What's the—" he began, in a normal voice, when an abrupt gesture cut him off. She held her hand up: Wait. Listen.

He listened.

To the rumble.

The skin of his scalp tightened, and a small frightened child in his soul began beating frantically at his self-control, desperate to get away from that sound. From that Thing.

Marianne started back down the tunnel. Esher listened a moment or two longer, stepping back under the shaft to look up. There was nothing to see. Just little noises, which might have been tunnel mice.

Twenty feet down the passage part of the wall had fallen in, creating a slide of dirt and rock. He caught up with her as she negotiated it, having had to take off the knapsack to squeeze through a narrow opening at the top.

"Come on," she whispered.

The glimmer of light on the other side led him up the ten-foot-high slide on his hands and knees, the dirt sliding and rattling underneath him, six inches back for every one foot forward. The gap at the top was barely wide enough for him to wriggle through on his belly, and his hat fell off and bounced down the other side, sending streamers of light arcing as it rolled. It propelled him through, on his feet and after it before he was even aware what he was doing, frantic to catch the hat before the lamp broke and left him alone in the dark.

"Not far now," Marianne said.

Esher paused in the act of brushing dirt off the lamp, inspecting the glass for cracks, and strained to listen. "Do you hear something back there?"

She gave him a haunted look. "Yes."

# 7

The first level of the Heartbreak Mine, a hundred and fifty feet down. Gil could hear the cage rattle to a stop, the wire door screech open. He brushed against the side of the shaft and listened to the pebbles drop, judged his distance, and let go.

He fell directly beside the cage, catching himself on the rail and staggering, and he lost the gun. Nearby it hit metal and bounced, and the marksman in him thanked God he had the revolver and not the automatic, which might have gone off from the impact.

Kostner was there, waiting for him; he could hear the man chuckling to himself, and he ducked and rolled and prayed he wouldn't fall into the next shaft. He was straining his eyes uselessly against the dark when the lights came on, an impact almost physical, and he cried out.

"You think you're going to stop me?" Kostner crooned. Gil could see him, a blurry figure fifteen feet away, between him and the shaft. He had something in his hands. "You and your friends think you're going to stop *me*?"

It was a pickax. Kostner held it high, the sharp points gleaming, and advanced on him. Gil back away, scrambling. The gun was against the near wall. He lunged for it and held it, steadying it as his vision cleared.

Kostner laughed and kept coming. "You think you can stop me, man? You think you can stop me *here*?"

Gil retreated. He was in a tunnel now, off the metal plates flooring the cave. A tunnel. His mouth was dry with old memories, even though he could stand upright and stretch out both his arms full length without touching the sides. This was not Vietnam, Charlie wasn't waiting for him. This was Nevada. He remembered the stories Mikey had told him; maybe this was one of the tunnels that led up instead of down, maybe there was a way out. But he couldn't think of that now. He had a man to kill—

Kostner's shadow, cast by the lights in the cave, stretched out and touched him, lapped at his knees. His finger tightened on the trigger. At this distance he couldn't miss. "Kostner!"

"You poor damn fool." Kostner's laughter was pitying, and the pickax came down, wedged in the dirt between them.

Gil had heard the sound of the green liquid before.

He had not heard the Beast.

Something geysered from the hole in the tunnel floor and spread like foam or fog, obscuring Kostner. It took a shape from the liquid. Gil saw it coming at him, heard the other man's laughter. He fired, repeatedly, and the laughter did not stop, until he was pulling the trigger against empty chambers and the liquid was boiling the tips of his boots, and Kostner still laughed.

He wheeled and fled down the tunnel.

# Three

## 1

"Not far now" was down another long tunnel, one that divided halfway along. After a moment's thought the young woman chose the left-hand tunnel, which sloped down at a steep grade for several yards before taking a sharp turn around a massive boulder and widening into a small cavern. Another, larger tunnel opening was situated across the cavern. A ladder shaft above their heads was matched by a squared-off hole in the ground. Someone had brought down a wooden rack for drills and other equipment; a small generator stood against one wall. Esher remembered Mikey talking about going from one end of town to the other under the ground, and for one irrational moment wondered if he could claw his way straight up to the safety of his hotel room. More likely he was under Gallita's house, or somebody's swing set.

"This is it." Marianne examined the rack. "We'll use these to set the charges." Grabbing a small drill, she looked thoughtfully at the generator. "If I started that up, we'd have better light—"

"No," Esher said frantically. "You can't drill. It'll feel it, it'll know!"

"I have to set the charges." She hefted the drill in her hand. "I could set it in a crevice instead."

"It's back there, I can hear it. Make it fast, whatever you're going to do—"

"I'm going to plant it down the shaft. And when it goes, everything's going to go with it—"

Soft, far away: *rumbling*.

"Do it!"

# 2

"All we have to do is light this." Marianne lit an automatic torch, and the flames hissed out, light dancing through the cave. Handing it to Esher, she lit another for herself. "It's a fifteen-minute fuse; that's all the time we've—"

*Rumble*.

"Hold it right there." The carbide lamps jerked up to converge on Harry Kostner, smiling, stepping off the end of a ladder at the far side of the cavern. With a gun in his hand. And behind him, the air, thickening like a cloak.

"It's the Beast—" David could not have told which of them said it. "The Spirit."

"You've been listening to that damn fool Gallita, haven't you, Esher? I told you not to do that. There's no Beast down here. There's gold, and there's silver, and it's mine! And I'm not going to let you take it away from me!"

Flecks of froth glittered from his mouth as his voice rose, and the cavern wall behind Kostner began to blur and disappear. Beside him, Esher could hear Marianne inhale, a sharp gasp. Esher tensed, seeking an opportunity to grab for the gun.

Kostner waved the gun at the ledges of rock around them. "You see this, Esher? This is silver! This belonged to my grandfather, and it belongs to me! It's mine, you understand? You ever *owned* anything, Esher? You ever reach out and grab and know it's *yours*? You can take it and you can make it and you can break it!" The gun went off and the two of them hit the dirt as it ricocheted past, off the rock and into the far wall. "I'm going to rip every penny out of this godforsaken ground and I'm going to take it away from here and live like a human being." His voice rose to a scream. "You ever lived like a human being? You ever *been* a human being? And it's all going to come from here and I'm going to take it all!"

Behind him the darkness towered, impenetrable, murmuring, swirling.

"It's growing," Esher whispered. "It's growing out of him!"

It was true. As they watched, the darkness took substance, growing larger, darker, moving faster and faster around Kostner as he grew more and more agitated. Half the cavern was swirling in darkness now, with the short, bull-like figure of Harry Kostner spotlighted by their carbide lamps. He was laughing now, and the gun was beginning to move in smaller circles, centered on the two of them.

"I've got to light the fuse! Distract him!"

*How?* Esher thought, but he stepped away from the girl and looked frantically around for inspiration.

And from behind the rock came an undersized, towheaded child to throw himself at the ranting Kostner, screaming, "It was you! You took Tessy! You bring her back! You bring back my sister!"

The noises behind him, Esher realized, sick. It had been Jeremy, following them. And all the while the Beast was in front and *waiting* for them.

"Jeremy!" Marianne dropped the fuse and raced for the child, and the darkness reared up above them all, roaring like a thousand earthquakes, taking Shapes. A vast Bear. A Badger with glittering silver eyes and claws as long as his hands. A Thing with wings that beat and swept the opposite walls of the cavern. A Child thirty feet tall with blonde hair and empty eyes. The face of Rick Zimmermann, with calm and empty eyes. A Rat. A Worm that arched over the struggling humans and came down again to change, and change, and change . . . Esher reached for Marianne and Jeremy and cried out as the darkness brushed his arm and an incredible coldness gripped him.

There was nothing left of them—Kostner, Marianne, even Jeremy were gone in the darkness. Esher retreated as the Beast turned to him, lazy speculation in the stone eyes, and claws reached out for him, and he ducked behind the rock, gibbering, dying already from fear, his mind shrieking for blessed oblivion.

Until his eye fell on the fuse, extinguished in the struggle, and looked up again to see the Beast change yet again, into Marianne, Jeremy, Kostner—and Rick, reaching out for him with awareness and the resignation that comes when death has been acknowledged.

He knelt and grabbed the end of the fuse and scrabbled for the lighter as the Beast changed back again to the Badger, a dirty yellow-gray mass swelling and filling every crevice of the cave, absorbing the light, roaring with the sound of a million tons of earth giving way. He snapped the lighter one more time and fled up the tunnel for his life.

He was starting up the last shaft when the dynamite blew.

# Epilogue

## 1

"Dave? Hey, about time I heard from you! What's going on out there? I got something off the wire services about another big disaster in Nintucca. Are we going to get a story about this?"

David Esher cradled one useless arm against his chest and looked around at the comfortingly artificial aluminum palm trees in McCarran Airport, Las Vegas, Nevada. His eyes were empty. "No, Steve. No story. We were wrong about Nintucca."

"Dave? David! Dammit, man, I went on the line for you with this!"

"I know, Steve." He fell silent, and on the other end of the line his silence was matched, redoubled. But he felt no urge to fill it up or explain.

After a time the line disconnected as Steve Migliori hung up on him. David Esher replaced the handset gently in its cradle, shrugged his bag onto his shoulder, and walked away. As he went he passed an open-air bar.

He never glanced up.

226

# 2

At the drilling site outside Nintucca, Paul Northhampton kicked the tire of the tanker and ruffled the papers on his clipboard. "Okay, let's give it another try . . ."

# 3

And at the Nevada Test Site, men at the control center watched a clock counting down, waiting for the Earth to rumble.

## ABOUT THE AUTHOR

Ashley McConnell is a former Air Force brat now living in Albuquerque, New Mexico, with the obligatory writer's cats. She has been a technical writer, a security administrator, and a contracting representative, and has published short stories in *Women of the West* and *Final Shadows*. She is particularly proud of the fact that like almost anybody else with the normal assortment of body parts, she can hit the side of a barn door with a grenade launcher. Really.